Secrets Below

Book 2 of the Secrets Series

By Amy M. Ward & Olivia Cayenne

Secrets Below

Book 2 of the Secrets Series

Copyright © Amy M. Ward & Olivia Cayenne

Cover art by Covers by Christian

Dear Secrets Keeper,

That's right! If you have read Secrets Above, you are now a Secrets Keeper! That makes you our favorite kind of person.

A Secrets Keeper has read Secrets Above. A Secrets Keeper feels a close bond with Lia and her friends. A Secrets Keeper has a strong sense of imagination and curiosity.

As a Secrets Keeper, we are sure that you have been waiting patiently for Secrets Below. You are anxious to find out what happens next with Lia and her friends. Well, you will have to wait just a bit longer for the rest of Lia's story. You won't be disappointed, though.

In Secrets Below, you get to know Lukan. His story takes place at the same time as Lia's. You will get to find out what exactly is going on above ground, while Lia is enduring the oppression of Terra Convex. As you read Secrets Below, keep in mind that what you are reading is happening parallel to Secrets Above. Lukan has his own fears, troubles, and oppression. He also has a tremendous sense of imagination, curiosity, and adventure.

We hope you enjoy Lukan's story. He is very special to us, and we have big plans for him in the next book in the Secrets Series, Secrets Revealed.

Much Love,

Amy M. Ward & Olivia Cayenne

Please feel free to send us your comments, questions, or fan art!

Facebook: https//www.facebook.com/wardarewriters/

Email: wardsarewriters@gmail.com

Website: wardsarewriters.com

Walking, I am listening to a deeper way.

Suddenly all my ancestors are behind me.

Be still, they say.

Watch and listen.

You are the result of the love of thousands.

-Linda Hogan

Native American Writer

PROLOGUE

Screaming.

I can hear screaming all around me. It doesn't matter how hard I press my fists into my ears, I can still hear the constant screaming. Fear overwhelms me, but I don't want to appear weak while my friends and family are fighting for their lives.

Howling.

Mixed in with the screaming is the howling. I want to help my father fight the monsters. Of course, I am old enough to know they aren't real monsters. No, they are only men pretending to be monsters; dressed in the skins of wolves that they have already killed in their madness; howling like wolves to add to the delusion.

I keep thinking about my neighbors that are being killed as I lay hidden. I need to help. Although I know that I am too young and too small, a plan comes to mind. A dangerous plan. A plan my parents would not approve. That doesn't matter right now. Right now, I need to help them fight.

When the monsters arrived, the screaming started. Before my parents ran from the house, my mother told me, very sternly, to stay hidden.

"They only want our boys! If they find you, you will be taken." I remember her whispering harshly as she put me in the hiding place. The look of terror in her eyes makes me shudder even now as I think about it.

As I ran to my hiding place, I could see that my parents were arming themselves. They forgot one of the guns, though. The gun that had been my great-grandfather's. It is considered an antique. Although my father has taken it out of its protective box many times to clean it and tell me the stories of long ago battles fought with it, he has never fired it. It seems to call to me as I remain hidden under the pantry. I had tripped over it as I ran to the farthest corner of my hiding spot.

I reach for the box, opening it quickly. As I grasp the ancient gun in my hand, I am surprised by the weight of it. I know nothing about loading guns with ammunition. I especially don't know anything about firing guns. This one seems very different than the ones I have seen others in the community carrying on occasion. I ignore the fear that holding the weapon adds and I begin to load them ammunition into it. Loading the gun takes several minutes, as my hands will not quit shaking. When everything feels right, I make my way outside of the safe place my mother had ordered me into.

The screaming and crying are louder, now that I am outside. The howling more hysterical. My hands continue to shake, and I am ashamed when I feel my eyes begin to well up with tears.

I can see my father struggling with one of the monsters. Although the beast seems quite large, my father seems to have the advantage somehow.

"Stop!" I hear my cousin, Domenic, say in a loud voice. Why isn't he hiding like the rest of the boys in town?

Looking over, I see that my aunt is being attacked. She is on the ground, her face already bloody. A monster is on top of her, striking her repeatedly with his fists. A strange gurgling growl rises from its throat. Fearfully, I raise the gun to my eye and put my finger on the trigger. I aim at the monster and pull the trigger.

The explosion is deafening.

The pain is excruciating.

I know I am screaming, but I am unable to hear myself. The ringing in my ears is incredible. I am confused as to what has happened. Turning in circles, I try to fend off the monsters with just my hands. There are no monsters, though. There is only blackness. I realize that no matter how hard I try, I cannot see.

"Lukan!" I am barely able to hear my mother scream my name.

I try to call to her, but the pain is too much. My thoughts begin to swim around in my head, and I feel, rather than see, my world turn black as the pain consumes me. Before I collapse, I feel my mother's arms embrace me.

*****

Some time later, I wake up to the pain again. A loud scream escapes me, and I begin to cry. My mother is instantly at my side. She tries to comfort me.

"Shh, it's okay. You will need to be still for this, Lukan. I need to wrap your head," She says calmly.

"Mom, it hurts!" I scream, raising my hand to my right eye where the pain is the most intense.

"I can mend your wound; you just have to calm down." She sounds worried which makes my panic rise.

"Where's dad? Are the monsters still here?" I ask frantically.

"Your dad is taking care of them." She begins to wash the blood from my eyes, sending slivers of pain through my head and face.

I yelp in pain, "Mom, tell me a story. The happy story about a safe place." My voice quivers in terror and agony. She has always had the ability to soothe my fears with her stories. Even though I had tried to be brave earlier, now I have no shame in retreating into the safety of her voice.

"Okay… Somewhere far away, there is a safe place. A place where people don't have to worry about the monsters. This safe place is deep inside the earth. They have food and water. In this secret place, there is a boy just like you. He's curious and brave… Because he's so curious, he wants to leave this safe place." She begins, as her hands continue to work.

"What's his name?" I ask, as my mother begins wrapping my head, covering my eye.

"His name is Alan. He's nine, like you."

"And three-quarters?" I ask weakly.

With my uninjured eye, I can see her smiling down at me as she answers, "Yes. He is nine and three-quarters years old." She knows that when a boy's age is about to go into double digits, the precise age is important to him. "Alan wants to know what it's like to feel the grass on his feet or hear the birds sing... But the people won't let him out. They know it isn't safe for the little boy. So, they tell him about the monsters. Monsters do not scare the little boy, though. He wants to go outside even more. He is curious about monsters. The people won't let him, though."

She is finished wrapping the bandage around my head. I can't help but wonder if my wounded eye is even still there? I can't feel it, only the pain.

"Why won't they let him go, Mom?" I ask, not ready for the story to be over.

"Because they know it isn't safe for a little boy. They want to keep him safe, so they keep him under their control with strict rules." She answers, "So he tries to find a way out. The other people beg him to stay. He's scared for them. The boy believes he can slay any monster he sees. So, he keeps looking."

She pauses and kisses the top of my head. Even though I try to be tough, the way my father wants me to be, I allow my mother to pull me into her arms as she continues.

"When he finds his way out, he is shocked by what he sees. He hears the birds chirping and sees the trees blowing in the wind. He is surprised to see other little boys like him. The people in his home only ever told him about the scary monsters. They wanted the little boy to stay with them, not so he would be safe, but so he could be controlled. They didn't like how curious or brave he was. They wanted him to be like everyone else. They wanted him to be scared of the unknown. Instead, he was only scared of *them*."

She looks at me with her piercing green eyes, "You're brave, Lukan, but you must be careful. I know you were scared for your father and the community. It's understandable that you wanted to help. But sometimes the brave thing to do is just wait and watch."

With pain continuing to pulse through my head, I nod, "Is Domenic okay? Merritt?" I ask about my cousin and best friend.

She hesitates, and I can see tears begin to form in the corners of her eyes. I begin to fear that my cousin had been killed. My mother calms my fears and answers calmly, "They are both fine."

Outside, the howls have ceased. Only to be replaced by the screaming sobs of the community. Lamenting for those Grayson has lost to the howling monsters begins. The grieving will not end until...

I wake up with a gasp. For seven years, the dream has been the same.

No, not a dream, I think to myself, *a memory.* A memory of the day the Howlers came to our community to punish us for hiding our boys after they found one playing in the meadow. Parents, tired of losing their sons to the Howlers, tried to rise up. The madmen were too much for our citizens, though, and they killed many that night, including my aunt and uncle.

Reaching over to my bedside table with one hand, rubbing my face with the other, I take hold of the leather patch and place it over the place where my right eye used to be.

Chapter 1

I hear her talking but cannot concentrate on her words. To be honest, I've made a choice to not concentrate on her words. I'm not exactly trying to be rude. Just trying to avoid the conversation.

Her name is Luetta. She is my mother. My father, Avis, lovingly calls her Lue. In this post-virus world of not-quite-primitive living and occasional madness, she is quite beautiful, with her stunning red hair, freckled skin, and green eyes. At the moment, she sits next to me, with her arms stretched as she passes me the serving bowl that is heaped with scrambled eggs. Her eyes are kind as she tries to read my face. Of course, she knows my response. She knows that I am choosing to ignore this conversation. Again.

Dom is talking enough for the both of us. He never quits, it seems. Early this morning, like most mornings, he was stalking in the woods while the rest of the community, myself included, was still dreaming warmly in our beds.

My cousin, Domenic, is the great hunter of our family. He is the son my parents wish I could be. Dom is a community favorite. Perhaps, he could even be considered a hero. He provides food by hunting the wildlife in the forest that surrounds us.

Everyone has a job to do in Grayson. There are very few hunters, but they are skilled and almost never return empty handed. As a young man, and cousin of the most efficient hunter in town, I am expected to join the hunters and be a provider for the community. As a one-eyed freak, however, I am nothing but a taker. I have nothing to give. Although I try to help those in need, I have made no real contributions to our society. Sometimes, I feel that the weight of the handicap of having only one eye is heavier than that of the hunters that our community relies upon.

Although our community of around 250 has never been on the brink of starvation, like other communities, we have had to provide for the Howlers on a regular basis. Luckily, the Howlers have never found our hidden food supply. It was determined many years ago that the only way to ensure our population's survival was to hide food away. Each family has a hiding place.

At the thought of the Howlers, my hand instinctively goes to the patch that covers the gnarled socket that once held my right eye. I suppress a shudder as I think of all the times the savage group, wearing wolf skins, howling like madmen, have come into our little town making their demands.

Each community has to contribute something to the Howlers. Some, like ours, supply them with food. Others will provide ammunition. There is one, I heard, that does nothing but tan the furs that the Howlers wear. Not the wolf skins, of course. The Howlers do those themselves, which is evident by the poor, raunchy quality. Most vests, pouches, belts, moccasins are from tanned furs. The community of Maness has some exceptionally gifted people that have taken on that duty.

All communities, though, are forced to supply the Howlers with soldiers. Once a boy gets to be a certain size, no matter his age, he is taken by the madmen. They are meant to be raised and groomed by the Howlers until they become part of their "pack." The Howler packs travel the countryside leaving destruction everywhere they go. They wear the skins of wolves and wreak havoc to intimidate the towns. Young boys help ensure that their numbers will always be large enough to command respect from the communities. Of course, the loss of a male presence in the towns leaves the citizens even more vulnerable. It seems that the Howlers want boys that are younger and younger every year. Because of that, we keep our boys hidden when the Howlers make an appearance.

Because of my disfigurement, they have never had any interest in me. With only one working eye, I wouldn't be any use for their army. All the other boys that are my age flee into hiding when the Howlers make their surprise visits. They hide among the antique vehicles that once made transportation easy. When the virus struck, vehicles proved to be of no use.

To make matters worse, Howler visits rarely end without violence. Sometimes even murder. My aunt and uncle, Dom's parents, were not the first to die at the hands of the savages. Nor were they the last. We never know when they will show up. It is always in the best interest of the population to have food in abundance, just in case.

"Lukan," my mother says quietly, still holding the bowl of scrambled eggs.

Taking the bowl from my mom, I give her an apologetic smile. My mom is accustomed to my daydreams. Her patience with me, my disability, and my constantly wandering mind is never ending. She flashes me a charming smile in return. After scooping two spoonfuls of eggs onto my plate, I keep my eye averted so as not to get sucked into the needless and recurring conversation. With my plate now full, I begrudgingly begin to eat, wondering if we will ever be able to have a meal without discussing how the food ended up on our plates.

"The buck is huge, Uncle." Dom describes, with a mouth full of food.

"Dom. Manners."

I try to hide the smile that threatens to emerge at my mom's gentle scolding of my cousin.

"Sorry, Auntie." Dom apologizes, still with food in his mouth. I doubt that he is truly sorry. The apology must be enough, though, because she doesn't chastise him for the second indiscretion.

Dom chews quickly. I try not to gag at the obnoxious sound as his mouth works the pieces of food into a suitable consistency to swallow.

"You eat like an imbecile," I mutter under my breath.

"Anyway, the buck is huge. He is at least a six and a half year old." Dom continues, ignoring my insult.

"You'll get him eventually," my father reassures Dom.

Looking around the table, I can't help but feel inadequate. Even though Dom failed to get the big buck he was after today, my parents treat him as if the trip was not a failure.

"Oh, thank you, Uncle. You have too much faith in my hunting skills. That old buck is a wise one." Dom acknowledges. "After breakfast, I am going to go check my snares. Hopefully, we will have some rabbit and squirrel to put in our food stores for winter."

As my parents soak up my cousin's humble remarks, I find myself glaring as I look across the table at him. It isn't that I hate him. I just wish my parents would find some reason to be proud of me. Their son.

"How about you, Lukan?" My mother asks, attempting to draw me into their conversation. "What are you going to do today?"

I look up from my plate to see her smiling as she takes a bite of bacon. Chewing my food slowly, I bide my time, trying to think of what exactly I plan on doing today that is even worth mentioning. Her radiant green eyes narrow as she patiently waits for my answer. We continue this staring contest as I try to figure out if she truly wants to know or if she simply feels it is her duty to ask.

"Are you deaf, son? Your mother asked you a question," my father barks.

I glance at him. "Oh, I heard her. I'm just trying to think if I plan on doing anything today that any of you would want to hear about," I reply, returning my attention back to my food.

"Lukan, we always want to know what is going on in your life. So, what is it today? Are you going to help Mr. Fisher with his lambs? Or maybe help Old Lady Mills weed her garden?"

I do plan on doing those things today, but when my mother says them out loud, it all seems meaningless compared to hunting. Honestly, though, what else can a one-eyed boy do?

Nodding, I feel my mouth start to form into a sarcastic grin as I look up again. "Yes, Mr. Fisher and Mrs. Mills need help today. I will also help Mr. Jarvis put new strings on two of his fiddles."

My mother is beaming; obviously, she is proud that her maimed son is at least of some value in the community.

"Later, Merritt and I will probably practice reading for a bit." I continue, "After that, I will go down to the creek. I will sit on my favorite moss-covered rock, and think about how much I dread dinner."

Her face has fallen. She is no longer beaming.

I hate myself for being so rude but yet I continue, "Because I know, I just know, that we will sit around the table and listen to Dom tell his exciting stories and dad will laugh and laugh." I pause to take in their reactions. They are not pleased. "Thankfully, I know that the meal you cook tonight will be delicious, mom. There is that."

Each of my family members stares at me. I'm not sure why they seem surprised by my words. They have heard something similar from me several times. It's usually at this point that my cousin says something witty to get the attention back on him. This time, however, he is frowning and shaking his head as he eats his food. I can tell that the wheels in his mind are turning; he wants to lighten the mood but seems unsure.

As I am about to take a bite of buttered toast, something makes me pause. In the distance, something has caught my attention. It is just barely audible, but it seems like I can hear...

I close my good eye and try to give the sound my full attention. There it is. It most definitely is...

Howling.

Dom opens his mouth to speak, but before he can get his words out, I shush him harshly.

"Lukan." My mother chastises.

I open my eye and announce, "Howlers! They're coming."

They do not question me. We have relived this nightmare many times. My father is instantly up from the table and looking out the window of our living room. My mother begins gathering the food and putting it away. She does so quickly and efficiently. Dom is clearing the table, taking the dishes to the sink. When the Howlers arrive, there can be no trace that we were enjoying a meal. They consider everything we have as their own. The Howlers know that we must eat to survive, to provide for them. However, if they knew how much food we had, it could incite a terrible punishment.

"There isn't time, Dom. Go now." I tell my cousin. He gives me a frightened look before grabbing his bow and bolting out the door.

He will run through the community towards the forest. Along the way, he will warn everyone of the imminent danger that will soon descend upon our home. When everyone on that side of town has been notified, he will join the other boys as they disperse into their designated hiding places.

Only I remain at the table; my eye remains closed as I continue to listen. I can sense the anxiety around me as my parents are moving through the house in emergency mode. In the far off distance, though, the Howlers continue their approach.

Standing, I make my way to the front door. My mom has joined my dad by the window. They don't ask where I'm going. They already know. I'm about to perform my one contribution to the community.

For reasons nobody can explain, I can sense an impending crisis. Most times, the impending crisis is the Howlers. A couple of times, it was a terrible storm. When the feeling hits me, it is my job to run to the area of our town that offers the best vantage point, warning the citizens that live on that end of Grayson as I run. Once the danger is in view, I will hurry back home to let my family know what they can expect and when.

As I open the door, my mother approaches, anxiety etched on her face. She gives me a quick hug.

"How long till they arrive, Lukan?" my father asks from the window.

I close my eye once more, listening for the distant sound.

"Half an hour," I answer. "Maybe less. I need to hurry."

I take a last look at my mother. It's obvious that she is close to panic. Her eyes are welling up with tears that threaten to escape, making my heart hurt for the fear she feels because of these madmen.

"Breakfast was delicious, mom." I acknowledge quietly before jogging out the door. I can't think of anything else to say to her. I don't wait for a reply or even look back. There isn't time.

Chapter 2

Jumping off the front porch of my home, I head west. I have run this route many times; too many times, to be honest. West on Hampton. Then I take a left and run up Franklin to an intersection. At the intersection, I will go to the first house on the right and announce the danger and then to the first house on the left. The residents of those homes will have the task of broadcasting to their neighbors.

Dom warns the residents on the east side of town because the houses on that side back up to the forest with the car cemetery. The boys that live in those homes will immediately flee and be hidden well before the Howlers arrive. I warn the few and far between houses on the west because they are on the way to the lookout point. There are only older adults that live on the west side.

It doesn't take long for the word to spread. I run past each house, yelling the warning. I shout it loud enough that if the resident is inside, I can still be heard. I begin to see people in their yards, several houses ahead. They have heard the commotion. As soon as they see me running down the road, they rush into their homes. Everyone in the community knows, if they see Dom or me running, danger is approaching, and they need to prepare.

My best friend, Merritt, is standing at one of the intersections. I don't dare stop to speak to her. She won't be offended that I pass her. We have been friends since childhood. We make brief eye contact. She nods and turns to warn the people in her neighborhood. I continue my journey.

It takes me about fifteen minutes to run to the lookout point. At the edge of our small town, I slow my running to a walk and eventually a crawl. I peek over the short rock wall that separates us from the field and forest beyond. The remnants of an ancient road snakes its way through the field and into what remains of the stone pillars that is the entrance to our town. I imagine, at one time, the pillars were a warm and welcoming sight to all who entered this community.

When the human population began to die out, the earth found her opportunity to take back what was hers. While the lunatics of the world were becoming consumed with grief over their dead loved ones, they destroyed the buildings and bridges. Ransacking. Looting. Taking what was not theirs, but somehow they felt obliged to take in their anguish. It didn't take long for the earth to take it upon herself to start uprooting the highways. Now, all across the landscape, there is green grass consuming the old pavement through gaping cracks.

As I chance a look over the rock wall, I can hear, before I actually see, a group of Howlers approaching. When I finally catch sight of them, I count about a dozen men dressed in the skins of dead wolves. That number gives me some optimism. That number means they are only here to make an announcement. Although they are howling and jumping and pushing each other around senselessly, these are just messengers. Crazed messengers.

I hurry home to inform my parents. They are standing on the front porch by the time I arrive. It's obvious that they are anxiously awaiting my report. My mother is wringing her hands nervously. My dad stands with one arm around my mom's waist to comfort her. With his other hand, he nervously strokes his graying beard. His face conveys worry, but it's obvious that he is trying to remain calm. Panic will only make our situation worse.

"What are we in for, Lukan?" My father asks, ready for the scouting report.

I take a quick glance over my shoulder before turning back towards my parents, "Just a messenger group." I reach over and give my mom's arm an affectionate squeeze to try to calm her nerves.

They both let out a sigh of relief. I don't feel that danger is completely out of the question, so I add, "But they seem to have gotten themselves all riled up."

Realizing what I am suggesting, my mom begins to tremble, while my dad lets out a grunt of disapproval. They know that even a small group of Howlers, when agitated, can be extremely unpredictable.

"It's odd that they would come this early in the morning," My dad says to no one in particular.

As soon as the words leave his mouth, we hear the howling.

"They're here," I announce needlessly. "Are we all set inside?" Since Dom and I took off to deliver the warning, my parents were left to clean up and hide our breakfast.

Nobody answers my question. My mom simply nods an affirmation as she and my father stare off in the direction of the town entrance. The howling is loud now. Families are beginning to gather outside on their porches and lawns. Nobody speaks. We all just focus on the madness that is approaching with their hoots and howls. I can't help but wonder what kind of damage our community will endure with the presence of this messenger group.

The Howlers round the corner and are in view of our home now. Even though they are at the end of our street, the stench from the dead wolves that they wear on their body is revolting. It's late summer and still much too warm to be wearing a fur coat, even if it is sleeveless. The heat makes no difference to the Howlers, however. Their filth-covered bodies, blanketed by the poorly prepared fur of dead animals, only adds to the putrid odor that emanates from these unwelcome visitors.

My mom gags slightly and looks away. In a vain effort to guard her against the hideousness of the approaching group, my dad steps in front of her. His act of chivalry is not lost on me. I also position my body in front of her. We have seen what these monsters do to the women of our community and the communities nearby.

The pack of howling chaos makes its way into our settlement. As usual, they have split up into smaller groups of two or three. They move through our community like an infestation. By the time they leave, our entire town will be contaminated with the damage they are sure to cause. Every home they pass will be affected. Some will suffer physically, others emotionally and mentally. Regardless, the remainder of the day will be spent cleaning up the mess left by the group.

Every citizen knows the routine. We are required to stand on our porches as the Howlers pass by, wreaking havoc on each property. If they pass by a bush, they rip it up. If they don't like the way an individual is looking at them, they will run up onto the porch and begin screaming obscenities. Or worse, pummel them with their fists. Once they pass, we are to follow them to the Community Building for whatever message they are here to deliver.

A few months ago, one of the citizens took it upon himself to break the routine. He hadn't been in our town for long but had been here long enough to have endured a few visits from the Howlers. Once, after Dom had run through with the warning that the Howlers were on their way, this man decided he didn't want to wait for them to pass by his home. His pride, at the time, was excessive. He took his family and waited for the Howlers at the Community Building instead. When the pack, much bigger than today's group, arrived at the Community Building, they were enraged. They demanded to know why the family was there. How did they know they were coming?

The man suffered a brutal punishment for breaking the routine. Not before watching what his wife and daughters had to endure at the hands of the Howlers, however. As the rest of the community had to stand by and watch this horrible display of brutality, my parents and I waited anxiously to see if the man or his family would reveal to the Howlers just how they knew the pack was coming. They never did, though. When we could finally talk about it, we decided that the family was so new that they probably didn't even know who had run through the streets yelling the warning. The prideful man and his family left town in the middle of the night. They have never been seen again.

Today, with a much smaller group inflicting mayhem, I can't help but feel that our citizens could stand against them. We greatly outnumber them and are much smarter than they are. My parents have heard me have this discussion with my cousin on too many occasions apparently. I can see them eyeing me and shaking their heads slightly.

As we stand on our porch, watching as a deranged man rips my mother's beautiful flowers and plants out of our yard, hate consumes me. I do not dare look at my mom. She loves fresh flowers and was pleased to have successfully replanted some bulbs she had dug up out of the field. Now, as she watches this obviously demented man rip up the bulbs, I can't help but remember her delight when they bloomed in the spring. If I look at her and see the tears that I am sure are threatening to escape, I don't think I will be able to stop myself from charging this lunatic. My father, sensing my outrage, catches my eye and subtly shakes his head at me.

The Howler that is destroying my mom's flower garden is a regular. I don't know his name, or that he even has a name for that matter. My family and I simply refer to him as Sprightly because of his quick and agile movements. He has moves that are unmatched in his group or ours. We have watched him climb trees or leap onto houses with incredible agility.

Sprightly is always in the messenger group. He isn't large like most of the Howlers. There isn't anything particularly menacing about his appearance. Most Howlers wear the badge of their battles, in the forms of scars or missing body parts like ears or fingers. And teeth. Lots of missing teeth in their group. Although he does sport the menacing tattoos that are customary for their pack, he seems free of scars. Usually, the men that ravage and ruin our town are covered in filth. He seems to take his appearance seriously. His wavy light-brown hair lays on his shoulders and seems clean every time he has visited our town. As I watch him, I try to think of a word that best describes him. The most fitting word that comes to mind, even in his flower-garden-induced rage, is "proper."

Even in his flower-destroying frenzy, he must sense my glaring. In one quick leap, he is on the porch and in front of me. His breath isn't as rancid as some who have tried to intimidate me before in this same manner. Although he is obviously very muscular, he isn't much taller than me. We stand, glowering at each other for several seconds. I am expected to show respect to all Howlers by looking down at the ground. I refuse. At this moment, I find myself distracted by his well-groomed mustache that curls up on both ends.

I can hear my mom taking in short, shallow breaths. She hates when I blatantly defy the rules that have been set upon us by these madmen. This Howler doesn't seem too agitated by my actions, though. In fact, during most of his visits, he appears to gravitate towards me. He never pushes me around or spits in my face, like he does the other citizens of our town. No, usually, he simply tries to entice me to anger with his taunting and menacing words. Surprisingly, while I glare now, his lips curve into a sly smile, revealing his rather gleaming white teeth. I continue to glare which causes him to smile bigger.

My parents and I flinch when the man leans his head back and lets out a thunderous howl. The others that arrived with him, now scattered all throughout our community, answer his call. He brings his attention back to me, still smiling. Before he jumps off the porch, he gives me a quick wink.

As we watch the Howler run towards the Community Building, we make our way down the steps and toward the street. Others join us along the way. Nobody speaks. The mood is incredibly somber. My mind is racing, and I can't help but worry about the boys that remain hidden in the forest.

We, as a community, are always thankful that the Howlers have never decided to enter the building. There is a large concrete patio in front of the building that is raised almost like a stage, giving the Howlers the perfect place to stand over us as we stand below them. If they went inside, we wouldn't be able to go back in for weeks while the stink remained.

Much of the town is already at the Community Building. I am relieved to see Merritt standing towards the back with her family. We make brief eye contact. I attempt a reassuring smile. Merritt nods with a slight tilt of her head and rolls her eyes. Her response to the Howlers amuses me. She seems to hold no fear for the group.

The menacing group is on the raised stage where the message will be delivered. Just like the previous times we have had to listen to their pointless messages, we stand silently and wait.

The Community Building is the largest structure in our town. I imagine that there were important meetings held here before the Langston Virus. Perhaps even concerts or plays. It was one of the first buildings to be repaired when the first of us settled here, ninety years ago. The small band of Langston Virus survivors felt they needed a central place to coordinate and plan how they would begin to rebuild the badly damaged town.

Almost as one, the crazed group on the stage, begin to howl, signifying that the meeting will begin. We wait for them to finish their raucous behavior. When they finish, the largest Howler of this messenger group steps forward and clears his throat loudly.

"Servants of Grayson," he begins ceremoniously. The other Howlers chuckle at his wording. "On this fine morning, we bring you news." His arms are open wide as if to welcome cheering from the crowd. He receives silence from us; hoots and hollering from his band of cranks.

The large man, wearing the rank wolf fur, doesn't seem to comprehend that our silence is a sign of insolence.

"Our humble pack," he continues, gesturing toward the Howlers that accompany him on the stage, "wish you to know that we have been granted a new Alpha." He pauses again for effect.

The community members only stare at him. Of course, our minds are racing. In my lifetime, there has only been one leader of the Howlers. The current leader is completely demented. Although nobody is entirely sure of the name given to him at birth, his pack calls him Ripley. We assume the name comes from his actions of literally ripping into the throats of those that oppose him. He has been known to murder his own pack members just because he was displeased with how they were ransacking the towns that they control. His face is covered in horrid scars, and some of his teeth are missing. A new alpha could be beneficial for us or quite the opposite. It could bring death to many.

My eye is on Sprightly. While the rest of the messenger group is smiling and gesturing towards us obscenely, he is looking at each one of us with a brooding gaze. His sly smile is unwavering. He takes short steps back and forth. He seems to have too much energy stored up inside his brawny body. There is something about his actions that is even more unsettling than those of the rest of his group.

"In two weeks, you will meet our new Alpha." A pause, "And you will show him respect." His voice thunders. Leaning forward, the speech-giving Howler places his hands on his knees as if he is speaking to a child. He lowers his voice to add, "It will be in your best interest to provide a gift for the new Alpha." His eyebrows are raised as if he is questioning our ability to understand his meaning. All too well, we understand what our "gift" is to be.

We understand that the Howlers require our teenage boys to join their pack. They need the numbers in their pack to maintain control of all the little settlements, communities, and towns that are being reborn after the Langston Virus. The pack moves from town to town, destroying anything of value.

The Howlers especially thrive on demolishing anything that gives them the perception that the community is beginning to prosper. For Grayson, it has always been our governing body. If the Howlers suspect that we have a leader, somebody governing us other than them, that person is killed, without question.

Some communities have attempted to repair the electric grid that was once crucial to the survival of our ancestors. When the virus claimed the world as its own, the grid was one of the first things to go. Either by the hands of maniacs bent on senseless destruction or simply because there were not enough people living to help maintain it, nobody knows. At the time, nobody cared. It was all about surviving the virus and then surviving the mayhem that followed. The why doesn't matter anymore, anyway. What is known, is the fact that the Howlers will not allow the power to be turned back on. If we took that step towards modernization, the fiends that now rule this world would begin to lose their grip on us.

"I expect that our new Alpha will look favorably on this rather insignificant colony if you mind your manners." The head messenger continues in a sing-song voice that grates on my nerves. His hands remain on his knees. In this parody, we are just children, and he is our parent lecturing us over eating our vegetables. More than anything, I want to leap onto the stage and bury my dagger into his belly.

Grayson is silent. As a group, we stare at the Howlers, blank-faced. The best thing to do is silently endure the rest of the ridiculous speech and pray these messengers leave without causing injury to our citizens or destruction to our town.

The speech-giving Howler must realize that there is nothing left to say. He has informed us of the new Alpha. He has given us a timetable to expect to meet said Alpha. He has advised us to be on our best behavior when the Alpha arrives. Without warning, he stands up straight and begins to howl. The other messengers join in. As one, the group leaps from the stage and begin their raucous exit from town.

From where we all stand, we can hear their howls. They echo through the streets. Nobody moves until their howls are barely audible in the distance. Eventually, we each begin to breathe again and decide it is safe to discuss the message or simply head home. Mothers of sons begin to beckon for their boys to return from the safety of the forest. The men gather to hash out what we have been told by the Howlers and how to prepare.

In the distance, I see Dom making his way out of the forest with several other boys. The mothers, including mine, rush to them, grateful they have returned unharmed once again. I, with my defect, will never know the feeling of my mother rushing to me as I crawl from my hiding place. I will never have to hide from the madmen. My disability keeps me safe; however, it also keeps me at a disadvantage.

The unease caused by the visiting Howlers, along with my feelings of inadequacy as I watch the boys of our community return to their families, is almost more than I can bear. Before I say or do something that will wound my family, I quietly walk away. I am well aware that nobody will rush after me.

Chapter 3

The rest of the day is uneventful. I manage to complete all the tasks I had set out to do. I helped Mr. Fisher with his lambs and old lady Mills weed her garden. Before lunch, I made it to Mr. Jarvis' house and restrung his fiddles. His fingers are beginning to feel the effects of his old age. Even though he can still play wonderfully, it has become too difficult for him to put new strings on his prized fiddles.

Merritt was busy helping her mother babysit the Coleman twins, so I wasn't able to read from the large Geography book as I had hoped. Merritt and I enjoy looking at the pictures and reading about far off places. Mostly we daydream about traveling the world. Well, mostly I fantasize about traveling the world. Merritt is perfectly content within the walls of Grayson.

The day I met Merritt, I was up in a tree. I climbed trees regularly before I lost my eye. Usually, the climbing occurred when Dom and I were playing a game where he would have to find me. I would scamper up the tallest tree in our town and laugh when he was too scared to come up after me. Back then, I was brave, and he was always whimpering. On the day I met Merritt, I wasn't playing a game or hiding. I was just gazing into the meadow beyond our walls, letting my mind wander to far off places.

When she was a young girl, Merritt's family had traveled here from a nearby community. I was just a child also. Much too young to pay attention to all the details. I do remember overhearing my parents talking quietly one night about an illness that had nearly consumed the town that Merritt's family had come from. There was talk in Grayson about the chance that the family could have brought the sickness with them. For some time, Merritt and her family were treated cautiously. The men wouldn't invite her father to meetings. The women wouldn't speak to her mother as she passed by on the street. As a child, without a great understanding of diseases, I felt the treatment was unfair. Although Merritt refused to join me in the tree the day we met, we became great friends.

During lunch, Dom tells us about his morning of hiding in the forest with the other boys. They had all made bets on what the message could be. Nobody had guessed that it was about a new Alpha. This news, although not completely dismaying, is still unsettling. Too many unknowns with a new Alpha. One thing is certain, though, as a Howler, he is nothing other than feral.

While my father and Dom discuss this morning's event, I keep a watchful eye on my mother. She appears to be listening, but her eyes are sad. Looking up, she notices me staring at her. A forced smile crosses her face before she turns her attention to the window. Following her gaze, I realize immediately where her mind is. Her flower garden.

Watching Sprightly rip at her lovely landscaping must have been more distressing than I had realized. Thinking about it now, though, I can imagine the frustration she must have felt. I remember the day she came home with her bundles of bulbs, wrapped in wet linens to keep them fresh until she could plant.

"What have you got there, Lue?" My father had asked her when she returned home with the bundle.

Beaming, she opened the linens to reveal dirt-covered bulbs. She looked at her husband with prideful delight but didn't say anything. Immediately recognizing her prize, my father wrapped an arm around her tiny waist and gifted her with an affectionate kiss on the cheek.

"Ah, yes. In a few months, you will have a yard full of pretties. For sure, my dear." My father affirmed.

"I hope so. I saw them in the field last spring and marked their spot so I could find it again after they withered." Her face was still lit up with delight.

My father's arm remained around her waist, comfortably, "If anyone can give them life, it is you." One more kiss on the cheek before he left out the back door to return to his chores.

As I had been sitting at the table, tinkering with an ancient piece of electronics that will most likely never be restored, I had been listening to their exchange.

"Tell me when you're ready, mom. I'll help you plant those bulbs."

"Thanks, Lukan." My mom acknowledged. "When it gets cold, we will plant them so they can sleep soundly during the winter. Hopefully, they will come back as beautiful as they were in the field."

My mom and I had planted them on a cold day. I was glad when the task was complete. Although I hadn't thought much about them since that cold day, I'm sure my mother watched the ground expectedly, waiting for them to begin their climb out of the dirt. Spring came, and to my mom's delight, the green leaves seemed to emerge overnight. All the bulbs that we had planted survived the transplant, and my mom found great joy in the colorful blooms during the warm months.

I am sure that even with the damage done to the flowers by the crazed Howler, the bulbs that laid buried safely below the surface remain unharmed. They will produce the beautiful blooms again next spring. Until then, I know she will be missing their beauty.

An idea begins to form, and I rush to complete my meal. The rest of my family also finishes up and we all pitch in to clear the table before we each head off in different directions. My mom is at the sink, running water to wash the dishes. Laying my empty plate on the counter, I thank her for the meal and rush off to bring my idea to life.

Leaving my house through the front door, I can't help but notice the destroyed flower garden. It appears that my mother has already begun to clean it up. Most of the bulbs remain safely hidden under the protection of the dirt. Others were not as lucky. Sprightly knew to rip the beautiful plants up from the base, exposing the precious bulbs.

I can't stop to think about this right now, though. The idea that came to me requires me to walk some distance, and I believe rain is coming. I hear thunder in the distance and realize that the wind has picked up a bit. The smell of an earth-cleansing rain is in the air. Mothers call to their children that are still kicking a ball in the street. They summon the kids to come in before it begins to rain on them. As I walk by on the street, dodging children in a hurry to get home before they get scolded, a few of the mothers acknowledge me with a wave.

"You better get home, Lukan. Those clouds look angry." Mrs. Pettigrew warns with a kind smile.

"Just out for a quick walk. I won't stay out long." I lie, returning her smile.

The street is nearly clear of children by the time I reach the end of it. I flip the hood of my worn-out jacket up onto my head and shove my hands into my pockets. I turn around to make sure nobody is following. Nobody ever is. For reasons I cannot explain, I get a strange feeling that my little neighborhood will look different to me after the rain finishes its cleansing.

There is a small rock wall that stands crookedly between me and the forest beyond. I easily leap over it and begin my journey into the familiar woods. The rain-filled clouds that are building angrily overhead make the path slightly difficult to see. Luckily, I have hiked this path enough that I am confident I can do it in complete darkness.

This particular game trail is my favorite. Just as the forest begins to thicken, seemingly closing in on the path, it opens back up to an expansive meadow. This meadow is where my mother found her flower bulbs. I know of another place where flowers grow that she has never seen. That is where I am headed.

Not many of the mothers from Grayson would find themselves on the meadow side of the rock wall. My mother possesses a refined fortitude, however. A short, crumbling rock wall may keep others in but not her.

Off the trail, to the right, there is a cliff. A thick line of trees hides it. At the bottom of the cliff, there is a lake that is the most striking color of blue. The sky should be jealous of the blue the lake possesses. I have dived off the cliff many times, into the unbelievably blue lake. It is highly unlikely that any of the other boys in my community can say the same.

To the left of the trail, across the vast meadow, there is a series of caves that I enjoy exploring. That is where I am headed tonight. I leave the path and make my way across the meadow. As I walk, I run my fingers along the tops of the waist-high grass. I realize that the flowers that grow wildly and in abundance have begun to wither. The season will be changing from summer to fall within a few weeks.

Before the catastrophe, the world measured time with watches and calendars. From the smallest milliseconds all the way to eons, with days/weeks/months/years in between. Now, although we do still keep track of years, the rest seems insignificant.

In the beginning, after many weeks and even months of running, time didn't matter. Only survival did. Once the communities began to settle and rebuild, time began being measured by the seasons. Each season is significant and valued.

As I near the edge of the meadow, I turn and look back at the trail that now lies almost out of my sight. Thunder claps and I begin to feel the first sprinkles of the impending rain shower. The cave isn't much farther ahead, but the sky is darkening, giving me a sense of urgency.

Leaving the meadow, I carefully make my way over some boulders that are already slick with rainwater. Another clap of thunder overhead and I fear I am out of time. I begin jogging, and the hidden mouth of the cave quickly comes into view. Well, not really into view. It remains in the shadows of the trees that seemingly guard it. I doubt that anyone else would see it if they didn't already know it was there.

With the cave now in view, I can also see the bountiful purple flowers that are nestled into the cracks and crevices of the rocks. These are wildflowers in the truest form. I doubt that any other human has had the privilege of being able to see these flowers as they grow without restraint amid the trees and large rock formations. This was my quest for this afternoon. To gather as many of these wildflowers as possible and take them back to my mom. I know the rich purple will make her smile.

The rain shower begins, and I step into the cave to wait it out. The extra amount of water the flowers are receiving right now will be good for them until I can get them home and into a container. I let out a chuckle as I am impressed with myself for not getting soaked to the bone in what is now a downpour.

Although grateful to be mostly dry, the cave proves to be much cooler than actually standing outside. I sit on the hard rock, my arms wrapped around my crossed legs. As I sit there, listening to the rain fall through the leaves just outside the mouth of the cave, I rest my chin on my knees. I relish the comfort and the seclusion the cave provides.

I realize that, at this moment, I feel peace. My mind wanders through the events of the past but seems to be unwilling to give up the peace I feel in this place, at this moment. Listening to the rain. Enjoying the solitude. As I close my eye, I feel myself begin to get drowsy, listening to the song of cleansing that comes as the rain wets the leaves and then tumbles to the ground.

"May I share your cave?" I hear a low gruff voice say, startling me from my near slumber.

Jumping up, I scan the rain-soaked forest in front of me, squinting my good eye. I can barely make out a broad-shouldered man standing in the downpour. His features are blurred by the rain that separates us, but it seems like he is wearing a thick fur coat and holding a stick that is as long as he is tall. Immediately, I am afraid. If he is a Howler, I am doomed.

"May I share your cave, friend?" He asks again, louder this time.

"Y-yes," I manage weakly, "Yes, sir." I hope that the manners my mother has taught me will win me favor with this Howler. It really is all I have to offer him.

The rain-soaked man makes his way into the cave. He uses the stick to tap the ground in front of him. Without taking my eye off him, I back towards the closest wall and lean against it. Although he seems large because of his broadness, the man isn't as tall as I first thought. As I stare at him, I wonder if his broadness is mostly just the incredibly thick fur coat that he is wearing. Although the coat is unnerving because it sets him apart as a Howler, the thing that intrigues me most about this man is the blindfold that covers both of his eyes.

"Thank you," he acknowledges, turning his head in my direction. I'm positive that I haven't made a sound since he entered, and yet, even blindfolded, he knows exactly where I am standing. He has a gentle smile, but it does nothing to improve my anxiety. I seem to have lost my ability to speak. The size of the rain-soaked, blindfolded man has left me dumbstruck.

"You don't need to be afraid. I'm not here to hurt you. I just needed to get dry." The man's voice is thick and raspy but kind. "My fur gets very heavy when wet," he says, indicating his coat.

I remain seemingly tethered to the wall as the man begins removing his large and obviously heavy fur coat. It is soaked, making it impossible for me to determine what type of animal it used to be. It doesn't reek of death like a Howler's fur would.

"I'm surprised you haven't built a fire," he comments as he uses the long stick to find a large boulder to drape his coat over. "That is easily remedied."

"Y-you're blind," I verbalize as the realization of his affliction becomes too much for me to contain.

The man continues to strip off wet articles of clothing as if he didn't hear me. Under the coat, his obviously handmade clothing seems dry, so they remain. Reaching up to his head, he removes his coon skin cap, revealing a head slick with baldness, but covered in tattooed markings.

"How about that fire?" he asks excitedly, rubbing his hands together.

"There isn't any wood in here. Nothing to build a fire." I reply.

"Hmmm," He groans thoughtfully, and begins rummaging sightlessly through the pockets of his shirt and pants. His hands finally find what they have been searching for and he pulls out a metal tin. Turning towards me, he shows me that the tin has some letters, printed faintly across it. They are so faint that I cannot read what it used to say. He is smiling and nodding as if I am supposed to understand and appreciate the meaning. I wish I did understand, but the meaning is lost to me. I wonder briefly how he, a blind man, knows what it says.

The man squats down and pats the floor of the cave with his hand. He searches until he finds a flat area. With incredible ease and efficiency, he removes a few items from the tin. I quietly inch closer to see what he is doing. Before I can get a good view, a fire is lit in the spot. He works at it for a few more seconds and then sits back on his haunches.

A clap of thunder echoes loudly through the cavern causing me to flinch. Without looking in my direction, he waves his hand at me and then motions towards the fire. It seems like a clear invitation to join him by the warmth of the small blaze. Hesitantly, and without taking my eye off of him, I move closer. He has his hands up to the fire to warm them. I am struck by his features. His skin is dark, smooth, and surprisingly clean. My eye is drawn back to the tattoos on his scalp. The design is difficult to make out in the firelight, but it appears quite intricate.

A content sigh escapes him, "That's better." He is rubbing his hands together. "I'm Helix. Thank you for sharing your cave."

"You're blind," I repeat after a few seconds. I'm not trying to be rude. I am just astounded at how easily he is able to get around and function without sight.

He simply nods an acknowledgment. His hands come up, and they find the back of his blindfold. He begins to untie it, and I realize that he is going to remove it, exposing what lies beneath. Apprehensive about what I might see, I avert my eye. I can appreciate the privacy he no doubt desires at this moment. Nobody, but my mother, has ever seen my empty socket, I can't imagine that he would want a stranger to see his dead eyes.

Even with my eye averted, I can see that the blindfold is off and discarded. I sneak a quick peek at him and am unnerved by the sight. Both of his eyes have been gouged out, leaving him with horrid scars. His wounds are very similar to mine. Covering my mouth with my hand, I attempt to stifle a gasp and am immediately ashamed of myself for peeking. He pulls another piece of cloth out of his pocket and ties it around his head, concealing his disfigurement once more.

"How did you know I was in here?" I manage to ask with all the courage I can summon. "You're blind."

A long, low groan, from deep in his belly, escapes him as he ponders my question.

"I could smell you," The mysterious man finally answers. He tilts his heavily tattooed head slightly as if he is looking at me sideways. His constant smile spreads further across his face as if he finds the statement humorous. "You don't smell bad. You just smell," deep inhale, "...different. Not part of the forest."

Astonished by his answer, I am also mesmerized by his deep voice. It seems to come from the deepest part of him and is always present, even when he isn't speaking.

"What is your name, friend?" He asks kindly.

I'm not ready to give away any information. I must ensure the safety of the community. Even though this blind man does not seem dangerous, he is a stranger nonetheless.

"Are you a Howler?" I ask, hoping to lead him away from any questions about me or my community.

Helix is shaking his head slowly, and I can discern his low groan growing from deep inside his belly once more.

"No. Not a Howler. Just a Wanderer," he finally answers. He doesn't seem perturbed by the question like I was afraid he would be. Actually, he seems mostly sad that I asked. The smile has diminished slightly but is not gone entirely.

I consider his answer and reaction for several seconds as I begin to feel the effects of the fire and its warmth. My eye never leaves this strange man. Wanderer? I can only assume that means he doesn't have a community to call his own. Is he hiding from something? From someone? How did he lose his sight? His answer has only given me more questions.

The man, Helix, remains on the cave floor. His smile returns as he looks up. Well, he isn't really looking up since he has no sight.

Rather, he is merely tilting his head up as if he is looking at the ceiling of the cave.

"The storm is almost over," he comments.

I glance to the mouth of the cave. Outside, the rain is still falling just as heavily as it was when he first arrived. It doesn't show any sign of stopping or slowing. I'm about to disagree with him when suddenly the rain does begin to slack off. I continue to watch him as he also hears the sudden change in the downpour. His smile is endearing. I am amazed at how white his teeth are. How does somebody that "wanders" stay so clean?

After just a couple of minutes, the deluge has turned into a sprinkle.

"How did you know?" He continues to surprise me. There can't be a logical explanation, only dumb luck, but still, the question escapes me before I realize I have even asked it.

Helix releases a raspy chuckle but doesn't answer me right away. We sit in silence for a while longer, listening to the last of the rain as it makes its way from the leaves of the trees onto the grass below. At this point, I can't tell if it is still raining or if it is just the leaves releasing the water they had been hoarding.

I continue to stare, but then feel guilty. I hate when I receive stares because of my missing eye. Helix, I'm sure, feels the same. So, I take my eye off his blindfold and focus on the tattoos that cover his bald head. The design is intricate and difficult to make out. From what I can see in the firelight, it appears to be several lines that intersect each other with dots that I imagine have significant meanings. Almost like a map. Why would he have a map on the top of his head? More importantly, why would a blind man need a map at all?

"Why are you tattooed?" I ask, summoning a voice of confidence, although I am still leery of him.

Helix releases that throaty chuckle again and shakes his head. This time, he waggles a finger at me.

"Nope. No. I have answered *your* questions. You need to give a little too." His cheeky smile turns into a noticeably fake frown. "How do I know you're not a Howler?" The smile returns, only it seems mostly mischievous. He knows I'm not a Howler.

"I'm not a Howler," I say quietly, slightly amused at his question but trying to suppress a smile.

"Good." He is nodding and smiling thoughtfully. "Good."

"Lukan," I answer, after some time.

"Lukan?"

"That's my name," I reply, still trying to fake confidence. "My name is Lukan."

"Hmmm," the thick groan of pondering again, along with the kind smile, "Well, Lukan. There is no need to be afraid of me. I am harmless."

His words send a chill up my spine for reasons I cannot explain. Although I no longer feel I have any reason to be afraid of him, I doubt very much that he is harmless. I imagine someone or something had a reason to blind him. My only concern is if that someone or something will follow him to me. Or worse, to my community.

The man, Helix, and I sit in silence for several minutes. The rain has ceased, and I have a strong feeling that I should be heading home. However, even with his blindness, I do not feel safe leaving first. I don't want to risk being followed. So, I remain.

The silence becomes thick, and I begin to get nervous. I continue to sit across from Helix, warming myself by the fire he started with almost nothing. Over Helix's shoulders, I can see the darkness begin to creep into the valley outside. I hadn't realized that it was so late in the day. My parents will begin to get worried if I don't come home before dark. More importantly, they will be angry.

Lately, I have had to endure several lengthy lectures about my poor attitude. Most nights involve my parents gushing on Dom and his impressive hunting skills. Next, I am asked when I am going to begin hunting. At which point, I say something snarky, and maybe even a little rude, depending on what kind of day I've had. This results in my mother's feelings getting hurt and my dad coming to her defense. I'm always sorry for my hurtful words as soon as I say them. Even before the lecture on respect begins, I am already punishing myself.

If they would just try to understand my point of view; I will never be a hunter. I can't. Not with only one eye. The more they push the subject, the more I don't even want to try.

As if reading my thoughts, the blind man surprises me with his deep voice.

"Were you hunting when the rain started?"

Always with the hunting. I roll my eye and shake my head in irritation.

I take a deep breath. "Why do you ask? Is that how you measure a man? By his hunting skills?" My frustration is building and, as the words escape my mouth, I realize that I really shouldn't be saying things to this strange man that could antagonize him.

Another deep breath. This time to calm my nerves because I am sure I have provoked him with my response. Surprisingly, he remains unchanged. His smile remains. I am surprised when he lets out another little chuckle.

"Actually, I was asking because I am getting a little hungry. I don't smell any freshly killed game, so I didn't think you were hunting." He pauses to reach behind him, producing a leather bag that I hadn't noticed until now. "I have some fresh squirrel in my bag. I would be happy to cook enough for the both of us." He pulls out three skinned squirrels that are wrapped in cloth.

I am dumbstruck. Part of me feels incredibly guilty for being rude. However, there is another part of me that is still leery of this man.

"You're blind. How are you able to hunt?"

Helix releases that rumbling chuckle again. "I've been blind for most of my life. My other senses have taken over. I no longer need my eyes to hunt." He skewers the squirrels one at a time and holds them over the fire.

"I find that hard to believe," I say incredulously.

"It's true," Helix says, turning the skewered squirrels, cooking them on all sides. "I don't have anyone to be my eyes. So, I have to rely solely on my other senses. They have never failed me."

I consider his words for several long minutes. Although I have already eaten, the aroma of the squirrels cooking over the fire pit is causing my belly to complain needlessly. I decide that I should begin my trek home while he is busy cooking his dinner.

"I need to get home," I say reluctantly.

"Of course. It's getting dark." Once again, I am amazed at his intuition. Before I can ask how he knows, he comments, "I can feel the air cooling off as the night begins to push the day away."

"Right," I say with a tone of doubt that I regret.

"Here. Take a squirrel for your trip, Lukan." He says, handing me a sizzling skewer.

"No, thank you. My mom will have dinner ready when I get home." I immediately regret my words. They make me sound like a weak child.

I make my way towards the mouth of the cave. My emotions are mixed. Although I remain on guard, this strange man has intrigued me to the point that I am sorry to be leaving his presence. I know I will never see him again and the thought makes me sad for reasons I do not understand.

When I reach the exit of the cave, I turn and add, "Thanks for wanting to share your dinner with me."

Helix turns a bit and replies, "You're very welcome. Thank *you* for sharing your cave with me. I am pleased to have met you, Lukan."

I have a hard time walking away. For reasons I cannot explain, I feel it necessary to say, "I'm blind in one eye. That...that's why I don't hunt."

He considers this for a few seconds. "That explains the shuffle."

"Shuffle?" I ask.

"The way you walk. You favor your sightless side slightly. Shuffle your foot a bit when you walk." He flashes the smile that makes his cheeks rise to the point of lifting up his blindfold. When he smiles, his whole face is involved. "I'm sure you don't even realize you are doing it."

He's right. I've never paid attention to how I walk. Now that he mentions it, though, it seems to make sense that I would move that leg cautiously.

Helix turns back towards the fire. Just as I am about to walk away, I hear him say, "If you want to hunt, if you have any desire at all to hunt, then you should, Lukan." Turning towards me again, "Your blind eye does not define you. Your good eye will not fail you."

I'm not sure what to say to this, so I stand there dumbstruck once again.

"Be safe, Lukan," Helix says, turning back to the fire once again.

Chapter 4

The sound of a rooster crowing wakes me up from a restless night. Opening my eye slightly, I can see that the sun has already come up. Strange that nobody decided to wake me up, I consider. I am thankful, however, for the chance to sleep in a bit.

After walking home on a rain soaked trail the night before, I was exhausted. The tall grass seemed to have saved most of the rainwater so that it could be shared with me as I walked through. By the time I reached my house, my pants were waterlogged and my shoes heavy.

My family had been just a bit curious, and somewhat irritated, about my afternoon and evening wanderings. Wanderings. If they knew about Helix, the blind Wanderer, they would most certainly be irritated. I imagine they would feel it necessary to call a town meeting to discuss the implications of a strange traveler so close to the community. The town meeting would get the people of the community riled up for no good reason, causing strife and anxiety for several weeks. For that reason, I kept Helix to myself.

The rooster crows again. I can also hear children laughing and women talking. It seems that everyone else in my neighborhood has begun their day. I guess I should too. Reaching for my eyepatch, I am reminded again of Helix and his grisly wounds where his eyes used to be. The mystifying ways of the peculiar man torment me. Sadness creeps over me as I realize I will never see him again. Surely, a man that considers himself a Wanderer does not remain in one place for long.

A soft knock on the door spurs me into motion. I jump out of bed, covering my eye with the patch at the same time.

"Come in," I say as I pull the bed covers up to my pillow and flatten them out neatly.

My mother is at the door with a smile, "Oh good. You're awake."

Seeing her now, I am reminded that I wasn't able to bring home the flowers as I had planned. Between the rain and my encounter with Helix, my mind had become preoccupied.

"Sorry I slept so late. I meant to be up earlier." I explain.

"No worries. I know you had a restless night." Her emerald eyes are bright this morning. The events from yesterday seem to be a distant memory.

I can't help wondering how my mom knows how little I slept. I know that I tossed and turned a lot in my sleep. Twitching and jerking, my legs felt like they wanted to continue hiking all night. Still, I feel like I managed to get at least a little rest. It certainly wasn't any reason for the rest of my family to be kept awake.

My face must convey my confusion. My mom adds, "You cried out in your sleep again." She has stepped into my room and opened the curtains, allowing the sunlight to shine in warmly. "Was it the same dream of the Howlers?"

I realize that I have no recollection of dreaming at all last night. However, the memory of the night the Howlers took my eye, as well as the lives of my aunt and uncle, haunts me most nights. Her statement doesn't surprise me.

My mind drifts back to the evening shared with Helix. Although he didn't act like any Howler that has ever terrorized my town, he still seemed to share a few of their feral traits. When I left him, I no longer felt fear of him. Surely if he were a Howler, bent on harming me or the community, he and his pack would have attacked early this morning while the town was still groggy from sleep.

When it seems clear that I am not going to answer her question, she comments, "Breakfast will be ready soon," and walks out of my room.

Once she is gone, I change into my worn-out jeans and t-shirt. There are very few original articles of clothing leftover from ninety years ago; from before the virus claimed most of the population. The world had to resort back to a primitive way of life. Most of the clothing now is handmade thanks to some wonderfully talented people in our community.

Twice a year, there is a swap meet in each of the nearby communities. It is a grand event that lasts for several weeks. Citizens of the towns will travel to all the others, trading items that they don't need for the things they do. That is where most of us get our clothing.

Other things are traded as well. Dried meats, fresh meat, vegetables, fruits, furs, furniture, tools. Everything we need can be found at the swap meets. My mom is famous for her dried fruits, herbs, and potpourris. She has been very successful with her trades. Her successful trading is probably why I am still able to wear the ancient clothing from before the devastation of the Langston Virus.

The Langston Virus killed off 96.23% of the human population, 1.78% proved to be immune, 1.99% were killed off by looting and other violent crimes. Those precise numbers are engrained into us beginning in our earliest days of childhood. I will never understand the selfishness of our ancestors. Also baffling to me is the fact that nobody thought to round those numbers up or down. Why so exact? All anyone really needs to know is that a man named Langston was obviously demented. He poisoned the earth, killing off almost the entire human race, leaving the rest to battle the deranged for survival. What the virus didn't kill, the lunatics did.

Our little town, Grayson, is one of many small communities that litter the landscape of what used to be considered the Midwest in America. In the past, boundaries had been set that indicated the different states. State lines are no longer relevant, though. After months of running, not just from the virus, but from those that had even more sinister intentions, a small group found what was left of a community.

All that was left were a few burned down houses, a half-demolished school, and the Community Building. The group had been on the run for too long, had to bury too many loved ones on the side of the road or in the forests. They decided this was as good a place as any to stop and attempt to set up camp.

My thoughts are interrupted by my father's thunderous laughter in the dining room. As I cinch up my moccasins, my belly begins to complain about being empty. I make my way into the dining room and find that my mom has started setting the table. My father and cousin are already seated. As I say, "good morning" to them both, I take my place.

Looking around the table, part of me wishes I had heard what had been so funny, instead of being absorbed in my own thoughts, as I was preparing for my day. Another part of me is relieved that I hadn't heard what I am sure was a gripping hunting story by Dom. All of his stories are all the same, in my opinion.

It was about this time yesterday that I had first heard the Howlers approaching. Closing my eye, I strain to listen for any danger that may be approaching. When I do, a thought occurs to me. What if my ability to perceive sounds from great distances is due to my loss of sight in one eye? Could it be that my sense of hearing has increased to compensate for my inferior eyesight? Helix certainly seems to have gained an edge with his other senses with the loss of his eyes. The possibility intrigues me.

I am caught off guard when I hear my cousin clear his throat in an attempt to get my attention. When I look over at him, he has a plate of scrambled eggs that he is trying to pass to me. I take them and give myself a decent portion. Although I am still fascinated by the idea of my other senses picking up the slack for my one eye, my grumbling belly is demanding to be fed.

As my family and I eat our breakfast, my parents and cousin talk casually among themselves. As usual, I remain quiet. I am aware of their subtle attempts to include me in their conversations, but with my stomach appeased with the hearty breakfast, my mind begins to wander back to the previous evening.

The whole ordeal was so strange. Not just the odd blind man, Helix, but also the fact that he called himself a Wanderer. I have never heard of such a person, but the idea of roaming the world without any defined destination is intriguing to me. If Helix can do it without any sight whatsoever, then surely a one-eyed teenager could too.

"Have you ever met a Wanderer?" I ask my family.

The conversation they were having stops abruptly. I had not been listening, so I have no idea how important it was. They look at me in confusion. It is unlike me to ask questions or prompt discussion. Their eyes narrow with uncertainty. I hadn't considered the unwelcome attention the question would bring me. It seemed pretty straight forward when I asked. Either "yes, I have met a Wanderer" or "no, never have."

Their staring makes me uncomfortable, and I return my attention back to my breakfast. Hopefully, if I pretend I didn't ask the seemingly ridiculous question, then my family will pretend too, and return to their conversation.

My hopes of them forgetting the question are diminished when Dom replies, "What is a Wanderer?"

This wasn't the way I saw this conversation going when it popped in my head. This is also the reason I don't carry a lot of conversations. They rarely go the way I plan. Trying to formulate the right response to my cousin's question, I don't answer right away.

"Lukan?" My mother prompts, obviously curious.

"A Wanderer. Um, a person that doesn't really belong to a community, I guess. So, he just wanders around, living off the land." I explain, trying to come up with the right words that will, hopefully, end the conversation. Shrugging, I return my attention to my breakfast.

"Why would a person not belong to a community? Were they exiled?" Dom asks, once again dashing my hopes.

Taking a deep breath, I answer coarsely, "I don't know. Maybe." The scar under my eyepatch begins to twitch slightly, so I rub at it briefly. "Maybe he just wants to be by himself."

"Well, I have never heard of anyone living like that." My mom says, clearly shaken by the prospect. "Why would anyone want to live alone? I can't imagine."

I feel my head do a combination of nodding and shaking at the same time. *Please let this be over now*, I pray silently. I am partially relieved when my mother and cousin begin to eat again. They are apparently done with this conversation.

My father has been silent during this exchange. He sits to my right, my blind spot, but I can feel his eyes on me, still. "Why do you ask, Lukan? What made you think to ask about Wanderers?" His low voice asks calmly.

My father is a man of reason. He is highly regarded in our community and respected in his home. Still, I'm not convinced that news of a blind man wandering the countryside, dressed in furs, will be received well.

"I dreamed of such a person last night." I lie.

His eyes are still on me. I feel them burning into the right side of my head. The twitching under my eyepatch continues, but I try to ignore it. I just want to finish my meal and find something to do outside.

"That must be why you were so restless in your sleep last night," My mother concludes. "Such a thing is quite concerning, but you have nothing to fear, Lukan. You will never be alone." I look up at her smiling face and can tell she is trying to relieve a fear that I don't carry, but I won't tell her that.

"I'm sure you're right, mom. That is probably why I was so restless," I answer.

Her smile remains, and her green eyes are shimmering. The way they sparkle reminds me of the lake at the bottom of the cliff. For a moment, I consider going there today and getting one last jump in before the water gets too cold. Before I get preoccupied with my cliff-diving plans, I flash her a smile that seems to ease her apprehension about Wanderers.

"Lukan, rest assured. There are no such people as Wanderers. We belong to a community for a reason, son. Safety in numbers. Anyone in their right mind would want to be part of a group." My father explains, matter-of-factly.

I simply nod. What else can I do really? He's wrong, of course, but saying so would only cause an argument.

My cousin and father resume their conversation about hunting as if I had never interrupted them. For once, I am thankful they are talking. I make a mental note never to mention Wanderers again. Or anything unusual, for that matter. The response from my family is proof that they will not accept such things. I hurry to finish my meal so I might escape before I am drug into the dialogue. Once finished, I ask to be excused and make my way to the kitchen.

In the kitchen, I scrape my plate into the compost bucket. As I rinse my plate, I glance out the window above the sink. The children of this neighborhood are kicking a ball in the yard next to ours. Mrs. Hobbs is taking laundry off the clothesline. Mr. Forman is repairing his fence. Normal, everyday life, here in Grayson.

My thoughts are interrupted when Dom approaches the sink where I have been daydreaming.

"You should come with me sometime, cousin." Dom comments. Of course, he is referring to hunting. It is always the same with him. "You wouldn't have to shoot anything. Just being in the forest would do you good."

Nobody realizes how much time I spend in the forest. I take in and let out a deep breath. We have had this discussion too many times.

Turning towards him, I shake my head in exasperation. His brown eyes are soft as they gaze into mine. I know he means well, but the pain of that night seven years ago, when I was unable to save his parents, is more than I can bear. My strength will never match his.

I can't hold his gaze. So many things I want to say but, honestly, they have already been said and haven't ever done any good. This time, I simply walk away.

******

The morning air provides further proof that the warm season is making its exit and fall is nearly upon us. The new season will bring with it, cool nights and frosty mornings, as well as the smell of wood burning in fireplaces and wood stoves for warmth. Most importantly, though, fall means harvest. All the produce is picked, cleaned and stored so that we might survive the harsh winter that comes next.

During the summer and winter months, life seems to slow a bit in Grayson. The summer heat is sometimes too much to bear, making it difficult to get much work done. Winter forces many into their homes, hidden away from the bitter wind and biting snow. These two seasons are often the cause of many quarrels. It seems that even the most warmhearted people are unable to withstand the effects that the heat and cold place on a person's mood.

When spring arrives, the people will begin to emerge from their seclusion. Although everyone is eager to reunite with neighbors and loved ones after being snowbound for several weeks, work must begin immediately. Gardens, crucial to our survival, must be planted. Fruit trees must be pruned back. Damage from snowstorms, repaired. Even relationships, marred by too many weeks of confinement, must be mended.

As we continually move from season to season, time seems to pass too quickly in our post-Langston Virus world. Our days are filled with tasks that lead us to the next task, and then to the next, so that we may survive. I've read stories and heard tales from our most ancient citizens about the ease of life before the catastrophe. Electricity provided power, making the use of human-power nearly obsolete. Our ancestors relied on such things to accommodate their life in such a way that when the calamity hit, those that survived the virus, were taken by death in other ways. They simply were not prepared to live life without the comforts that they had taken for granted.

"Hey, Lukan." I hear a familiar, fluid voice.

In a large tree to my right, is my closest friend, Merritt. I chuckle as I see that she is sitting on the lowest branch, just barely off the ground really. With wide eyes and an open-mouth grin, she is gazing at me with a questioning look as if to ask if I am proud that she at least climbed the tree. Merritt has a tremendous fear of heights. She has scolded me for cliff-diving on numerous occasions.

"Nice climb," I say sarcastically. "That must have taken you some time." I reach out my hand to her. Merritt takes it comfortably and jumps from the tree.

"Sixteen years, actually." She is smiling broadly. She is very proud of her small accomplishment.

I shake my head in fake disapproval. "You should have waited for me. We could have climbed it together. I've told you it's safer to climb in pairs."

"I know you, Lukan. You would have become impatient with me and climbed ahead. Leaving me behind to fall to a certain death." Merritt jokes, her brown eyes beaming with delight.

I glance over at the branch that she had been perched on, "I think my front porch is higher than that branch." I return my attention back to her mesmerizing eyes. "You would have survived the fall."

Merritt giggles and we begin walking together down the street. She talks nonstop about everything she has been doing the past two days. The Howlers visiting, the weather, the quarrel her parents got into, the dreams she had both last night and the night before. Her constant chattering doesn't annoy me, however. Her voice is pleasing and seems to calm my nerves. I listen without interrupting her.

While Merritt talks, we walk. She hasn't asked where we are going. She simply walks along beside me. When we reach the short rock wall, the place where I always cross into the world beyond, I stop and wait for her story to end. It does, eventually, and she looks around.

"What are we doing, Lukan?" Merritt asks, confused. She knows this is my exit from town. Although she has been beyond the walls a few times, she is afraid and has only done so because I asked her to relentlessly. I don't plan on asking her this time. She already climbed a tree today; I won't ask her to watch me jump off a cliff.

"I'm going out," I answer nonchalantly.

"I thought we could read together today. We didn't get to yesterday because of the Howlers and then the twins. When I finished, you were gone." Her eyes are pleading.

"We can read when I get back. I won't be gone long." I glance out across the wall and realize that I hadn't meant to be gone so long yesterday. Of course, I hadn't considered that I would meet a blind man in a cave either.

"I just need to pick some flowers for my mom." It isn't exactly a lie. I do plan on getting the flowers today since I didn't get to yesterday. Merritt doesn't need to know that I also plan on jumping into the blue lake. It would just make her worry. She is eyeing me as if she doesn't believe me. She knows me too well.

"Sprightly ripped up her flower bed yesterday," I explain.

Merritt, along with everyone else in the community, is all too familiar with Sprightly and his tendency to destroy anything that comes into his path.

Merritt nods slightly, and I feel like my half-lie has worked. She backs away from me a few steps and says, "Come find me when you get back so we can read."

I smile and nod. She turns and begins walking back the way we came. I watch for a few seconds before I start to cross the small wall.

I have one leg over the wall when I hear Merritt say loudly, "If you come back all wet, I'm telling your mother you went cliff-diving." Shaking my head, I realize once again that nothing gets past my best friend.

Chapter 5

The chill in the morning air is invigorating, and I feel my speed pick up as I make my way to the cliff. Behind me, in the distance, the sounds of the town are fading. The people of Grayson are beginning their day. Everyone has a job to do. No doubt Dom is preparing for another hunt. He won't have any time for hunting as harvest nears and then winter arrives with a blast of bitterly cold fury.

As I continue on the path, toward the cliff, I continually glance in the direction of the cave where I met the blind man the night before. I can't help wondering where he has wandered off to. So strange to live in isolation, with only the forest to keep you company. Strange, but intriguing.

As much as I would like to return to the cave today, just to see if Helix left any trace of his existence, there is no time. If I'm going to dive today, I must do it early enough that I will be dry before returning home.

The line of trees that seemingly guard the cliff, and the prize below it, come into view. My heart quickens as I begin to prepare myself for the initial leap into the air. Even though I have jumped from the cliff more times than I would ever admit to my family or Merritt, the leap is the most difficult. Once that is accomplished though, the feeling of the wind in my face, taking my breath, is exhilarating. As I plummet and the lake gets closer, I will hold my breath for the surge of cold water that will most certainly try to steal it away when I crash into its peaceful waters.

I enter the tree line at a brisk pace. Exiting just as quickly and with anticipation, I am stopped suddenly by what I see. The cliff is just in front of me with the blue lake below; however, sitting tranquilly in the very spot that I leap from, sits Helix. Seeing him here, I feel both delight and annoyance.

For several minutes, I do not move. I consider whether I should approach or leave Helix here in his solitude. If it is peace and quiet that he desires, then I certainly do not want to interrupt that. As I imagine Helix finding this spot, I can't help but wonder how he didn't simply walk off the cliff in his blindness.

In the daylight, I can see that he is wearing clothes made from hides and other materials. His fur coat, obviously quilted together from several different animals – but not wolf - and a couple of leather pouches lay next to him. More than anything, I am mesmerized by the markings on his head, down the sides of his face and back of his neck. What I couldn't see last night in the cave is revealed to me today. Although I still can't decipher the meaning.

"Lukan, please join me," I hear Helix say in his low voice, startling me from my bewilderment.

I remain planted where I stand next to the tree line. Once again, I am fascinated by the abilities of this blind man.

"Let me guess...you can smell me," I reply, moving toward him.

Laughter erupts from deep in his belly.

"No. Not this time. You came crashing through the trees. I thought I was about to be trampled by a herd of deer." Helix pauses as I sit down next to him. Moving his head in my direction, he adds, "It was that shuffle that told me it was you." A warm smile is spread across his face, revealing extraordinarily white teeth that I hadn't seen in the light of last night's fire.

I can't help but smile back at him. Even though he cannot see me, he seems pleased. He nods his head once with a satisfied grunt and returns his attention back to what I know is only blackness for him. We sit together for several minutes. My mind begins to become cluttered with all the questions I want to ask this strange man that sits next to me. As I glance over at him, I see that he is still smiling slightly. He seems perfectly content to sit in silence, so I keep my questions to myself.

After a while, the silence becomes too much for me, though, and I am ready to dive. "I thought you were a Wanderer." I finally comment. "Why aren't you...wandering?"

Another chuckle from Helix. "I will get back to it. This seemed like a good place to enjoy the sunrise." He tilts his head as if daring me to say something about him being blind and not being able to enjoy the beauty of a sunrise. In the small amount of time I have spent with him, though, I have no doubt that he is well aware of the beauty that is all around him.

Sitting on the cliff with Helix is comfortable. Oddly enough. It doesn't feel as though I just met him the night before. We sit together, for quite some time, in a contented silence. The sun is steadily gaining height in the sky. It brings warmth with it that will be sure to last only a few more weeks. My mind begins to wander, and I imagine diving off the cliff and what Helix's reaction would be to such nonsense.

"What are doing on this cliff, Lukan?" Helix finally asks, breaking the silence.

I contemplate how I will answer this. If Helix was a member of my community, I would be afraid to tell him. Since he isn't, I don't see any harm.

"I came out here to...jump off this cliff." I try to say it bravely, so he won't think it is some mischievous teenage act but rather something to admire. Suddenly, I realize that maybe he thinks I want to kill myself by jumping off a cliff, so I clarify, "Cliff-diving. It's just for fun, really."

"Cliff-diving." Helix considers with his broad smile beaming. "*That* sounds dangerous..." He leans towards me and adds, "...and extremely fun."

Smiling, I nod but then remember that he can't see my head bobbing in agreement, so I say, "It is. There is a lake at the bottom of the cliff. It's deep enough that even jumping from way up here, I have never touched the bottom."

Several more minutes of silence. Not complete silence, of course. The birds are singing their happy song. Tree frogs are complaining to each other about the birds singing. There is a bit of a breeze that blows gently through the pine trees behind us, making the needles whistle. As I take in the sounds around us, I find myself staring at his markings. The more I study them, the more I am convinced they are some sort of map.

That groan that is part of Helix is barely audible but present, all the same. "Are you ever scared when you are diving from this cliff?"

"No, I enjoy it," I answer with a slight shake of my head. "I guess I'm mostly scared that my mom will find out. She wouldn't approve." I try to force a laugh, but the thought of my mother's scolding's for such nonsense makes me nervous.

"I believe you enjoy it, Lukan. There must be some part of it that scares you, though. That really gets your heart beating. What scares you when you are cliff-diving?" With a chuckle and a teasing elbow, Helix adds, "Besides the wrath of your mother."

I think for a minute and then answer honestly, "The leap. That first step is always the scariest."

"Ah, yes. That first step. Taking that first step towards a free fall of unknowns. That is always the scariest thing. But once you do, once you take that first step...that leap, there are no more unknowns. Because after that one step, you are staring at the end result full-on. It's just a matter of getting from the first step, to the goal. What is the goal?"

I feel like he is trying to say something important to me. I'm just not grasping it yet. "The blue lake. The blue lake at the bottom of this cliff is the end result. That's the goal."

A snicker escapes Helix. "That is the goal when cliff-diving. But what if we weren't talking about cliff-diving, Lukan. What would be the goal if we weren't talking about cliff-diving?"

I ponder his question for several long minutes. He quietly allows me this time to consider my answer. My hunch is correct. We aren't talking about cliff-diving. Helix is much wiser than I had first perceived. His last words to me last night were about my inability to hunt. He clearly wants to revisit my insecurities.

Quietly, I admit, "To become a hunter. To provide for my family, my community."

"Lukan."

"Yes?" I answer, curiously.

"That is a good, strong name. Did you know that it was the name of a brave warrior?"

I remain silent.

"It's true. Lukan Augustus was his full name. He was an archer without compare. When he was a young boy, a rival clan stole him away from his family, from his village, after they heard what a successful hunter he was. Forced into his new life, Lukan became the group's primary hunter. The people that had stolen him were brutish but lazy."

"Were they Howlers?"

"No, this was long ago. The Howlers haven't been around that long." Helix answers with a chuckle. "As Lukan grew up with his enemies, hunting for them, providing for them, they didn't realize that he was also in constant communication with his own people. For years, they had been working together to build an army. An army trained by Lukan in the skills of archery. An army set on destroying the rival clan. Oh, Lukan hunted and provided. More importantly, though, he gained the trust of his enemies. With all that he provided, they were unaware of how much he loathed them and what his true plans were."

Admittedly, Helix has my attention. I would expect a story to attempt to inspire me to have the courage to hunt with only one working eye. The story he is telling doesn't seem to be designed for that though.

"The time finally came. The enemy's camp was nestled deep inside a vast forest. The trees were thick all around them giving them the illusion that they were protected. What they hadn't considered, however, was that the trees also provided the enemy cover when planning an ambush. Lukan left to hunt that morning but returned, quietly, with his home clan. The goal was in sight. He picked the perfect day for the attack. You see, the wind was galing that day. Whipping the trees and the tents around wildly. In all the chaos of the howling wind, the enemy didn't hear Lukan, and his army, surround them in the forest."

Helix pauses, but I am eager to hear how the story ends. "And?" I say impatiently. "What happened?"

The smile that is seemingly plastered on Helix's face spreads widely. He is obviously pleased with himself for telling such a captivating story.

"Well, with Lukan's subtle signal, that first step, his army began firing arrows into the camp. Not one shot missed. So, not one survivor left. They defeated their enemy before their enemy could even understand what was happening. It took years of patience, planning, and training. Their perseverance paid off. Their enemy was defeated."

We sit in silence, and I go over the story again and again in my head. I try to pick it apart to understand what significance it has for me. Although I don't know Helix well, I am convinced that everything that comes from his mouth is intentional and full of meaning.

Finally, I comment, "So, was Lukan blind in one eye or suffering from some other sort of disability?"

Helix laughs, "No, nothing like that. I just wanted to tell you a story about a kid named Lukan." He continues to laugh. He gives my shoulder a playful slap.

Looking out over the landscape, I begin to feel silly for thinking that the story was any kind of motivational speech or lesson. I shake my head at my own ignorance. Helix stands slowly, and I worry that he may tumble over the side of the cliff. I jump up quickly. He stretches with a satisfied groan.

"I've become stiff from sitting here so long," Helix comments with a chuckle. He begins to gather his belongings, and I can tell that our time together is over.

Not wanting to see him go just yet, I ask quickly, "What was the signal? Lukan's signal? To start the battle."

"Ah, yes, the signal. He shot one flaming arrow up into the sky. When the rest of his people saw that blazing arrow, they knew it was time. Just one shot started it all...and ended it all."

Helix is walking away, and somehow, even though the story had nothing to do with me, I do feel invigorated. Inspired even.

Oh, something for you just over there behind that rock," Helix says, motioning with a nod of his head toward a large rock a few feet away from where we had been sitting. "Take the first step. Your goal is in sight, Lukan. You just have to leap."

I realize that our conversation has come full circle. We started and ended our time together by talking about cliff-diving. Smiling, I walk to the rock that Helix had indicated. I am shocked at what I see. More importantly, I realize that our conversation was never about cliff-diving at all. There, nestled in between the rocks, Helix has left me a handmade bow and a quiver full of arrows. Looking up to question such a gift, I realize with just a bit of sadness, that Helix is gone. He has resumed his wandering.

Chapter 6

"Lukan, where did you find these?" My mom gushes as I hand her the flowers I picked. Her green eyes shimmer as she fights back tears of joy for receiving such a gift. The moment, for me, is both delightful and awkward at the same time. Smiling, I shrug and try to back away. She will not have it, though. My mom brings me in for a warm embrace, still clinging to her freshly picked purple flowers.

My dad must sense my discomfort at such a display of endearment. He comes to my rescue. "Lue, you better get those flowers in water quickly. They will begin to wither and your time to enjoy them will be short."

Releasing me, my mom thanks me once more before turning to the sink to pump water into an empty jar. My dad gives me a wink.

"Well done, Lukan. It's been too long since your mother received fresh flowers." My father acknowledges. With a wink, he adds, "You're making me look bad, son."

After my mom gets the flowers settled into their jar, she begins to set the table for dinner. I have been gone most of the day, and my empty belly complains loudly about the lack of attention it has received. While I wash up, I can't help but reflect on the events of the past couple of days. The Howlers message about a new leader, Helix, and now a new bow, complete with a quiver full of arrows.

Because my family had such a reaction when I asked about Wanderers, I decided not to bring home my gift from Helix. Instead, I took it to the cave where I first met him. Once inside the cave, I realized that the cave showed no indication that Helix had ever built a fire, or that he was ever there at all. I found a good hiding place for my new treasure and hurriedly rushed back out. Before leaving the area, though, I picked the arrangement of purple flowers for my mom. I was hoping the act would ease her sadness over the loss of her flower garden. Judging by her reaction, I believe it did.

My family gathers around the table and begins to pass the food around. My mother enjoys cooking. It is evident with every meal. Tonight, she has prepared venison chili. She serves buttered bread, still warm from being baked this afternoon. Chili is generally eaten during the cold winter months. Although grateful for the dinner she has prepared for us, we all look at the meal questioningly.

"I'm hoping that preparing the chili will entice fall to arrive earlier," she explains with a smile. Fall is her favorite season. My mother loves the changing colors. To be honest, I do too.

"Not too early, Auntie," Dom remarks. "Our smokehouse isn't quite full yet. I need a few more days of good weather to hunt before the harvest."

Dom knows that once harvest time arrives, everyone in the community, including our great hunter, will be too busy to do anything but tend the garden vegetables. Fall doesn't seem to last long before winter arrives with its biting wind, forcing everyone inside. Dom's hunting days for this year are coming to an end quickly.

"I can help you hunt, Dom." My parents and cousin seem as shocked to hear those words come out of my mouth as I am to have said them. Dom sits across from me, glass to his lips, staring at me over the rim. On my left, my mother squints her eyes as if the glare from the lantern that sits in the middle of the table is too bright for her to comprehend words. My father sits to my right. My blind side. I dare not look at him, but I have no doubt that he is also staring at me.

After what seems like an eternity of everyone staring at me, although I know it has just been seconds, I drop my fork exasperated. "What?" I ask a little too demandingly.

Dom is the first to break the silence. "You want to go hunting?" He asks slowly, finally sitting down the glass that he has been holding to his mouth since my declaration.

"I'm not so sure, Lukan." I didn't expect my father to be contrary about this. It has always been my assumption that he would want his only son to be a hunter. Something to make him proud. His words confuse me.

Sensing my confusion, he adds, "Hunting isn't a game, or something to do because you are bored." He pauses and then continues cautiously, "Or because you are seeking attention."

His statement sets my blood on fire. I've never been one to seek attention. If anything, I have tried my best to stay out of the way. Doing just enough in the community to earn my right to live here without being a burden. My anger is about to boil over into hateful words when my mother speaks up.

"Lukan, your dad isn't implying that you have ever done anything to gain unwanted attention." As she speaks, she glares at my father. He realizes his error and turns his attention back to his food, rather than argue with her. Nobody in the house wants to bear witness to the wrath of Luetta – wife, mother, aunt.

I give her a small smile and then turn my attention to my cousin. The ultimate decision will lie with him since he is the hunting expert of Grayson. He continues to eat. I assume he is also wary of my mother's displeasure.

"Sure, Lukan. I would love to take you hunting. I've wanted to take you since we were boys." Dom's excitement grows with every word. He may, in fact, be sincere about wanting to take me. "You can follow along for a few days. If you find that you like it, we will gather the supplies and then over the winter we will make you a bow and arrows."

I avoid eye contact with my cousin. I dare not betray my secret gift from my secret friend, that is hidden in my secret place, just yet. Better to delay the panic that information will inevitably create.

Although, I do believe Dom will be impressed with the craftsmanship that Helix put into the weapon.

As I laid the bow and quiver in its temporary hiding place, I couldn't help but marvel. Each arrow was exactly the same length, with handsome, stiff feathers for the fletching. I stood in awe, once again, of the capabilities of the blind man.

"What are we to do if the Howlers show up while you are hunting, Lukan? How will we know they are coming? Who will warn us?" My father resorts to another tactic to keep me out of the woods.

I hadn't considered this, and for a minute I wonder if he makes a valid point. When the thought occurs to me that I have actually spent a lot of time outside our walls, supposedly leaving the town unprotected, I nearly blurt the words out. I clamp my mouth shut before any damage is done, though.

"The Howlers won't be back for more than a week from now. The town will be fine, Avis." My mother interjects calmly. "Besides, it shouldn't be up to a 16-year-old boy to keep this town safe. Just like it shouldn't be up to a 16-year-old boy to be the sole hunter of our town." She says this matter-of-factly, between bites of chili.

With that, the matter is decided. No other points can be argued. Mother has spoken, given the look, and returned her attention to her meal. There is nothing more for my dad to say. He glances at Dom and me, obviously conceding. When he returns his attention back to his meal, Dom smiles at me proudly. It's obvious that my cousin is delighted that I will be joining him in the woods.

The rest of the evening is spent making plans. Dom and I will camp at night and hunt during the day. He goes through my closet, only half-full of clothes. He picks out the most suitable items, which are meager, for camping, hiking, and hunting. His eagerness builds until he is almost giddy with excitement. I hadn't realized that my presence, while he hunts, was so important to him. After he gets me all packed up, he shows me his camping bag. It contains all the necessities for an extended time in the wilderness. While his excitement grows, so does my trepidation. My mom busily gathers food for Dom and me. Enough to last three days. Dad pretends like he is disinterested in our plans, but seems to linger wherever we are in the house. The evening also consists of listening to Dom retell many of his favorite hunting stories. I begrudgingly listen before I announce that I should head off to bed if we are to get an early start.

******

Dom and I are up, and on the path that leads out of town, well before daybreak. The light of the full moon illuminates our way. There are lanterns in our packs, but the path is brightly lit. We agree there isn't any need to unpack them just to put them back again when the sun comes up. The air is much crisper this morning than it was even yesterday. Our pace quickens once we are out of town, and I wonder if the pressure of bringing home enough game to last the winter is the cause.

Although we walk the same trail I have traveled countless times, I am just a guest on this expedition. I allow my cousin to take the lead. The tall but withering grass is heavy with dew. If not for the leathers tied over my pant legs, my trousers would certainly be soaked within minutes of stepping into the meadow. I make a mental note to thank Dom for letting me borrow his extra set.

There is very little discussion as we walk. The only sounds are the animals just beginning to wake up, as well as those heading off to bed after a night of hunting. A hoot owl can be heard in the distance saying good morning and good night to the rest of the forest. Once he is comfortably snoozing in his nest, a hawk will surely take his place hunting the meadow for field rats, squirrels, and rabbits.

As we hike, I can barely discern a sliver of the day begin to edge its way over the horizon. Realizing where we are, my mind wanders to the blue lake that lies at the base of the cliff that is just beyond the trees. My eye is fully accustomed to walking in the moonlight, making it possible to barely discern the trees. Which means, just past the trees on the other side of the trail is...

"Hey, Dom." My voice seems loud after walking in silence for so long, and I startle myself.

In the dark, I can see that Dom has stopped and is looking around. I'm not sure if he is looking for the danger that must have made me speak or if he is trying to find me in the dark. His eyes finally settle on me, and I can see annoyance and confusion on his face.

"What?" He whispers harshly. I hadn't realized we were supposed to whisper.

"Um, can we make a slight detour?" I asked, whispering now.

"What? Why?" Dom clearly wasn't expecting to veer from the plan. He glances at me, back at the trail and then me again.

My words fail me. I hadn't thought this through. It takes me a few seconds of stuttering before I finally just take off in the direction of the cave, hoping Dom will follow or stay put until I return with my own weapon. After a few steps, I can hear him following. There will be a lot of questions, but part of me seems almost relieved to be able to share at least a few of my secrets.

The sun is rising quickly now. Although still dark, the darkness has a certain tint of daylight in it. The two seem to be battling for possession of the day. The darkness is sure to concede, allowing the sun her time to shine her warmth across the earth. As the pink hue of morning sneaks further up into the sky, I can see the tree line that hides the caves.

I thought that Dom might begin to ask questions, but he remains silent. He is walking beside me now, glancing around. Once we are on the other side of the trees, the mouth of the cave is in front of us. It beckons to me, and I wonder if Dom feels its pull the way I do.

When I hear Dom suck in a breath, I smile because I know that he does, in fact, feel it.

Smiling, I look over at my cousin. His mouth is wide, but his eyes are full of curiosity and wonder. I nod towards the cave with a gesture of welcome, and we hurry towards it. He sees the remaining purple flowers and realizes that this is where I found the ones that now adorn our dining room table.

At the mouth of the cave, I pause. "Dom, listen, there is something in here that I need for our trip. Please don't ask any questions. You just need to trust me."

Narrowing his eyes at me, trying to comprehend my meaning, he studies my face. I do not move from my spot at the mouth of the cave. Finally, he nods in agreement, and I turn at once to retrieve my weapon.

The bow and quiver of arrows are right where I left them. I hadn't doubted that they would be there but seeing them here, gives me a sense of relief. Not wanting to waste any more of our trip, I snatch up my weapon and go back outside where Dom is patiently waiting. When he sees what I have, his eyes widen. It's obvious that his mind is filled with questions. He honors my request, though, and stifles them all. I can't help wondering how long he will be able to allow them to boil inside before he can no longer contain his curiosity.

Dom's eyes dart from me to the bow and back again. Finally, with a confident look, he nods, gives my shoulder a squeeze and starts back towards the trail. With my new weapon in hand, I can't help but smile as I follow him. Our hunting trip has officially begun.

*****

The excitement I felt when we set out this morning diminished to nothing more than frustration as we trekked through the afternoon and into the evening. Now, as we sit huddled underneath a makeshift canopy of items provided by the forest, listening to the rain and feeling the occasional cold raindrop rolling down my back, my frustration has turned to anger.

Dom's mood seems unchanged by the torrential downpour and cold wind. To pass the time, he ties and unties knots in a short piece of rope, staring out into the gray landscape. He is humming a happy song that does nothing to lift my spirits. Dom sits to my left, giving me the opportunity to glare at him with my good eye.

When my cousin first decided it was time to make camp for the night, after a full day of hiking, I was relieved. My feet were aching, and my stomach was empty. Complaining, I helped him find what we needed to set up a canopy to sleep under. Grumbling, I gathered sticks and dried leaves for a fire. Through all my moaning and groaning, though, Dom patiently instructed me on what to collect and why.

In all my journeys from Grayson, exploring, I felt like I had gone quite far from home. Farther than anyone else, I had assumed. After today's hike, I realize how wrong that assumption has been. At one point, during the hike, I began to feel panicky. My imagination began to run rampant with images of crossing paths with a group of Howlers.

"In all my time out here, I have never seen a Howler," Dom commented when I voiced my concern. "They have no reason to be in the woods."

"Why not?" I asked, curious as to why he would know such seemingly important information about our enemy.

"With the communities providing all their needs, why would they need to waste their energy in the woods?"

His logic made sense and my nerves were somewhat set at ease.

With our temporary shelter in place, and our fire burning steadily, Dom began to prepare our dinner. After a day of eating the dried fruits and meats that my mother had packed for us, I was delighted when Dom pulled smoked rabbits and potatoes out of his pack. The potatoes were tossed into a small pan and placed on a rack over the fire. The rabbits were skewered and set onto a makeshift rotisserie. I sat watching Dom work carefully and meticulously. It became apparent to me that there was far more for me to learn about hunting than could be accomplished in a 3-day trip.

While our food cooked, Dom and I discussed what could be expected over the next couple of days while hunting. He went into detail, the act of scouting and stalking. It seems that there was much Dom had left out of the stories that he told around the table back home. There, he only gave the highlights. Here, he spoke of things like rubs, scrapes, and even dung. Each held valuable information that was vital to a successful hunt. I listened intently, fascinated at how much there was to learn. All this time, I thought that Dom just went out into the woods, saw an animal, released the arrow. There was much more to it than I had ever realized. The more he spoke, the more unease I began to feel. I was starting to feel like I wouldn't be able to be a hunter after all.

"Have you shot that bow yet?" Dom asked as we ate.

When we had retrieved the bow and quiver from the cave, I had asked for no questions. Now that I know a little more about the process of hunting, I can understand why Dom asks. Looking up at him, over the skewered squirrel I am enjoying, I merely shake my head. I hope that the fact that I haven't shot it doesn't give Dom the same sickening feeling that is beginning to creep over me.

"Have you even tried to pull it back?"

Again, I shook my head slowly.

Dom held my gaze for several seconds. I imagine he was starting to realize that his one-eyed cousin was right all along, I am not meant to be a hunter.

Finally, Dom continued, "I know you asked for no questions, but I have to ask..."

"Why?" I blurted out.

"Lukan, bows are custom made to fit its archer. Were your arm length and pull-back strength measured? If you haven't pulled that bow back, then I am assuming the answer is no." His face conveyed worry.

Shaking my head in frustration, I looked down at my food. "This is too much. I'm not a hunter. Never will be."

"You're not a hunter now. You can be though." Dom said with too much confidence in me. It did nothing but grate on my already frazzling nerves.

Looking up at him, I could see that he had returned his attention to his meal. I wanted to tell him of Helix, my friend that gifted me with the bow. However, after the reaction I received when I mentioned it to my family, I decided against it. He wasn't ready for that revelation yet.

"First thing in the morning, we will test out that new bow of yours," Dom said, looking up at me with a smile. I simply gave him a nod, already dreading the morning because I knew that this would be a test I could never pass.

Chapter 7

"This is a fine bow, Lukan," Dom says with a broad, approving smile, as he tests the weapon by pulling it back several times.

Even though I don't know the qualities of a "fine bow," I smile with delight.

Dom hands the bow back to me and picks up the quiver. He examines each arrow and explains the craftsmanship involved with building an arrow that will fly accurately and efficiently. Apparently, my gift from Helix truly is something special. I try to seem humble, but inside I am beaming with pride.

After setting up a primitive target area, Dom demonstrates how to hold the bow, notch an arrow, pull back, aim, and finally release. Each step sounds simple enough, but my arms tire quickly as I practice. Luckily, I didn't lose any of the arrows that Helix made for me. They all hit the target area, just not the center that Dom referred to as the "the kill shot." He is patient as I struggle through the session.

After what seems like several hours, we decide to take a break and hunt small game to help feed us during our trip. My arms tremble with fatigue, but Dom ensures me that he experienced the same thing when he first started. His encouragement gives me hope that maybe I can be considered a hunter someday.

"Dom! Do you see that?" I ask, looking off into the distance as Dom skins the rabbits and squirrels that he successfully snared.

"What?" He remains focused on the task at hand.

"Smoke," I answered, pointing.

Still not looking up, Dom answers with caution in his voice, "I never go that way."

His answer perplexes me. I can't help but question his reasoning. "Why not?"

"Howlers."

"Is that their camp?" Suddenly I understand his caution. A shiver snakes its way up my spine as I consider that we may be in Howler territory.

"Not sure. Like I said, I never go that way. I don't want to chance it. Besides, who else could it be?"

I consider this, "Another community maybe." As I say it though, I realize that it may, in fact, be Helix camping just over the ridge. I don't want to do anything to disturb the solitude that my new friend obviously relishes.

"Not sure," Dom repeats.

"You said the Howlers don't come into the woods. I'm sure it is just another community...or something."

"Probably."

The smoke in the distance seems to have put my cousin on edge, so I decide to drop the subject. I watch in silence as he cleans the animals that will soon be our dinner. He works in silence for a bit longer.

Suddenly, the shifting wind causes me to choke. "Ugh. Something stinks."

Covering his face with his arm, Dom nods. "It's the smoke. It always smells like that. That's why I think it may be Howlers."

"What could they be burning that smells so bad?" I ponder.

"I have no idea," Dom replies, finally looking in the direction of the smoke. "I'm done here. Let's hike back to camp. I don't think we will be able to smell it from there."

I agree with him and help gather our supplies. Before I follow Dom back to camp, I take one last look over my shoulder, at the billowing smoke that carries the rancid odor. Although the unknown makes me anxious, I can't help but feel that the smoke isn't from Howlers or Helix but from something my people have never encountered before. A feeling of dreadful curiosity creeps over me.

*****

"Shhhh!" Dom whispers harshly.

I have lost track of how many times Dom has made that sound at me today. Apparently, even my walking through the forest is too loud for hunting. I give him an apologetic smile that he does not return. He is beginning to lose his patience with me.

To me, it seems that my steps are very quiet. The ground is still wet from the downpour we received last night. Whatever sound I am making as I walk, is terribly aggravating to my cousin.

We have been "stalking" a deer for quite some time. Since daylight, actually. I never saw the deer, but Dom is confident that we are on the trail of a nice sized deer that will be a great addition to the smokehouse and help our community get through the winter.

As we sit behind a log, Dom scans the forest in front of us. In the trees above us, the squirrels are barking in irritation at our presence. Apparently, their barking is also a warning to the rest of the animals because there are none to be seen.

After what seems like hours, Dom turns to me, "I think we should split up."

I may be blind in one eye, but I'm not simple-minded. I realize that I am a tremendous hindrance to the task at hand. This is probably the most important hunting trip of the season, and I am only getting in the way. However, the thought of hunting without him as my guide unnerves me.

My mind begins to swirl through all the scenarios, most of which end in me becoming lost in this vast wilderness and meeting my demise at the hands of Howlers.

Dom interrupts these thoughts, "See that trail over there?"

I look in the direction he is pointing. Without looking back at him, for fear that he will see the anxiety on my face, I simply nod.

"Follow that trail until it reaches a large oak tree that has a curve right above the base." I look back at him and can see that he is indicating the curve with his finger. "You can't miss it."

I nod again, this time looking at him.

"When you get to the tree, take the trail that veers off to the right. That trail is long and winding but will lead you right back over there." He points to a group of trees nearby. "It makes a big loop."

My head continues to bob up and down as I try to pretend that I understand what is expected of me.

"Walk slow, Lukan. The slower, the better because they can hear you but you won't ever know they are nearby."

I shiver as I imagine that he is speaking of Howlers even though I know he is talking about the deer that he is trying to kill to help feed our community.

"As you walk, you will really be pushing them in my direction, and I can get my shot. This is called a 'drive' and is a very efficient way of hunting. I've just never gotten to do it because I never had a partner." He says this last part with a smile and gives my shoulder a pat.

I try to return the smile. I look back at the trail that will lead me away from the only person that knows his way around this part of the forest. When I turn back to voice my concern, I am startled to see that he has already moved into position. The rest is up to me. The burden is almost more than I can bear.

With a deep breath, I finally find the courage to leave my spot behind the log. Gathering my bow and quiver, I make my way to the trail that Dom had indicated. The squirrel that had been complaining about us is now quiet, as are all the birds. The only sound in the forest is the crunching of leaves and fallen twigs under my feet. I am immediately aware of how much noise I make when walking. It takes me several minutes and steps before I find a suitable way to move through the woods. I begin taking each step carefully and methodically and soon find that I can no longer hear my footfalls. It doesn't take long before the woodland creatures reemerge from their hiding places.

By the time I reach the crooked tree that Dom told me about, my legs are burning from the effort of making quiet footsteps. I take a few seconds to take in the sight of the strangely shaped tree before I decide that a brief rest will probably do me some good. As I sit on the ground, leaning against the tree, my belly reminds me that I haven't paid it any attention for several hours. I rustle through my leather bag for some dried fruit.

As I enjoy my much-needed break with some rest, water, and a little snack, I look around the forest that surrounds the large oak tree. It is quite serene, and I find myself relaxing from the stress of the unknowns that surround me. Trying not to think about the fact that I have no idea where I am, I remain focused on the task. Drive the deer to Dom and let him do the rest. Surely that isn't a chore that I can muddle.

Leaning my head against the tree, looking up at the leaves as they tremble in the slight breeze, my mind wanders back to the foul-smelling smoke we had seen in the distance. The odor seemed familiar although I can't quite pinpoint the origin. There seems to be a prickling in the back of my mind that is trying to warn me of something. I shrug it off to my fear of Howlers. Once again, I try to put the smoke and my fears out of my mind by taking in the beauty around me.

I refocus on the crooked tree. The shape of it reminds me of stories that have been passed down from generations before. Stories from the past of a primitive people that roamed this land long before the Langston Virus. Hundreds of years before. These people were known to take young trees, bending them in such a way to serve as a guide as they roamed the wilderness. I imagine these incredibly resourceful people of the past turning this tree into a marker to indicate something important to those who followed behind.

The faint sound of a twig breaking interrupts my imaginings, and I spin around quickly. My breath catches in my throat as I see a large buck strolling towards me from the direction I am supposed to be 'driving' the deer. I wonder briefly why Dom hadn't shot the buck since that is the direction he came from. Surely, he had walked right in front of my cousin, the experienced hunter.

The majestic buck meanders through the forest without any concern. Every once in a while he lowers his nose to the forest floor and sniffs or eats whatever delectable thing is in his path. Always, though, his ears rotate back and forth, listening for any sounds of danger. At one point, he approaches a young tree, sniffs it, and then begins striking it with his massive antlers. Although Dom had described this act to me, I watch the display, dumbfounded. He rubs at the small tree viciously with his antlers for several minutes. When he is satisfied that the now sad looking tree has been appropriately flogged, he backs away and continues searching for food. From my vantage point, it is easy to see the damage done by the buck. A large place on the tree is now bald of bark and glistens in the sunlight.

My heart thuds in my chest and I force myself to focus on the buck. He seems to be headed straight for me, and I am at a loss of what to do as he approaches. I am supposed to be driving him towards Dom.

From the corner of my good eye, I can see my bow as it rests against the tree. It beckons to me as if it is a living thing, ready and willing to be used for its purpose.

With very little confidence that I will be able to hit my target, I reach for the bow. When I do, the buck senses my presence and stiffens. I freeze. For several minutes, the both of us remain in this statue-like position. The deer doesn't move at all. Not even his ever-flinching ears and tail stirs. I also remain stone-still, with my arm still stretching towards my bow. The muscles in my arm begin to burn, and I wonder how long I can stay in this position.

At once, and without warning, the buck jumps to his right and bounds off into the forest. He is racing off in the same direction he had come. Realizing that this is the perfect time for the drive Dom told me about, I grab my weapon and race after the large buck.

As I run, bow in hand and quiver draped across my back with a leather strap, an odd sensation seems to wash over me. My mind goes back to the Native Americans that bent the tree I had just been resting against. Is this how they hunted their food? The pictures that Merritt and I have seen in the ancient books of the past show half-dressed men and women with long black hair. Some of the pictures showed these people, their skin kissed to a rich bronze by the sun, working around their village. Children played around the teepees with mat-haired mutts. Mothers worked diligently on preparing and cooking the food that the men brought home to them. I imagine the native men of this area, racing through the forest as I am now, also with their weapon in hand. The act gives me a distinct sense of freedom and something that I can only describe as nostalgia.

Even though I can't see him anymore, the noise the brute makes as he crashes through the forest is intense. I try to follow the raucous sound, hoping I won't lose his trail and that he will turn towards Dom's direction, giving him the shot he needs. As I think it, though, the buck veers toward the meadow instead of deeper into the woods, where Dom waits. My heart sinks as I realize that I have failed at my first drive.

The buck exits the forest and enters the wide meadow. Abruptly, he stops. Ducking down behind some fallen trees, I hold my breath and pray that he doesn't realize that I followed him. I watch for several minutes, trying to control my heavy breathing. Although the large animal remains on edge, alert at the edge of the meadow, it's evident that his nerves are beginning to settle. With one last wary look over his shoulder, a few more ear rotations to hear what may be coming up behind him, and a couple more tail twitches, the big buck takes a few more tentative steps into the meadow and away from the trail.

I'm torn. My assignment was to drive the deer down the trail and towards my cousin. The buck is close enough that, even though I have only shot my new bow a few times, I feel I can get a good shot off. My only hesitation, besides doubting my own skills, is the reaction I may get from Dom. He is the community hunter. It should be him that takes the shot, not the one-eyed community freak.

For reasons I don't understand, I think of Merritt. In my mind, I see her smiling warmly at me. The thing that strikes me the most, as I remember the beauty of her face, is just that…the beauty of her face. Merritt and I have been best friends since we were young kids. I have never thought of her as beautiful. Fun. Witty. Compassionate. Smart. Those attributes define Merritt to me. I guess she has always been beautiful to me, but for whatever reason, at this moment, I long to look at the beauty of her face.

As the sun shines down on the buck, his majestic antlers gleam over the tall grass of the meadow, interrupting my daydreaming. I push the thought of Merritt to another place in my mind that I will visit later. I refocus on the buck. His worries seem to have faded away as he leisurely nibbles at the grass around his hooves. I continue to watch him, and my hopes of driving him to Dom also fade away. He is slowly meandering his way further into the meadow. Glancing over my shoulder, back at the trail, and then back at the buck that is getting farther away with every second I delay, I finally make the decision that I will do my part for the community and bring him home to the smokehouse.

By the time I decide to take the shot, notch an arrow and bring my bow up, the distance between us seems too great. To make a shot that I am comfortable with, I will have to leave the cover this tree fall provides. I look up and see that the buck is increasing his distance from the forest. All his worries have seemingly disappeared giving him a false sense of safety.

I am not a hunter. However, there is a part of me that is screaming right now. *Let him keep walking!* Two scenarios roll through my mind as I let him keep walking. Either the big buck will simply walk out of my life and I can keep my misjudgment to myself, or the late afternoon sun will be so bright out in the meadow that he won't notice when I move towards him to get a good shot.

I am not a hunter. Everyone knows this.

I choose to let him walk. The farther away he gets from me, the more his red-brown hair shines in the sunlight. I decide to follow. Apparently, the hours I spent learning how to walk slowly on leaves and twigs has paid off because he never acts like he hears me stalking behind him. He continues to stroll and eat, making me think that I might be able to get a good shot off. I follow at a slow pace, crouched low to the ground to try to remain hidden.

When I reach the edge of the woods, I stop. I rest on my knees and pull my bow up. The buck isn't that far in front me. He remains oblivious to my presence. I lower my bow and watch as he raises and lowers his head several times, looking around and nibbling at the ground. This seems like the right time, so I raise my bow with the notched arrow already in it. Taking aim at the spot Dom told me is the "kill shot," I take a deep breath and pull the string and arrow back as one. The buck remains in the same spot. I release my breath and then the string, letting the arrow fly. The arrow finds its mark. I know this because the buck jumps straight up into the air, kicking his back legs out at nothing. He dashes off across the meadow in an instant, and I lose sight of him.

My breath is coming in short gasps. An incredible tremble overcomes my body. I'm not scared. Far from it. The excitement I feel is exactly like how I feel when I am cliff-diving. For a moment, I am reminded of the story Helix told me of the archer that shares my name.

My heart is pumping hard and fast. A strange laugh, something like a nervous giggle, escapes me while at the same time I feel sorrow. I have no doubt that I have just taken a life.

I think I might have closed my eye when I released the arrow. I opened it again just as I watched the arrow penetrate. Blood. Lots of blood. The trembling continues, but I regain my focus and attempt to see which direction the deer went when it bolted away. It couldn't have gone far after losing so much blood.

Taking a few deep breaths to calm my nerves and return to the task at hand, I stand up and make my way to where the buck was standing when I made my shot. He must have been farther out in the meadow than I had realized when aiming because I seem to walk forever before finally finding a pool of blood. There are a couple of mature trees in this part of the meadow. I find my arrow, now soaked in blood, at the base of one of them.

As soon as I see the evidence of a clean shot, I gasp and cover my mouth. I've done it. I actually hit something on my first hunting trip.

Now to find it. I know it cannot be considered a successful hunt until the meat is hanging in the smokehouse for my community to enjoy. The nervous giggle returns. Reining in my emotions once more, I begin to follow the blood trail. I've heard Dom tell stories about trailing wounded animals. He spoke of the wide range of emotions that haunted him until he would find the animal finally surrendered to its wounds. I know that my hunting trip is far from over.

Chapter 8

Blood droplets glisten in the late-summer afternoon sun. With each step, I am both hopeful and anxious. Hopeful that I will find the buck, dead, with the next step; anxious when I don't. I begin to doubt the shot. Begin to fear that maybe I just wounded the brute and will never find him.

Stopping, I look around. I'm surprised at how far into the meadow I have gone while tracking the deer. I begin to wonder if I should make my way back to Dom, who is oblivious to the events that have transpired in the past couple of hours. Hopefully, he won't worry and will simply go back to the campsite. If I don't find the buck soon, that's where I will go. By then, the sun will be setting.

Just as I decide to resume the search, a larger pool of blood catches my attention. My heart, which had slowed to a reasonable pace, quickens again at the thought of finally finding my quarry. The grass is extremely thick in this area, and I nearly give up the quest when, finally, a large lifeless shape catches my eye.

I know immediately that I have found him. It's obvious, even from this distance, that he's dead. The sight of his once magnificent body, now lying lifeless, causes me to pause. Even in death, he is still magnificent. I am seemingly frozen where I stand, half-expecting the buck to jump up and run off. I am fully aware, though, that he will never reign over the forest again.

I have taken his life.

As I begin to fully comprehend what I have done, I slowly approach the lifeless animal. Slowly, I lower myself down to the ground next to him. Respectfully placing both hands on his still-warm body, I close my eye and say a sincere "thank you" to the buck for his sacrifice. I assure him and the forest that what is being provided to my community will always be greatly appreciated.

*****

Cresting the hill, I can see that the sun is setting quickly. I concede to the fact that I will not make it back to the camp before nightfall. Thankfully, the skies are clear, and I needn't worry about another torrential downpour dampening my mood. Looking down at the buck, I can't help but feel pride.

Now I understand. All the times Dom told his stories, I could never grasp why he was so enchanted by the endeavor of hunting. Now that I am reliving each moment of the hunt, my heart still thumping with excitement, I understand.

I imagine what it will be like when I return home with this prize. Hopefully, my parents will be proud of their son and his first kill. Proud that I am able to provide meat for the community.

My arm aches with the effort of dragging the beast back to camp. Switching arms to get a better grip on the blood-sticky antlers, I notice something odd out of the corner of my eye. The setting sun, blazing pink and purple, is shining not only from the sky above but also glinting from the ground. Between blades of grass, I can see traces of pink and purple reflecting.

It almost looks as if...

But it can't be...

Releasing the antler, allowing the buck's head to fall, I shake out my arms that have become stiff from dragging the beast. Looking down at my bloody hands, I realize how badly I need to find a creek. They remain sticky and red with the blood of the old buck. I walk over to the area that intrigues me and squat to the ground to inspect the oddity further.

Squatting over the area that now also holds my reflection, a gasp escapes me as I realize that my first notion was correct. For reasons I cannot comprehend, a window is hidden in the grass. Not hidden really, because it is much too large to be concealed. Somehow, though, while hunting and then tracking the buck, I had missed the window. As I study the area, it becomes apparent that the buck had been standing on the window when my arrow founds its mark. Splatters of blood remain on the window, just past where the grass ends.

Standing to my feet, I take in the sight. The window appears to be made of something stronger than any of the glass windows in town. It isn't large. Probably the size of the double doors that are at the front of the community building. Dirt smears, leaves and other bits of debris are scattered across it.

To my right, I can see a blood-smeared trail cross the corner of the window. I must have drug the buck across this area. It would have been in my blind spot, which would explain why I hadn't noticed it. Now, though, I am mesmerized by it.

Concentrating more on the window, trying to see past the brilliant sunset reflection, as well as the disheveled one-eyed boy that stare back at me, I can barely discern that there is a room below me. Placing my hands on the window to brace myself I quickly realize that I need to use one to shield my eye from the rapidly setting sun.

The room is pretty unextraordinary. Small, dark, lots of pipes. One door. Although the room is dark, illuminated only by the setting sun, I can discern that there is a blanket lying on the floor. The scene both confuses and intrigues me. A window in the middle of the meadow is odd enough; however, the blanket that is obviously well-used, lying on the floor in a room full of pipes is beyond explanation. Could there actually be somebody living beneath the ground?

In the distance, I can hear my cousin. He is shouting my name. His voice sounds concerned with just a bit of annoyance mixed in. Understandable. It's been hours since I left his side and took off to drive the deer towards him. I'm sure he is wondering where I've been all day.

After the conversation I had with my family about Wanderers, I don't think they would be open to the idea of another world under our feet. I want to get far from this spot before responding to Dom's shouts. Returning my attention to the buck, I grasp his antler once more. With one final look at the window, now reflecting a purple hue as the sun bids the landscape goodnight, I make a silent promise to myself to return soon and inspect it further.

Dragging the large animal once more, I see Dom at the edge of the woods. I beckon to him with a shout and a wave. He is relieved and somewhat perturbed when he sees me. Mostly, though, I think he is relieved. He would not want to receive my mother's fury if anything were to happen to me on my first hunting trip.

Wanting to surprise my cousin with my first kill, I drop the beast once more and approach Dom. As I get closer, I can see that his hunt was rewarding, as well. He has also killed a buck. My thoughts go to my parents and how thrilled they will be that both of their boys had a successful hunt. Surely, with what is already in the smokehouse, the community will have enough food for the winter.

"Dom! Nice job!" I commend as I approach.

Dom glances at his kill and then looks back at me, "Where have you been?" There is a hint of irritation in his voice. "I've been looking for you for hours. I had to field dress this animal myself."

I consider his words for a second, "Don't you usually field dress the animals you take by yourself?"

Dom takes an exasperated breath and then lets it out slowly, "Yes, but I wanted to show you how to do it. It's part of hunting, Lukan."

Smiling, I acknowledge, "I have something to show you, cousin." Walking away, I don't wait to see if he follows.

I can hear his footsteps behind me in the tall grass, and it reminds me of how irritated he was earlier today when my footsteps were too loud. Stopping just short of my prize, I turn to Dom and then motion for him to look ahead. He hesitantly walks forward. When Dom sees what I have killed his jaw drops and his eyes widen.

I can't help but beam when he looks back at me. He doesn't say anything, but it's obvious that he is shocked that I killed something on my first hunting trip. I thought he would be happy, but his body language says otherwise. Although he is certainly surprised, he also seems perturbed. His mouth is now shut, and his eyes seem almost defeated.

"I found the crooked tree and was eating a snack. He walked in on me. Surprised me, really. I waited for him to go in your direction so I could do the drive the way you told me." Dom just stares at the buck while I explain myself. "When he started heading off into the field, I decided to go after him." I pause, waiting for any sign that he might be listening. He continues to stare at the buck, blank-faced. "He gave me a good shot, so I took it." I begin to think maybe he is slightly jealous because the buck I killed is much bigger than his. "I thought you would want me to take the shot. You know, for the community."

Dom finally looks up at me, "Yes. Of course, for the community." He stumbles over his words as if he has just come out of a trance. "You did good, Lukan. Really."

"Thanks, Dom." I return. "I had a good teacher," I add with a smile.

He returns my smile, although weakly. "How did you know to field dress it?"

"You talk about hunting all the time." I chuckle. "Although it might not seem like it, I've been listening."

"You did good," Dom repeats, but his voice sounds distant.

I try hard to determine what could cause such strange behavior but nothing comes to mind. As Dom stares at the buck, I stare at Dom.

Finally, he says, "Let's head home. We have more than enough meat."

I nod as Dom walks back to his buck. Dragging our spoils, we make our way out of the meadow and into the already dark forest. Although still curious about Dom's reaction, I can't help but be elated with my success.

One last look at the meadow. I feel drawn to the window; trying to imagine what or who could be living under us. I consider telling Dom about it but decide it is best to keep it to myself. My consolation is knowing that I will return to this place in a few days to investigate the window further.

Chapter 9

After spending another night in the forest, we arrived back in Grayson with our spoils. We were delighted to be able to add to the smoke house which now holds enough meat to last our community for the winter. The trip back home was uneventful. However, the exhaustion from the ordeal weighed heavily on us.

When Dom and I got back to our camp the night before, we had the arduous task of skinning out the deer, removing the antlers, and quartering up the meat that would be stored in the smokehouse. Every bit of the deer will be reused for another purpose. The hide will be turned into jackets, shoes, pouches. The antlers will be repurposed into hairbrushes, knives, or other utensils. Every part has another purpose for man that it didn't have for the deer. We waste nothing.

With that job behind us, we gathered material from the forest and made a gurney to make carrying our spoils much easier. Dom knew exactly what to do and how to make it. He commented several times that he was glad that he would have help carrying it all out. Usually, he is forced to carry one end and let the other end drag, slowing his pace tremendously.

"We'll be home for lunch," Dom commented happily as we had begun our hike home. His mood showed significant improvement since the night before.

Dom showed me how to package everything up tightly and then fasten it to the two long tree limbs that he said would be perfect for this task. I did as he showed me and soon we were ready to head home.

Dom was right. We were back in Grayson before lunch. I was tired and ready to eat a warm meal at home, but there was still plenty to do before that could happen. It took us some time, after arriving in town, to distribute all our goods. The meat went to the smokehouse.

The skin went to the tanner. When we dropped the antlers off with Mr. Edwards, he beamed with pride and gave me a congratulatory slap on the shoulder. He promised to make something special for me since it was my first kill. The extra attention made me uncomfortable, especially when I noticed how Dom reacted. His face conveyed something I had never seen from him upon returning from a successful hunt. I attribute his mood to the exhaustion he must feel.

We received several greetings and congratulations as we walked the street to our home. The news of our successful hunt had spread quickly. Waving, smiling, and thanking those that congratulated us, we continued home. Both of us were ready to eat and get some rest.

"Well, you don't look any different now that you're a hunter," a familiar voice teases from our right. When I look in that direction, I see Merritt standing in the community orchard. She holds a basket filled with the peaches the orchard provides. Even though she is feigning disgust, a smile flirts with the corners of her mouth. With one hand on her hip, she continues, "But you sure do smell different." She fans her face and makes an exaggerated face of disapproval as if a terrible odor just blew her way.

When I see her standing there, the thoughts I had of her while hunting come rushing back. For the first time, while looking at her, I am struck by her beauty. Her brown hair which hints a red hue when the sun shines on it just right has thick, bouncy curls that I feel like I have never noticed before. Or perhaps I have noticed.

I have to look away as I feel my face begin to blush. When I do, my eye goes straight to Dom. He is staring at me with curious eyes and raised eyebrows. My face indeed blushes as I begin to think that maybe he has read my thoughts.

"You must have taught him well, Domenic." Merritt acknowledges. Only my parents and I call him Dom.

I return my attention to her as Dom replies, "Really didn't have to teach him anything. He's a natural." To me, he says, "See you at home, Lukan. I'll tell Auntie you'll be along shortly." I nod, and he begins to walk off.

"See you later, Domenic. Congratulations." Merritt calls after him.

"Thanks, Merritt."

I watch him walk away, wondering about the emptiness in his voice. Merritt saves me from my worry, though, "That's a nice bow you have there, Lukan."

In all the excitement of my first kill, on my first hunt, I had forgotten that I would have some explaining to do about the bow. Attempting to distract her, I ask what she has been doing while I was away. Her face conveys that she suspects that I am changing the subject, but she goes along with it. We have known each other since we were little, Merritt knows me well enough to realize that she will get another chance to get the scoop on my new toy.

Although I would love nothing more than to be in Merritt's presence for the rest of the afternoon, my belly complains loud enough that even she can hear it.

With a grin, Merritt says, "You better go eat lunch." She begins to walk away. She looks over her shoulder and adds, "Get some rest and then come tell me all about your first hunting trip."

I watch her walk away and wonder why my thoughts are far from appeasing my grumbling belly or getting rest. No. My thoughts are on Merritt and the way she ran her hand through her hair when the breeze blew it into her face slightly causing the faint shades of red to shine through. These thoughts are strange and almost disturbing to me even while being pleasant and warming. With a huff, I try to shake them from my head and finish walking home.

*****

As my family and I sat down for dinner on the night that the community's hunter and his apprentice returned home from a successful hunt, I wondered if my parents could feel the tension in the air as heavily as I felt it. Dom was hesitant to retell the story of killing his buck and seemed to focus on his food with an unusual intensity while I told my story. My parents listened as I recounted the whole trip for them but appeared to look around the table nervously.

By the time I had reached my home this afternoon after talking with Merritt, Dom had already eaten his lunch. He spent the rest of the day catching up on his chores and resting. My dad had been out all afternoon, but my mother was home when I arrived. She met me at the door, gathering me into her open arms with a loving embrace and a squeal of delight. I allowed her motherly affection until the embarrassment of so much attention became too much and then I gave her an, "Ok. Ok, mom." She quickly released me from the bear hug but still held me by the shoulders as she looked into my face with pride. It seemed like joyful tears were threatening which added to my discomfort. Still, I couldn't help but smile at her tenderness.

"Don't tell me anything," my mother instructed with fake sternness. Her smile returned, "Wait until your dad gets home and tell both of us at the same time."

A nervous chuckle escaped me. This feeling of importance is unfamiliar to me. I felt my head do an awkward nod/shake combination as I grinned with embarrassment. Although exhaustion seemed to be trailing me, my empty belly was in control. My weary legs carried me to the dining room. I was delighted to see that my mother had already set a plate of delicious smelling food at my place. I had thought that the food would refuel me like it did out in the woods. That was not the case though. When I finished eating, I felt even more tired. My mom was in the kitchen when I walked in to rinse off the empty plate.

"You look beat, Lukan. A twenty-minute nap would do you good."

I thought about this for a minute, "What about my chores?"

"They will be here when you are rested up." She said with a smile.

I considered her suggestion and realized that I would be much better suited for the rest of the day with just a little bit of rest. With a tired smile, I thanked her for the meal and went to my room to lay down.

Two hours later, I reemerged from what could be considered the best sleep of my life. Although groggy, my body felt refreshed and ready to tackle my chores. I put my eyepatch on and then my moccasins. My mind went back to seeing Merritt, and how she fanned her face at the stench I had brought back from the forest. My mom would question a bath this time of day, so I decided against it and simply changed into clean clothes instead.

The rest of the afternoon was filled with doing chores that had been left uncompleted while I was away, as well as helping my elderly neighbors do theirs. Each one wanted to hear the story of my first hunt. At first, I was embarrassed. After recounting it for the fourth time, though, it had become much easier.

When I returned home that evening, the clean clothes I had put on were now dingy from working with Mr. Fisher's lambs and helping Ms. Mills pull the last weeds of the season from her garden. I had hoped to see Merritt while I was still clean, but once I became dirty again, I prayed that I wouldn't. This thought baffled me. I have never cared how I look to her. For that matter, I've never cared how she looked. Honestly, she has always been full of beauty and grace. Not only her hair, eyes, lips, and the subtle crease between her nostrils. There was more to her beauty than that, for sure. Merritt had an inner beauty that was reflected in the way she cared for others.

"Dom, the question of the night is," My thoughts of Merritt are interrupted by my father. I look up from my dinner to see him smiling warmly at my cousin. Everyone at the table waits to hear what the 'question of the night' is. With a chuckle, my dad continues, "Did you see the buck you have been stalking? The big old fella that has been so elusive."

An awkward silence descends upon our dinner table. Both of my parents look at my cousin, waiting for an answer. Knowing what we killed for the community, I return my attention to the food on my plate. His reply takes longer than it should, and I look up at him once more.

Without looking up, Dom answers, "I did, Uncle."

This answer surprises me. It seems like Dom would have told me if he had seen it. "Really? When? Where was it?" For once, I am happy to be able to join in on the conversation.

Dom looks up at me now, "He's in the smokehouse. You shot him." His face is a mixture of sadness and defeat.

With this revelation, his odd behavior is explained. Dom has been after the old buck for months. He has worked hard, scouting and stalking. After all this time, he takes his one-eyed cousin on a hunting trip, and his chance of getting the buck is lost forever. Naturally, he is disappointed to have lost that opportunity.

The happiness I felt earlier is now replaced with regret. I struggle to find the words to convey my sorrow. It seems like all I can do is shake my head, moving my mouth in an effort to prime the words from my throat.

My mom must sense my struggle and attempts to come to my aid, "Dom, of course Lukan would not have known. You can't blame him."

Dom glances at my mother and, with a sad smile, says, "I know, Auntie. I know. It's just… I don't know..." He lets out a deep sigh and returns to his meal.

"Domenic, the animals of the forest are meant to be used for the good of the community. Not for the sake of our vanity, but for the interests of survival. You must remember that. That buck was meant for the community, no matter who took it." My father explains with stern, yet compassionate, eyes. Looking at me now, he adds, "You will do well to remember this too, Lukan, now that you are going to be hunting for the community."

This last statement catches me slightly off guard. I hadn't considered that I would be expected to start hunting for the community. Somehow, I feel like being able to bring something home from my first trip had little to do with skill. A tremendous weight seems to settle between my shoulder blades as I contemplate the magnitude of providing for the people of Grayson.

Chapter 10

The next few days pass quickly. It seems that harvest time crept up on Grayson just in the couple of days Dom and I were gone hunting. Now, with the smokehouse full of meat provided by the forest, the community can focus on gathering up the fruits and vegetables. Not only is this time of year busy because of the harvest, but this is also when the men begin making plans for any repairs that need to be done before winter arrives. Women take the winter clothes from storage and check for any mending that needs to be done. There will be a swap meet soon which also requires preparations.

Dom didn't have time to hold onto his sour mood. There was too much to do. The leaves on the trees had gone from green to red, reminding us that there is no time for self-pity. As I thought about this, I wondered if that is what my family thought of me in the years that followed the night that I lost my eye.

I had spent much of my life hating myself for letting my aunt and uncle get killed. If I hadn't attempted to shoot the gun, and then lost my eye as a result, they most likely wouldn't have been distracted by my screams of pain. All the years that I sat at the table, loathing Dom and his hunting stories, I blamed my insolence on the fact that I was handicapped. Now, I am beginning to think that maybe having only one eye isn't as much of a disability as the guilt I have been carrying for the night the Howlers attacked.

The sounds of another day beginning coax me from my bed. I've been lying awake for quite some time, letting my mind wander where it wants before I begin my day. I shake the thought of Howlers from my head, and another memory returns to take its place.

'If you want to hunt, if you have any desire at all to hunt, then you should, Lukan. Your blind eye does not define you. Your good eye will not fail you.'

The words Helix spoke to me on that rainy night I met him in the cave, return to me now. The memory makes me smile. At the same time, I wish I knew where Helix was so that I could tell him that not only did my good eye not fail me, neither did the bow he made. He would enjoy hearing about the buck walking in on me, and then me attempting to stalk it. I believe every aspect of the story would amuse him, even finding a window in the field.

The window!

With so much to do, I hadn't given any more thought to the window. I hadn't talked to my family or even Merritt about it. I told myself I wasn't going to. Not only because I didn't think they would believe me, but also because I didn't want them to worry about what it could mean. Now that it has crossed my mind again, I decide that I should probably go back and investigate it further.

It will take me most of the day to get back to it. The trip will most likely require that I camp overnight. In order to leave town overnight, I will have to come up with a reason they will believe. The explanation eludes me, though, as I stand in my room looking around as if it may be hiding in one of the dimly lit corners.

"Lukan. Breakfast." Dom beckons me from the other side of the door.

I decide to give this matter more thought with a full belly. Within a few seconds, I am seated at the table with my family. My mother has prepared another delicious breakfast for her men. There isn't much talking as we indulge in the bacon, eggs, and fried potatoes.

As our bellies begin to fill, the conversation about our plans for the day begins. For the last few days, I have been making my way through this end of the community asking what each citizen needs, in order to prepare them for winter. Dom did the same thing at the other end of town. There are roofs that need to be repaired, fences that need to be mended, trees that need branches removed before any possible ice storms bring them down onto nearby homes. With this list, several of the men will coordinate and assist however needed. We discuss the needs as we finish eating.

My mother brings up a need that is out of the ordinary, though. "Mrs. Clifton needs some supplies. She is running low on a few of the plants she uses to make the medicines." My father, cousin, and I look at her curiously. This is an odd request.

Mrs. Clifton is our town doctor. Just like the doctor before her, she relies on the healing powers found in herbs and plants. Before the Langston Virus, medicines were engineered in laboratories. When the virus killed the majority of the human population, those that survived resorted to the primitive ways of the Native Americans. Without medications, built by people to help sustain them, those with specific knowledge turned to the earth.

Redstem as an inflammatory. Mint for rashes. Devil's Nettle to aid in blood clotting. Colic Root for, well, colic. Catbrier for arthritis. Just a few examples.

Mrs. Clifton has never asked anyone to retrieve these things for her. She has always done it herself. None of us would know what these plants even look like.

Looking up from her meal, my mother explains, "Her ankle is badly sprained, or she would go get them herself. Lukan, I told her you would help her."

"I don't know which plants she needs." I retort.

"Well, I told her about the lovely flowers you had brought me. She said that what she needs would be close by that area probably. Or by a water source. I think that's what she said."

This is it! The believable excuse was just given to me by my own mother. I almost smile at the thought of it. Of course, I can retrieve the needed plants. I would check the cave and by the blue lake, retrieving the plants, and then make camp close to where I shot the buck. I will be able to spend the next morning investigating the window further before returning home with the medicinal plants Mrs. Clifton needs.

Without trying to sound too eager, I shrug and say, "I can go back to where I found your flowers and see if what she is looking for is there. If it isn't, I have a couple of other places in mind where I can look." Looking over at my mother, I see that she is smiling and nodding. Obviously proud that her son will be the one to bring medicine to the community.

What comes next may erase her smile, though. I return my attention to the food left on my plate and try to say the words nonchalantly. "It might take me a couple of days, though. I will probably have to camp one night. Maybe two." I worry my family can hear the excitement in my voice.

I look up in time to see my parents exchange a questioning look. Without using words, they are asking each other if they are comfortable with their one-eyed son camping outside the walls alone. My mother frowns. My father purses his lips, shrugs, and nods.

"I believe you've proven yourself in the forest, Lukan." When my dad says this, I think of all the dangerous things I have done beyond the walls that my family doesn't know about.

"You should take your bow." Dom comments without looking my way. "You should never leave the walls without a weapon."

Although I never leave home without my knife, I agree that taking my bow along will be wise. The thought of going back out and investigating the window causes me to rush through the rest of my meal. After washing my plate off in the kitchen, I thank my mother for the meal and head to my room to pack. Through all of this, my imagination runs wild with possibilities of who or what is living beneath our feet.

*****

It took me longer to get to the window than I had anticipated. I took too much time at the caves. The plants that Mrs. Clifton needs were easy enough to find but they were in such abundance that I spent several hours carefully digging them up and preparing them to be transported. I had always thought that all the greenery in the forest looked the same. Whenever I started looking for something specific, though, I could see the distinct differences in each plant.

Mrs. Clifton had been surprised and delighted when I showed up on her doorstep with my pack and announced that I would be going to fetch her medicine. She took the time to show me pictures of each plant from a book that looked very much like an antique. While our town's sweet doctor described each plant to me, it was evident the respect she held for the medicinal powers they provide. With a hug and extra food for my journey, Mrs. Clifton thanked me and bid me good luck on my quest.

When I arrived at the caves, I couldn't help but smile as I hurriedly but carefully gathered as many of the plants as I could find. It seemed that Colic Root and Devil's Nettle were in abundance in that area. I smiled as I thought that I would be able to collect these plants anytime I visit the caves, now that I know what I am looking for. Our town will never run low again. I didn't want to diminish the supply. When I had two sacks filled; I decided to head toward the window. I knew I could search for the other plants as I hiked.

When I crossed the short rock wall in search of the medicinal plants, I was just a little worried that I wouldn't be able to find my way back to the trail that Dom and I had used when hunting. However, once I was beyond the caves, the trail beckoned to me. It laid ahead of me like a carpet revealing the way to my quarry.

Since I wasn't in stalking mode, it didn't take me long to arrive at the spot where Dom and I had camped the first night of our hunting trip. The sun was high in the sky and shimmered through the leaves of the tall trees. I considered stopping in this spot for a quick lunch, but the excitement of getting to the window spurred me forward on the path.

As I hiked the trail, the memories from just a few days ago come rushing back to me. I reached the log that Dom and I had hidden behind before he sent me off to attempt a 'drive.' The sun was beginning to set, and the air was cooling rapidly. I decided to make camp in this spot for the night.

The crackling of the campfire that burns in front of me now is warm and comforting. After a full day of hiking, my body is tired and welcomes the warmth it provides. Although still uncertain, and a little uneasy, about what the window holds, I find a strange comfort knowing that it isn't far from here. I will be able to spend time tomorrow investigating it. Leaning against the log that Dom and I had used as a deer blind just a few days ago, I let my mind wander with the possibilities.

"May I share your fire, Lukan?" the throaty voice I recognize as belonging to Helix asks from the darkness.

The first time I heard this voice, I had been afraid of the man I now consider my friend. I smile now as I realize how delighted I am that I will be able to tell him about my first hunting trip. The fact that, even in his blindness, Helix knows who is sitting at this campfire baffles me.

"What was it this time, Helix?" I ask in amazement. "I'm sitting so it can't be the shuffle when I walk. I imagine I smell like the woods since I have been part of them all day."

The groan and chuckle that I am accustomed to resonate from deep inside Helix as he appears from the tree line. With his guide stick clicking on the ground in front of him, he makes his way to the campfire with ease. I briefly worry that he might walk into the fire. Quickly, I realize that my fears are unnecessary. Helix, even in his blindness, is much better suited for the forest than I am.

"To be honest, I didn't know it was you. I was just hoping it was you," Helix explains, still chuckling.

This statement astonishes me. "What if I had been a Howler?" I ask, horrified at the thought of what a Howler would do to the blind man.

With his hands, Helix finds the log and sits next to me. I notice that his smile has diminished slightly. "There are no Howlers in this area. They don't come this way."

I consider his words as Helix removes his coonskin cap. I can't help ask, "What do you mean? They don't come into the forest?"

"They don't come into *this* forest." Helix answers in his usual grumble.

His answer only leaves me with more questions. I don't want to annoy him, but I can't help but ask, "*This* forest? What's wrong with this forest?"

Helix doesn't answer right away. I can hear his customary groan growing from deep in his belly as he contemplates the best way to answer me. His pause causes a chill to crawl up my spine.

Finally, just when I am beginning to think he will not answer at all, he does.

"The voices."

The chill in my spine turns to a shiver as I wait for Helix to elaborate. When I look at him again, the kind smile that I thought was a permanent fixture on his face is now gone. Something dark and brooding has replaced it. I've heard people say that the eyes are the windows to the soul. As I sit here now, looking at the man with no eyes, I realize how true this statement is. I feel lost without the ability to read his mood by not being able to look into his eyes.

I decide to change the subject. If Helix, the Wanderer, stays around, I'm sure I can broach the subject of "the voices" again.

"What are you doing out here, anyway, Helix?" I ask as I poke the fire with a stick.

His smile returns and he groans his answer, "Wandering."

Nodding, even though he can't see me, I smile at his answer. "Of course." I chuckle.

Helix chuckles too, and I'm glad to be able to sit by the fire feeling comfortable with my new friend.

A thought occurs to me, "Oh, by the way, thank you so much for the bow." I say, remembering that I never had a chance to thank him.

His smile grows. "You're very welcome. I hope you have many happy hunting trips with it."

"I already have. My cousin and I just returned from a hunting trip a few days ago. I got a buck on my first trip."

Helix releases a booming laugh and gives my shoulder an affectionate slap. "Very good, Lukan! Very good. I knew you would be a fantastic hunter."

The rest of the evening is spent recanting the tale of my first hunting trip. Helix wanted to know every detail. I was happy to tell him the story. Although I gladly relayed the details of the day, I decided to leave out part of the story. The window. I want Helix to see me as strong and competent. I don't want him to doubt my sanity.

As the night wears on and weariness begins to creep up on me, I make the decision to wake earlier than Helix and make my way to the window. I don't want to explain where I'm going or why.

*****

I wake before the sun.

Expecting to wake to cold ashes in the fire pit, I am pleasantly surprised to find the fire stoked and burning warmly. Helix must have stoked it early this morning to keep it going. As I wipe the sleep from my eye, I look around to thank Helix for the warm fire. My blind friend and his meager belongings are gone. A strange feeling of sadness returns as I fear I may not see him again. The feeling quickly subsides when I realize that it seems like Helix is always popping up when I least expect him.

Not wanting to traipse through the forest in the dark, and not wanting to waste a perfectly good fire, I pack up my campsite slowly and eat the breakfast my mother packed for me. Although the warmth of the fire is relaxing, I feel myself becoming anxious as I think of what Helix said the night before. I ponder his words, "the voices." What could he have meant by that? What are "the voices" Helix spoke of, and what is the real reason the Howlers don't come into this forest?

The sunrise begins flashing pink and peach through the leaves of the tree, telling me I should get going. I'm eager to explore the area around the strangely placed window at the edge of the woods. I also need time to gather more medicinal plants for Mrs. Clifton before heading home.

To ensure that it will not spread to the surrounding forest, I cover the fire with dirt. Before I leave the area, I look back to ensure I have left no trace of my overnight visit. Satisfied, I begin my hike to the window.

The forest somehow feels different to me now. I cannot explain the feeling, but it's almost as if I am part of it. I can't help but wonder if it's because I killed the buck. The words Dom said to me that night, after the successful hunt, replay through my head.

As he showed me how to cut out and cook the backstrap of the deer, he explained, "It's the most tender part of the deer," Dom explained. "This is the only part of the deer you want to keep for yourself."

The thought gave me an instant feeling of guilt. "But we hunt for the good of the community," I recounted.

"We do," Dom acknowledged, "and they will get the rest. The backstrap, though," he continued, holding up the slab of meat, "is a gift."

"Gift?"

Dom nodded, "Yes. A gift from the forest for the respect you showed to its creatures. A gift from the deer for outwitting it in its natural habitat. A gift from the earth for doing your part to ensure the survival of your community."

I have been consuming venison since I was a child. I have been exploring the forest since I could walk. Now, though, the world feels different to me. I feel almost…dauntless. Like the forest is part of me now and I am part of it. My steps are more confident. My ears are more attuned to the sounds around me. Standing on the trail, I close my eye and take in a deep breath. Breathing deeply, the smells around me.

The wind shifts and my tranquil moment is interrupted by the horrid odor Dom and I encountered a few days earlier. At the time, Dom was obviously uneasy about the source. He didn't know anything about it and didn't seem at all curious. I, on the other hand, will not be able to think of anything else until I learn more about it. I make the decision to investigate the foul smoke once I learn more about the window.

I continue on the trail and eventually come to the edge of the woods. Although it remains hidden, I know the window is through the grass just up ahead. I peek through the trees and scan the grassland. The meadow is empty of any dangers, it seems. In the sky, a hawk shrieks as it begins its hunt. Although I cannot see them, I know that there are rabbits and mice that are scurrying through the grass.

Leaving the canopy of the trees, I walk into the field. The window, reflecting the morning sun, beckons me from the grass. Looking down on it, I also see my reflection, as well as the trees behind me. It's difficult to see the room below, so I squat down and shield my eye.

When I first found the window, several days ago, the room had been empty except for a well-used blanket that laid in the middle of it. Today, though, something else is in the chamber. I am astonished to see that lying on the blanket, is a drawing.

A sketch.

I had come here hoping to find evidence of life underground. This sketch is that evidence. People are living inside the earth. It must be some sort of compound, I imagine. How far does it go? Could it also be underneath Grayson?

I return my attention to the sketch on the blanket. Leaning closer, I try to discern what the drawing is. A nervous laugh escapes me as the image becomes clearer to me.

A buck.

More questions fill my already boggled mind.

Does the image of the buck mean that the person that drew it saw me with my kill? Somebody must have seen when I shot the buck. Why else would they try to communicate with me using the image?

Why are they trying to communicate at all?

I decide that the why isn't important right now. The why will be revealed later, I'm sure. Right now, I need to continue the conversation as best as I can. Looking around, I try to come up with a method of communication. Not knowing if the person can read or write, I decide to continue in the primitive method we have already established.

Taking an arrow from my quiver, I lay it on the window. Not just any arrow. Since the person below seems to have knowledge of my hunt, I leave the arrow that killed the buck. It is still covered in his blood. Dom had warned me not to clean it.

"Washing away the blood of your prey will seem like you are ungrateful for what the forest has given you. Keep it as evidence of what you have accomplished." He had said.

It seemed a bit superstitious to me, but I didn't argue. Leaving the bloody arrow now doesn't seem the same as washing away the evidence of the buck that gave his life for the community. Besides, I reason in my mind, I will come back for it after I'm sure the person below my feet has seen it.

Standing back up, I stare into the window. I try to imagine the person who left the sketch and what they must have thought witnessing the buck being shot. They must think I am a monster. I hope I get the chance to explain.

The wind picks back up, and I am struck with the horrendous smell once more. The odor is so pungent that I am forced to cover my mouth and nose with my arm. I decide that now is as good a time as any to find the source of the stench.

When Dom and I had been hunting, I had noticed the smoke before the stench reached us. Today, the odor seems thick, but I haven't seen any smoke. I try to remember where we had been the day we saw the smoke in the distance. I decide that my best course of action is to go back to where we had camped on that first night and then follow the trail. I consider that the odor may actually be Howlers, but my curiosity is greater than my concerns. With one last look at the window, I walk away with just a tiny amount of dread at what I may find.

As I retrace my steps on the hiking trail, my mind wanders chaotically between the window, Howlers, Helix, putrid smoke, hunting, and Merritt. They all fight for position in my head while I scan the horizon.

The window had been the most perplexing. Now, however, the window really isn't all that puzzling to me anymore. The person that left the sketch has taken the place of the window in the category of "strange things I have witnessed in the woods." My mind can't seem to find a reasonable answer as to why a person (or people, perhaps) would be living underground. Did the Howlers drive them into the earth?

At the thought of Howlers, I begin to get anxious as I think of them returning in the next few days with their new Alpha. The scariest thing about them getting a new leader is the unknown. With their last leader, it took time, but we learned what to expect from him. We all knew to keep our eyes averted, to walk behind him, and never to speak unless spoken to. Any of those actions would result in serious, sometimes fatal, consequences. It is highly unlikely that their new Alpha will be any less maniacal than an of the leaders of the past.

The trail seems familiar now. Even after only hiking it a few times, I travel the path with ease. I am surprised by how much I wish to go hunting again. The day of my first hunt replays in my head giving me a sense of longing. Every aspect, from stalking in the morning until indulging in backstrap that night, is a cherished memory.

Squirrels bark at me as I walk the trail that they feel is meant only for the animals of the forest. Perhaps they are right. When the Langston Virus flooded the world with death, the forests seemingly reawakened from a long hibernation. As humans became scarce, the creatures of the forests reclaimed their lands. They rebuilt their homes and retook their natural habitat. While the human race was sent back to the primitive life of our earliest ancestors, the animals thrived.

While I walk and let my mind wander, I happen to catch something out of the corner of my eye. Looking down, I realize that not only did the animals thrive, but the plants did too. On both sides of the trail, and scattered throughout the forest around, the plants that bring the healing powers Mrs. Clifton sent me after are growing in abundance. I smile as I think of how pleased she will be with what I have found.

I get to work immediately collecting the plants. The stench in the air is thick, and I find myself holding my breath and requiring frequent breaks. As a brief escape, I hold the plants up to my nose, relishing the rich aroma of the earth around me. With my mind temporarily distracted with the lush carpet of greenery that will bring wellness to my community, I am startled to look up and see Helix standing just off the trail. Not surprised, really. He has a way of appearing when I least expect it. It's almost as if he emerges from the earth with the sole purpose of keeping me guessing.

"I'm starting to think you are following me, Helix," I say, with a smile, as I return to my work. I know there is no need to tell him where I am in the forest. His keen sense of hearing will lead him straight to where I am working.

"Lukan," Helix acknowledges with gladness in his voice. "What are you doing in this part of the forest?"

I consider how to answer his question. He already knows that my trip is based on finding and collecting the plants for Mrs. Clifton. I had told him that when he surprised me at my campfire. I wonder what his response would be if I told him that, even though I am doing what I came out here to do, I am also on a mission to determine the source of the sour smelling smoke. Mulling it over in my mind briefly, I realize that Helix is most likely well aware of the stench on the horizon. Not only is he gifted with a keen sense of hearing, but his sense of smell is also acute. I have no doubt that he has experienced the odor just as I have.

"At the moment, I am digging up some Devil's Nettle for our town doctor," I answer while I work. "When I finish, I will be in search of the origin of the foul odor that is making it difficult to breathe without gagging."

As I suspected, Helix has also been assaulted by the foulness. When I look up again, he has a piece of fabric wrapped around his face, covering not only his damaged eye sockets but also his mouth and nose. I take in the sight with a slight feeling of unease. The scene really is quite strange. The broad, bronze-skinned man, with his tattooed head and neck, wrapped up in a quilt of animal furs, with his entire face covered with fabric. Even though I know he cannot see me, I try not to stare.

"It is an obnoxious smell, isn't it?" Helix asks behind his makeshift mask as he walks towards me.

"I think it is coming from smoke," I comment. Finished with the digging, I stand to gather the linens I need to wrap the plants up for transporting.

"Smoke?" Helix inquires with a throaty groan.

Placing the linen-wrapped plants in my pack, I explain. "I saw smoke when my cousin and I were hunting. As soon as we saw the smoke, the horrible odor hit us."

Helix is thoughtful. He is silent except for the growl that comes from his belly. Standing, with my pack draped across my back now, I wait patiently for him to sort through his thoughts. After some time, the silence becomes awkward.

Just as I am about to bid Helix farewell, he seemingly resurfaces from his deep thoughts, and surprises me by asking, "Mind if I tag along with you, Lukan?"

My first thought is one of selfishness, and I immediately feel guilty. Although I enjoy time spent with Helix, I fear he will slow down my trek to the smoke. As I run through all the reasons why he shouldn't tag along, he surprises me once again by seeming to know my thoughts.

"I can follow the sound of your footsteps," Helix comments. "You don't have to worry about being slowed because of my blindness."

The guilt weighs heavier. I shake my head in disgust with myself. Helix has shown me nothing but kindness. He crafted a bow for me without even knowing if I could use it. I repay him by trying to shun him? I am ashamed of myself.

"Of course, you can tag along," I reply, hoping Helix doesn't pick up on the regret in my voice. "I would really enjoy your company."

Helix grunts his thanks, and we set off to find out what has corrupted the air in the forest. Walking along the game trail, I try to make my footsteps loud so to help Helix stay on track. I glance over my shoulder often, to check on his progress. Of course, I am only slightly surprised to see that his steps do not falter as he follows me.

We walk for some time when the deep rumble of Helix's voice interrupts the sounds of the forest. "Did you know that long before the Langston Virus, men used to ride horses to get where they needed to go? Wouldn't it be nice if we had a couple right now?" He asks with a chuckle.

The question surprises me. Although I have never seen a horse, there are pictures in the Community Building of horses grazing in meadows. As a child, I had asked what the majestic animals were. My mom explained that they were "wild horses that used to live freely in the wilderness." A dark look of sorrow crossed her face, and I dropped the subject without asking the questions that coursed through my mind.

I wonder if Helix will be as sorrowful if I asked him the questions I was unable to ask my mother. I decide that if he didn't want to talk about horses, then he wouldn't have brought up the subject.

111 | P a g e

"What happened to all the horses? I've never seen a real one. Only pictures."

Behind me, on the trail, I can hear Helix's thoughtful groan before he answers, "Howlers."

His reply is simple but leaves me with more questions. As I walk, I wait patiently for him to elaborate. When he doesn't, I prod, "Howlers?"

"The Howlers felt that they couldn't keep control over the communities and towns if the people were able to travel freely back and forth on horseback. In order to remain in authority, every community, every town, was bombarded with Howlers on a mission. A mission to take the horses." Helix pauses and I assume the subject has depressed him and he doesn't want to discuss it further. He surprises me when he continues, "For a few years, the Howlers used the stolen horses to travel to the towns. They could easily ride into town, create mayhem, and then simply ride away. After a while, though, fewer of the Howlers were riding horses. Most were walking again. Until eventually, no more horses."

"What happened?" I ask, reluctant for Helix to speak the answer that was scratching at the back of my mind.

"They ate them." Helix answers with sadness in his voice.

Although not surprised by his answer, I am disturbed by the thought of it. I want to ask more, but I also don't want to irritate my new friend with my curiosity. With an abundance of cattle, pigs, poultry, and forest animals, why would Howlers choose to eat such magnificent creatures?

We walk on in silence, both of us lost in our own thoughts. The silence is comfortable, and I find the sound of our footsteps comforting after hearing such an unsettling story.

"That is repulsive," Helix comments from behind me. I turn to see what he is talking about. He places his arm over his already covered mouth and nose.

I must have gotten used to the odor. Just as I am about to say that I can't smell it, it hits me. Nauseating, yet sweet. Fighting the bile back down into my gut, I cover my face.

"We're close," Helix acknowledges. Although he cannot see me, I nod in agreement.

I look around and see that we are near the edge of the woods. Beyond the trees, I can see a clearing.

"There's a field ahead. Do you want to continue or do you think it's the Howlers?" I say the last part in almost a whisper.

Helix is shaking his head. "No," He groans. "Whatever is causing that stench is not a Howler."

The way he says it sends a chill up my spine. I am reminded of what he said the night before about the Howlers avoiding this forest. I make a mental note to ask him more about that statement later.

"Well, then, if you want to continue, let's go find out what stinks so bad," I reply.

Helix nods his response, and I head towards the meadow. Helix follows. Even though he seems confident that Howlers do not visit these woods, I am not convinced. I try to keep my footsteps just loud enough that Helix can follow easily.

The sight I am met with when we exit the woods and enter the meadow is perplexing. Before I can describe it to Helix, I try to understand what I am seeing.

Helix gives me time to wrap my head around the scene and find my words. Eventually, he says, "Lukan?"

I shake the fog out of my head and answer with a stutter, "There is a pipe sticking out of the ground. It looks to be made of some sort of thick metal. Covered in rust. It is as tall as a tree. Smoke is coming from the top of it." My words are muffled as I bury my mouth and nose into the crook of my arm in an attempt to stifle the horrid stench that seems to be pumping from the ground.

Beside me, Helix is also trying to stifle the musky stink. It's too much though. The smell is so thick and rich. Almost like it can be tasted. I can barely hear him groan as he tries to process what I just described to him.

"Helix," I say as the realization hits me. "This is a chimney."

Most of the homes in Grayson have fireplaces, so I am familiar with a chimneys purpose. However, the chimneys in Grayson have never radiated such foullness.

"Whatever they are burning down there, it definitely isn't wood." I ponder aloud.

"'They'?" Helix asks. I immediately realize that I will have some explaining to do. For a blind man, he never misses anything.

I try to think of how to explain my wording when I decide just to come out with it. "I believe there are people living beneath the ground," The words sound crazy when I hear myself saying them out loud. I shake my head in defeat.

Expecting Helix to laugh at me, I am surprised when he replies, "There *are* people living underground, Lukan." His voice is low and deep, lacking the lighthearted softness that I'm used to. "And that smell is the odor of death going up in smoke."

His revelation is much more startling than mine, and I can't help but stare at him. His face is unchanging. Turning, he begins to walk back the way we came from.

"It would be wise for us to leave this place." He doesn't sound anxious, but his voice does carry a hint of concern.

I trust his instincts. After one last look at the oddly placed chimney in the meadow, I join him on the trail. The placement of the chimney is as strange as that of the window. I have a suspicion that the two are linked even though they are quite a distance away from each other.

Because I'm still not sure that the chimney doesn't belong to the Howlers, I wait until we are some distance from the meadow before speaking. When I do, I ask Helix quietly, "What do you mean? How do you know there are people living underground?"

Helix doesn't stop walking, and I am surprised that he is able to stay on the trail without me leading him. With each step, he taps his staff on the ground. The sound of it adds to the eeriness that has fallen over the forest. For several minutes, Helix is silent as he makes his way down the trail with sure steps. I give him time but grow increasingly impatient with each step.

I pass Helix so that he doesn't have to work so hard to stay on the trail. After some time of hiking and hearing Helix striking the ground with his staff, I realize that the only sounds I hear are my own footsteps. Turning, I see that Helix has stopped and is standing on the trail, motionless. Slightly alarmed, I quietly walk back towards him. His face is still covered with the cloth to filter out the putrid odor, and his head is slightly tilted. It's almost as if he is in a trance and a cold shiver begins to snake its way up my spine.

"Helix?" My voice sounds shakier than I intended.

"Do you hear it, Lukan?" Helix whispers, raising my anxiety level even more.

Standing in front of him, I look in all directions but remain silent, listening for whatever sound Helix is hearing. I hear nothing. My greatest fear, while being away from home, is that the Howlers will show up in Grayson and I won't be there to warn them of the impending danger. My mind races back to Helix's story of the Howlers stealing and eating all the horses in this region. The cold shiver grips me and turns into an anxious tremble as I look around the forest.

Still, I hear nothing.

"Voices," Helix says almost in a hiss.

Chapter 11

Helix sits, brooding, as flames spit and crackle in front of him. The night has turned much cooler than expected, and we are relishing the heat provided by the campfire. Our journey away from the oddly placed chimney in the meadow, although uneventful, was brisk and ripe with apprehension. I never heard the voices Helix spoke of. At times, it seemed like I was hearing footsteps approaching us from behind but after looking over my shoulder several times, I decided it was just my antsy imagination getting the better of me.

Sitting next to Helix now, I glance at him repeatedly. His words have been few since he spoke that one word, "voices." There was an edge of haunting in his whisper. When I asked him if he was hungry, he grunted with a nod. Same thing when I asked if the fire was warm enough for him. I notice that every so often, he will turn his head this way or that. It's almost as if he is listening to, or for, something. My nerves remain on edge as the only sounds I hear are those of the nighttime forest animals and Helix's occasional groan.

The ordeal almost becomes too much for me to endure. I contemplate returning home tonight to escape the madness that seems to have taken over the forest and my friend. As I organize the possible excuses I can use to leave, I am interrupted.

"Do you ever feel as if the weight of this environment we live in is too much?" Helix asks in a quiet, sorrowful voice. "Do you feel like maybe it is a thing? Predatory? Digesting us through fear and intimidation?"

I stare at him, narrowing my eye as if to help me understand his question or more important, the reason for the question. This question is unlike him. I get the feeling that, in his blindness, he is able to see into the secret hiding places where I store my fears. I am well aware of his acute senses but is it possible that he is keen to the emotional well-being of those around him also?

117 | P a g e

Nodding at first, I whisper a meek, "Yes."

Helix grows silent again, and my nerves are nearly undone as his cryptic words play over in my mind. I do not take my eye off him.

"Helix, what's going on?" I finally ask.

"The ones underground," Helix begins wearily. "They are living life below us just as we are above them. Work. School. Relationships. Surviving. Possibly even thriving."

I consider his words. They are the words I have wanted to hear since I found the window in the meadow. Before I expose my secrets though, I want to find out what Helix knows.

"The voices?" I ask.

Helix nods with a grunt. "I hear them sometimes. Not loud, of course. I don't think anyone else can hear them. You couldn't."

"But you said the Howlers don't come into this forest because of the voices," I comment. "So, they must be able to hear them, somehow."

"I don't think so anymore. I used to. Today when you couldn't hear them, I realized that I had been wrong. After finding the chimney, I believe the Howlers stay away because of the smell of death."

The noises of the night seem to become louder and more ominous. An owl hoots nearby and then embarks on a hunting trip. Somewhere in the darkness, raccoons are playing and making a raucous. Meanwhile, a tremble has overtaken my body. The campfire, although still hot, gives me no comfort.

"The voices and sounds I heard coming from the ground near the chimney were wretched, Lukan. Full of affliction and misery." His voice cracks as he recalls. "I fear that our underground neighbors may be enduring oppression more monstrous than the Howlers."

I consider his words and how to proceed with this new information. "There is a window in the ground," I say with great hesitation.
117 | P a g e

Helix's head twitches slightly in my direction. "Window?"

"Yes. It's above a small room. Not far from here. I accidentally found it during my hunting trip."

"Did you see anyone on the other side of it?" His voice is getting more excited.

'No. Nobody was there. Just a blanket on the floor." I hesitate briefly and allow him time to absorb what I've said before I add the next part. "I went back to it earlier today. There was something new." I try to judge his reaction. Helix waits for me to continue. "A drawing of a buck. It was just laying on the blanket below the window."

Thoughtfully, Helix leans back against the log. He ponders my words. I can't help but wonder if he is going to chastise me for being a foolish teenager.

Finally, he says, "Interesting." He draws the word out slowly in his low voice. "It appears that someone below us is attempting to open the lines of communication."

I'm nodding in agreement, even though he cannot see me. This was my thinking also.

"Would you mind taking me to the window?" Helix asks.

Considering his blindness, I can't help wonder what he thinks he will be able to ascertain from the scene but I agree to take him. "Sure. We can go first thing in the morning. After that, I have to head home, though. The community is waiting for these plants, and I'm sure my family is worried."

"Of course," Helix replies. "It's dark right now, isn't it?" He chuckles at himself for becoming overly eager.

I chuckle. "Yeah, a little." I imagine it would be somewhat unsettling not knowing if it is daylight or dark. Helix chuckles too, and the sound of his booming laugh sets me at ease.

*****

"Would you mind being my eyes, Lukan? Describe what you see." Helix requests as we approach the window. As we leave the crunchy leaves of the forest behind us and enter the much quieter meadow, I offer my arm to assist him through the taller grass. He graciously accepts my help.

"The window is just a little further. The grass, although withering with the approach of the new season, is still thick. There are a few pine trees nearby that I believe shade the window during the heat of the day."

We have approached the edge of the window. From this vantage point, I can see into the small room that is lit brightly by the morning sun. What I see below me robs me of my words.

"Lukan? What is it? What do you see?" Helix asks. I hadn't realized that I had dropped my arm from his grasp. He stands awkwardly, waiting for an explanation.

"Something new," I answer, with a grin.

Helix takes a stiff step forward, and I return my arm to help him. "What do you see?" He repeats.

"I think it's a name."

"A name?"

"Yes. Written on parchment. 'L-I-A'." I explain, still trying to understand it myself.

There is a pondering groan coming from deep inside Helix's chest as he considers what I'm telling him. "Lia."

"What does it mean?" I wonder aloud.

"I think it means that somebody named Lia is trying to communicate with you. Perhaps you have found a friend in the underground."

I kneel down on the window and Helix follows suit. I watch as he gingerly touches the thick glass with his large bronze hands.

"What should we do? This seems important." I acknowledge as I realize the significance of what I'm seeing. "This could be a safe place for us, Helix. This could be our fortress from the Howlers." My voice becomes slightly squeaky with the excitement that is building. "Do you hear voices right now? Here?"

Helix is quiet for several seconds before he answers with a groan. "No. No voices." He pauses before he continues. "I don't believe it is the safe haven you wish it to be, Lukan. I'm sorry. My fear is that the room that is below this window is somehow connected to the death chimney."

His words shatter my hopes but also cause a vibration of fear to pulse through me. I don't want to believe that the person leaving these simple messages is a part of the horror of the chimney. For whatever reason, I feel the person on the other side of the window, living life underground, has an important message.

"I'm going to write my name as an answer," I declare, looking around for something to use. I settle on the earth, wet with dew, as my answer. Digging my fingers into the moist ground, I get a substantial amount of mud and return to the window. Just as I am about to write my name in the middle of the window, Helix puts his hand on my arm.

"Wait, Lukan," Helix says calmly. "When your friend below looks up at your name, it will be difficult to read."

"I can make it look plain enough," I counter.

"Of that, I am sure. However, you will need to write it backward. If not, from below it will read, N-A-K-U-L."

I ponder this for a few seconds, trying to imagine what words written correctly on this side of the window would look like from the other side of the window. I determine that Helix is correct and write my name backward. The act is rather awkward as I write each letter backward. Once completed, the word I have written looks unnatural and I shake my head.

Suddenly, Helix stands up. Looking up at him, I can see that his face is etched with alarm.

"What is it? What's wrong?" I ask.

"I believe you are in danger." Helix tilts his head. After spending time with my blind friend, I have confidence in his acute sense of hearing. I give him the time he needs to discern the danger.

Closing my eye to block out any distraction, I listen intently for any sounds of impending danger. I hear nothing but the birds and bugs of the forest.

"Is it Howlers?"

Helix nods. "They are far, but I fear for you, being away from home, Lukan." Helix remains calm, but his grumbly voice is thick with concern. "You must go now."

"I don't want to leave you out here without any protection, Helix. Besides, you said they don't come into this part of the forest." I counter.

"They aren't heading to the forest, Lukan. I believe they are headed towards your home."

Helix's words strike me like a knife. Grayson is most vulnerable when I am away. They have no warning in my absence. Although my hearing is not nearly as keen as Helix, I am able to give the community at least a small advantage over the madmen that terrorize us.

Without another word, or glance back, I grab my bow and race away. Tree branches and briars strike out at me as I crash through the forest. I am barely aware of the squirrels that bark at me when I rush by them on the trail. I try to calculate how long it will take me to get back to Grayson at this pace. All the while, praying that I reach my community before the Howlers. While I run, I am constantly battling images of horror in my head as I imagine what will happen if the Howlers arrive before I can warn the people that have counted on me for so long. The boys of our town will be playing in the streets or sitting in their homes as their mothers go over their lessons with them. All will be vulnerable to the assault of the Howlers. These thoughts spur me forward with more determination.

After running for what seems like just minutes, I am surprised when I break through the tree line and find that I almost to the caves. Stopping, I listen for any sounds that will tell me if I am too late to warn the people of Grayson of the approaching threat. My heart is thundering in my chest. With my eye closed, bent over with my hands on my knees gulping air, I begin to discern the familiar sounds of chaos and destruction.

In the distance, but much closer than I had hoped, the Howlers are approaching loudly. They chant and howl. Although they are much too far for me to determine their location, it is evident they are headed straight for Grayson.

No time for rest. I speed off towards home to begin the task of alerting the citizens of what is coming their way. The tall grass, still slightly wet with dew, lashes at my pants. Grayson comes into view, and I can clearly hear children playing, mothers chattering and men tinkering. Roosters continue to crow, and the lambs are bawling for their mothers. Everything seems to be as it should be in Grayson.

Everything is about to change.

Chapter 12

"Howlers!" I shout the alarm as I jump the short rock wall into town.

There is usually a method to sounding the alarm. These extreme circumstances require the process be altered. Typically, I start at the other end of the road. Today is anything but typical. When the fine folks at the town entrance see me and hear my cry, while delighted that I have made it home safely, they are quite surprised by my abrupt entrance.

"Lukan, welcome ba-," Mr. Lee begins.

"Howlers! Spread the word quickly!" I cut him off without stopping or slowing down. I make a mental note to apologize later for my rudeness.

As I continue to run down the street toward my home, I can hear Mr. Lee shouting the warning to all those nearby. I am home within a minute and leaping onto my front porch. Crashing through the door, my mom looks up from her mending, in alarm. Her lovely face flashes a brief smile of relief before being replaced by dread.

"Dom!" My mother beckons my cousin without taking her eyes off me.

Dom is instantly at her side. She is still staring at me while she puts away her needle and threads. Dom follows her eyes and realizes that I'm standing at the door breathless. I simply nod, and he immediately understands what is happening. Dom grabs his bow and quiver and is gone in an instant, off to warn the rest of the town and usher the boys into their safe places.

My mother approaches, already trembling. I attempt to comfort her with a hug, but there is still much of the town that needs to be warned.

"How close?" she asks, and then adds, "Your father is already at the Community Building with some other men. We felt like the Howlers would be back soon with their new Alpha."

"I'm not sure. I've been running for quite a while." I answer, still trying to catch my breath. "Prepare the house and then wait for me. I'm going to see how much time we have."

My mother gives me a quick nod and an attempt at a confident smile. I turn quickly towards the door and go back through town, retracing my footsteps. The street is quiet now as I run toward the entrance of town. Mr. Lee did an excellent job relaying the message for me.

Arriving at the entrance to Grayson, I crawl up the small hill to get a better vantage point. I can hear the maniacs hollering and howling, but they are still too far away to see. That gives Grayson a little time to prepare and me time to catch my breath.

"Rumor around town is you brought guests back with you," I hear the familiar fluid voice of Merritt say from behind me.

I turn towards her and see that she isn't cowering like I am. As I remain hunkered down low, she stands tall, looking across the meadow. She is full of confidence that I wish I could equal. Her warm smile calms my nerves a bit.

"Everyone else is running away and hiding from the howling," I remark. "Not you, though. You run towards the danger." I turn my attention back towards the direction the Howlers are approaching. "Why is that?"

Merritt joins me in a position of stealth. "Because that's where you are. Facing the danger," she says quietly, causing my heart to thump chaotically. I try to shake off the involuntary reaction I have when she is around.

Merritt is on my good eye side. In my peripheral, I can see her scanning the expansive meadow. The breeze, barely able to be felt, plays with the dark curls of her hair. The reflection of the earth in her brown eyes reveals tiny green flecks that I have never noticed before. At this moment, when I should be scouting the enemies approach, I find myself mesmerized by Merritt.

Oddly, I feel the incredible urge to relinquish all my secrets to her at this very moment. My strange new friend, Helix. The window, and the strange communication it has produced. I want to spare her the image of the chimney, though. Merritt is too flawless to be blemished with thoughts of death billowing from the ground.

As I open my mouth to speak, the howling becomes louder. Although still out of sight, the vast number of Howlers approaching is loud enough that they can be heard. They sound frenzied, which makes my skin crawl. I look over at Merritt and realize that she is staring at me with wide eyes. Her confidence has wavered a bit.

"They're getting close," I say, attempting to keep the fear from voice. "There are more of them than usual."

"I hear them," she says in a nervous whisper.

Even though the Howlers are still beyond our view, Merritt and I back away from our vantage point in a crouch and make our way back into town.

"I feel pretty lucky to be seen walking with the most popular guy in Grayson, you know?" Merritt says with a smirk that is all her own. "I just hope you don't forget about me with all the love you are sure to get from your admirers." She winks at me and grins.

"Popular? I wouldn't say that at all." I retort. "I'm just the one-eyed kid that can hear just a little bit better than everyone else. What makes you think I am so popular all of a sudden?"

"Well, first you added to the smokehouse, and then you brought back medicine." She answers with a proud smile.

The medicine!

My heart sinks. In my haste to return home to warn the townspeople, I left the crucial bundles of plants behind. I have no words for my failure.

"What, Lukan? What is it?" Merritt asks. Apparently, my face has betrayed me.

I drop my head in disgrace. "I forgot the plants back at the...I dropped them and ran when I heard the Howlers." Not a lie, exactly. Just not the entire truth.

Merritt is silent, and I attempt to gauge her reaction to my failure by glancing at her as we walk. She looks at me and smiles.

"I don't see how that is a problem compared to what is coming this direction right now. You know where you left them, right?"

I nod.

"Well, then you can go get them when the Howlers leave." Her confidence in me is almost too much to bear, but I manage a small grin.

Her smile is never ceasing, and even with the horde approaching, I feel no fear for my own life. Only worry for her safety. Howlers have been known to snatch young women away from the communities for their own evil purposes. These poor women are never seen again. More than likely, they are treated savagely and then killed. I shudder to think of Merritt in such a situation.

"Would you do something for me, Merritt?" I ask quietly.

"Maybe. Depends on what it is." Her answer doesn't surprise me.

"Would you go into the woods with the other kids? Please? There's time."

Merritt is quiet, and I can tell she is considering my request. Finally, she answers, "No." That answer doesn't surprise me either.

Although incredibly fearful of heights, my best friend has never shown a fear for Howlers. I have watched as they ransacked her home, bullied her family, and even killed her dog. All the while, she watched with narrowed eyes of fierce animosity. I'd like to think that is why the Howlers have never gotten close enough to her to actually cause her harm. When angry, her eyes seem to have the power to gnaw at a person's soul.

I feel no need to argue with her, so I drop the subject. We continue to walk into town, following the ancient path left by our ancestors. For a brief second, my mind wanders, and I imagine cars being driven in and out of Grayson. For many years, skeletons of old vehicles littered our town. The elderly enjoyed having them around. It reminded them of the days before the virus. When that generation began to succumb to their age, the younger generation started the cleanup process. With tremendous effort, the antique cars and trucks were pushed into the forest at the other end of town. Now, the automobile graveyard serves as an efficient hiding spot when the Howlers visit.

Merritt and I reach her home where I must leave her with her family. As is customary, each family must remain on their porch as the Howlers enter and spread through the town like a sickness. Nobody is allowed to leave their porch until the Howlers have passed through. Merritt takes my hand in hers briefly and gives it an affectionate squeeze. I wonder if she is aware of my body's reaction to her touch. We share a nervous smile, and I watch her join her family.

"Thank you, Lukan," Her mother says kindly.

I'm not sure if she if referring to bringing Merritt home safely, or my trip to retrieve the medicinal plants. Whatever the reason for her gratitude, I blush and nod awkwardly.

By the time I reach my home, my father has returned from the Community Building. He greets me with a squeeze of the shoulder and a kind but anxious smile. My parents assure me that Dom was successful in relaying the alarm to the rest of the community and all the boys are safely hidden away.

"If you hadn't returned when you did..." My mother wonders aloud.

"Shhh, Lue. It's alright now. Lukan is home, and the boys are safe now." My father consoles her. "And you brought the medicinal plants." He adds proudly.

My face must convey my failure. When I don't answer, I see panic spread across the faces of my parents.

"When I heard the Howlers, I took off running and left the plants. When the Howlers leave, I will go get them." I explain.

"They will be withered by then," my mother says with hopelessness.

"I packed them right. They will not wither," I hope I sound convincing because, to be honest, I fear they are dead already. "Besides, the forest grows them in abundance. I can get more."

"You can't leave again, though," she continues. "Think of the consequences of your absence."

"Mom, after they leave, they won't return for several weeks." I try to assure her.

Before she can respond, the sound of howling maniacs interrupts us. The assault on our community has begun. I can hear my mother take in a breath as we move to the front porch where the Howlers will expect us to wait.

Although they are loud and disorderly, the Howlers do not leave the street as they make their way to the Community Building. Even without witnessing the act, I know that there are small groups of Howlers breaking off and going down each side street in Grayson performing the same task. Gathering up the families of the town and leading them to the Community Building.

The same group as always makes its way toward my home. They lead their own parade down our street, passing by each house. The citizens are expected to fall in line behind them. A parade of oppression led by the demented.

As they approach, I spot the Howler we call Sprightly. Images of the energetic and agile fiend wreaking havoc on my mom's flower garden during his last visit race through my mind. I find myself staring icily at him as he passes by. Without stopping his march, he returns my glare, but a sly grin begins to form beneath his mustache. The look is unnerving, but I refuse to drop my gaze.

Sprightly lets out a hysterical cackle before throwing his head back and releasing an equally hysterical howl. The Howlers around him follow suit. I have no doubt that the act is meant to unnerve me. For the most part, they have succeeded. Still, there is a defiant part of me that seems to be trying to work its way to the surface.

I feel myself begin to move toward the edge of the porch when I feel my father's hand on my arm. "Your responsibility is much greater than your desire to concede to anger, Lukan." His voice is firm but kind.

When I look at him, he nods towards the street in front of our house. I follow his gaze. The citizens of Grayson are following along behind the Howlers in a strange sort of dismal parade. Amidst the crowd, I see Merritt and her family. She gives me a weak smile that I return. Looking back at my father, he nods encouragement and releases my arm.

In those brief seconds, with just a couple of gestures and a few words of wisdom from my father, I was gifted with an incredible amount of understanding. The realization of my role in the community, in my family, and possibly the future of Grayson came crashing down on me. While the weight of it is tremendous, and the undertaking difficult, I trust the reward will be profound.

My father senses my understanding. He takes hold of my mother's hand and, as a family, we join Grayson in the march toward the Community Building. As we walk, I can see Merritt's dark hair, the sun shimmering on the thick curls, revealing brief glimpses of the red that tends to stay hidden.

A thought occurs to me. A thought that would have made me nervous just a few days ago or even a few hours ago. A thought that, now, seems to give me the confidence to walk with my head high for the first time in my life.

It is time for the people of Grayson, my people, to meet Helix.

Chapter 13

With the larger group of Howlers descending upon Grayson, comes the putrid odor of their cloaks made from wolf skins. Even with the breeze, the stench of death and sweat radiates from the stage of the Community Building. I am reminded of the smoke stack in the meadow and the offensive smell that pumps from the ground.

"Good people of Grayson," a Howler on stage begins, interrupting my thoughts. I am surprised when I look up to see the one my family and I call Sprightly addressing the crowd.

Although the menacing Howler has always been present during their tumultuous visits, he has never addressed the crowd. He is best known for his acts of destruction and his agile movements that earned him the nickname, Sprightly. I have witnessed his nimble abilities in amazement as he ran up the side of a house, swinging his body onto the roof and then jumping back to the ground while performing incredible flips and twists. Many times, he has climbed some of Grayson's largest trees in just a few quick steps.

His tattooed body is short and lean but muscular. Although his long hair is always tied up behind his head with twine, today he has adorned it with a feather. Most Howlers wear the customary wolf skins, heavy and thick, adding the stench of death to their own putrid body odor. Sprightly's wolf skin, however, is thinner and without sleeves. I imagine the reason is to show off the muscles that define his tattooed arms.

"Today marks the beginning of a new journey for our pack. For our family. The passage of our Alpha is complete," With the wave of his hand, he motions towards Ripley. I hadn't noticed him until now.

Usually, Ripley demands our attention with his booming voice and his dramatic arm movements. If he doesn't feel that is working, then he will pick someone from the crowd and have his pack thrash the poor soul until he is left bloodied and broken. Today, though, Ripley stands towards the back of the stage, arms hanging limply at his sides. His face conveys desolation.

Sprightly looks at Ripley with a look of compassion before summoning him to the front of the stage. Hesitantly, the leader of the pack makes his way to Sprightly. Although he towers over Sprightly, his fear can almost be felt by the crowd. His trembling is apparent to all those observing, and I feel a chill in the back of my neck.

Sprightly has to reach up to put a comforting hand on his Alpha's shoulder. With a comforting tone, he says, "Thank you, Ripley, for your service. I, for one, will never forget what you have taught me."

Removing his hand, he takes a few steps away before he continues, "I will never forget the night I was finally old enough to understand the story my mother told me, time after time. I had always thought she told me that story to keep me from acting out." His voice has lost its tone of comfort. A tone of resentment replaces it.

"You know the one, Ripley. The story about a little boy that wandered off from his mother and little brother." His voice has a bite to it now. "But, but, instead of just letting him go. Letting the wilderness have him. What did you do, Ripley?"

Sprightly had been pacing, but now he jumps at the lumbering Howler. "What did you do? You went after the little boy. Oh, you made his momma think you were worried about him. You told her that you would find him and make everything right."

Sprightly is shaking his head, and the chill that was in the back of my neck has turned to a cold sweat.

Turning to the crowd, he continues, "I will never forget the part of the story when my Alpha found my brother in the forest. My mom told me that she had been so glad that he had been found. He hadn't gone far. He was safe...but there were consequences. Ripley disfigured him. Right in front of her. In front of our mother. Made her watch. Then he drug her back to camp without her mutilated son."

His voice is charged with rage and shakes as he attempts to control his emotions. "I will never forget how she described the screams of my brother as he laid on the ground twisting in pain. I will never forget my mother crying uncontrollably as she told me about being forced to watch her boy being tortured and then left to die."

Sprightly walks closer to Ripley. "You taught me that there are consequences for our actions. You taught me that the life of a child means nothing when the Alpha's rules are broken. My favorite thing that you taught me, though, is that life can be blown out like a candle." He makes a blowing sound and then adds, "I will never forget what you taught me."

With great agility, as if climbing a tree, Spightly scales Ripley's tall body. Before Ripley can react, Sprightly places his hands on both sides of the Alpha's head and, with one quick motion, snaps his neck. Both Howlers came down together. One dead. One alive.

The crowd stands horrified, but unmoving, at the spectacle. We have witnessed Sprightly killing before, but we have never seen any of the Howlers kill a leader. Sprightly is clearly as deranged as the others in his pack. With his emotions at their peak, we all fear what his next move will be and who will be the next victim of his wrath.

"Good people of Grayson," Sprightly begins once more after catching his breath. His sly grin is back, but it makes me feel no less concerned. "Welcome your new Alpha." He opens his arms up as if he is preparing for an embrace. He bows to the crowd in an awkward and dramatic way.

"Bow to Gallner, your new Alpha!" One of the other Howlers bellows out.

Confused, the citizens of Grayson look around anxiously. A few are nervously bowing, but most are not. I keep my focus on the one I have always referred to as Sprightly. Although he has always seemed feral, I always had the impression that he was just acting out. Like a boy in adolescence. Now that I know his real name, Gallner, a feeling of dread creeps over me. I fear his true personality will be revealed to my town.

"No, no, Lehman," Gallner interjects. "We are a family. A pack. There is no need for bowing." The Howler, Lehman, looks at Gallner with confusion.

"These good people will show their respect for me in other ways." Gallner's eyes land on me. The thin mustache that grows beyond the corners of his mouth begins to curl upwards slyly.

Everyone around me must sense Gallner seemingly staring through me. Even with my eye not leaving his, I am still able to perceive anxious glances in my direction from those around me. I hear my mother gasp. This seems to be some sort of stand-off between he and I. Although I do not understand the meaning, I am unwilling to relent from it.

"You," Gallner finally says, pointing a finger at me.

Unsure if I am being beckoned to join him on stage or if he merely intends to harass me where I stand, I remain planted. It feels safer in the crowd, among my people. With tremendous grace, Gallner jumps down from the stage and approaches. The crowd parts hastily to let him through. His smile broadens as he gets closer. The stench from his cloak reaches me before he does.

"You," he repeats, standing in front of me now. "I have use of you."

My heart has crawled into my throat and is thumping loudly. I try to control my breathing so not to show the maniac that stands in front me any fear. We continue to stare at each other, and eventually, his smile disappears.

Quietly, into my ear, Gallner says, "Be careful, child. I will suffer no queasiness over making an example of a one-eyed boy." Leaning back, he looks at me with upraised eyebrows. Clearly, he is conveying that I need to understand that he is threatening me. I do.

"What use could you possibly have for me? You said it. I'm just a one-eyed boy." I try to keep the sarcasm out of my voice.

With a forced chuckle, Gallner's devious grin returns. "Oh, this is perfect for you. You are going to be my eyes and ears of this community. Well, just *eye* and ears, I guess." He laughs boisterously at his jeer towards me. When he sees that he isn't getting a reaction from me, he continues, "You see, these men here, they convinced Ripley that there isn't anyone in charge. You people just do whatever you like without a leader. Do you really expect me to think that there someone in charge? Someone that everyone goes to when decisions need to be made or when things go wrong? Ripley was ignorant enough to fall for that. I am not" He pauses to gauge my reaction. "Just like the kids. How am I supposed to believe that you are the only child that has been born in the past ten years? Why is that?"

"Maybe because your pack killed so many the night I lost my eye. Maybe because everyone that was left alive after that night, decided it just isn't worth it to bear anymore kids in a world like this, with a pack of feral dogs roaming around." I answer with a biting tone.

Gallner seems unaffected by my snide remark. He nods and sucks in his bottom lip as if he is in deep thought. "Maybe so. That would explain it. It doesn't matter, though. There is more to this little town than Ripley was willing to see. I saw it, though. I can see it now in your one blank eye." He says the last three words slowly to rile me into a reaction. I have punished myself enough for my disability, the words of a Howler are meaningless to me.

"What is your name, freak?" He asks, still attempting to gain a reaction from me.

Nearby, I can hear my mother attempting to stifle a cry and my father soothe her. Although I am unaffected by his spiteful words to me, the thought of the burden this exchange much be having on my mom brings my blood to boil. I try to maintain my composure, but my anxiety has turned to anger.

"Lukan," I answer curtly.

"Lukan," Gallner says slowly. "That's a good, strong name."

"I've heard." He doesn't seem to hear the snarkiness in my voice.

The actions of my mom are not lost to Gallner. Looking over at her and then at me, his smile turns menacing. He walks over to her. She is looking down at the ground, trying to make her fear invisible. Gallner puts a finger under her chin, raising it gently so that she is forced to look into his eyes. I stand amazed, and slightly perturbed, that my father is able to allow a Howler to put even a finger on his wife.

"Is that one-eyed boy of some importance to you?" Gallner asks with kindness in his voice.

Silent tears streak my mother's face, and I attempt to swallow my heart back into my chest. All she can do is nod. The wretched Howler places an arm around her shoulders and gently leads her over to where I am standing. A tremble has taken over my body as I attempt to restrain my anger. Gallner's smile is large now.

"Alright, Lukan." He continues, with his arm around my mom's shoulders. "This is what I need. Observe and report. Simple, right? Observe what is going on in your community. Report to me when I return." Gallner shrugs.

"Not sure how I can help you with that," I reply. "There isn't anyone in charge. We all work together to make decisions. We all help each other when there is a need. *That* is what people in a real family do." I pause. "Besides, do you really think the men of this town would want a one-eyed boy lurking around every mundane conversation that is taking place?"

"It's true. You are hideous with just the one eye," Gallner acknowledges thoughtfully. "Still, I believe that you know things."

I shudder as I think to myself that indeed I do know things. I know that there is a whole world living beneath our feet. I know that there is a Wanderer named Helix. I also know that if I act quickly enough, I could fetch my bow and shoot Gallner in the back as he leaves Grayson. I do know things. Just not the things he thinks I know.

"I know you are the man for the job, Lukan."

"Have you considered that because you are ordering me to do this while they are all listening that maybe they will begin to avoid me? How am I supposed to learn anything after you just announced that I will be reporting to you?" I ask as I see the hole in his plan.

Gallner's arm is still draped over my mother's shoulders. He smiles and nods, "I have considered that. I *want* them to know that you work for me now. I *want* them to know the consequences."

"Consequences?"

"When I come back, if you don't have anything interesting to report back to me, I will begin taking the women. You see, it is time for me to do my duty as Alpha and find a mate. Time for me to do my part to repopulate the earth," He glances at my mother, crying silently under his arm. "Might even start with this one."

I taste bile as I try not to lunge at the madman.

"Careful, Lukan," Gallner says, sensing my rage. "I'm giving you a chance to prove yourself. Don't ruin it by acting out." His voice is taunting. "Get that cleaned up," he orders, pointing to Ripley's lifeless body. "The stench of it will attract predators."

I stare at him. In my mind, I am telling him to clean up his own mess. For the sake of my mother's sanity, though, I simply nod.

"Oh! I do so love my job!" Gallner exclaims and then begins to howl. His pack of ferals joins in on the howling.

Gallner's howl must have been the signal that the meeting is over. As one, the group of freaks jump from the stage and with Gallner leading, run through the town towards the exit. As is customary, their destruction can be heard as they make their way out of town. My father and I don't wait for them to leave. We immediately embrace my mother. She clings to her husband and sobs into his shoulder.

Looking through the crowd, I finally find Merritt. Her face conveys a mixture of fear and relief. Without any thought or apprehension, I go to her. As I make my way through the crowd of murmuring men and silently sobbing women, I keep my eye locked on the girl with the shimmering brown eyes. We embrace each other when I finally reach her. She trembles in my arms. I realize that this is the first time I have ever shown her affection. I feel no shame in it. My wish is to be able to keep her from such fear.

The same thought keeps recurring; almost pounding in my head. It seems to course through my body. I must find a way into the underground world. Even with the chimney of death billowing putrid smoke, I still sense that there is safety below us. This is the only way to save Merritt, my family, the citizens of Grayson.

Chapter 14

"No. I won't allow it." My mother says, almost in hysterics. She blocks my bedroom door with her petite body. She knows I won't go past her; I know that she can't stand there all day. We have been at this argument for several minutes.

"Mom, I have to. Mrs. Clifton needs those plants. I have several laying in my pack in the meadow that probably withered, but I know where there are a lot more." I explain once more as I gather a few things. I am thankful that Dom is letting me borrow his pack in case I have to stay overnight.

"Send someone else," she recounts. "Tell them where the plants are. Draw a map. Do not go." Her lip is trembling as she fights back tears.

The ordeal with the Howlers and their new Alpha, Gallner, has taken its toll on her emotions. Since they left, she has said very little. The whole town seemed to be in shock over the ordeal. Many families abandoned their chores and locked themselves in their homes for a full day. I felt that the men of the town should have a meeting and discuss what had transpired. My father said that everyone needed time to deliberate before calling a meeting that would only be fueled by emotions.

To busy myself, and because nobody else seemed to want to perform the task, I spent the rest of the afternoon disposing of Ripley's corpse. With the help of my cousin, Dom, I was able to get the body into the woods, dig a hole and bury the former Alpha. There was no ceremony. No words to help his spirit find its way into the afterlife. Just shovels of dirt tossed onto the man with the now crooked neck and wide lifeless eyes.

With that task completed, I feel as though I have two options. Either stay and brew like the rest of the town or go into action. For reasons I cannot explain, I feel my time for sitting by, and watching are over.

It is time for me to act. First, though, I must finish the task that was set before me with the plants for Mrs. Clifton.

"Let him go, Lue," I hear my father say from the hallway. Turning, I see that he is standing behind my mother. She turns to face him.

"It's too dangerous. The town cannot expect this from him, Avis," she retorts.

"The town expects nothing from him except for what he can offer. This is the service he has to offer at this time." He places his hands on her shoulders affectionately.

"Mom, I will be back soon. Tomorrow morning at the latest." I approach her, and she turns back towards me. Tears threaten to fall from her already tear-drained eyes, but a smile quivers at the corners of her mouth. "I know the way there, and I know the way back. You know that I can hear them long before they can hear me." I attempt a reassuring smile.

With a quick glance at her husband, she concedes and steps aside, giving me a clear passage from my room. Gathering my pack, I walk through and head out the front door. Although I have every intention of getting the plants, my secondary mission for this trip out of Grayson is to find a way into the underground world.

Grayson is quiet this morning. The sun is steadily climbing into the clear blue sky, yet the streets remain empty. The visit from the Howlers still weighs heavy on the community. Usually, there would already be men doing chores and children just beginning to play in the street.

Just as I am about to cross the short rock wall, I hear Merritt. "Want to see what kind of trouble we can get into?"

Smiling, I turn towards her. "You? Get into trouble?" I scoff.

"Oh yes. I am quite the mischief-maker. Things have changed a lot since you have been out doing your part to save our town," she answers as she approaches. "Where are you off to this time?"

"Going back to get the plants I left behind." I take a seat on the rock wall, and she joins me. The gentle breeze blows the scent of her hair in my direction. I perceive mint and lavender. The smell is comforting.

"How's your mom today? I know the Howler visit was rough on her." Merritt asks with genuine concern in her voice.

I ponder her question, recounting in my mind my mother's despair over the course of the past couple of days. "Well, she isn't very happy that I'm leaving town again."

"I imagine not," she says quietly, watching her own feet scoot dirt around.

"She'll be okay, though. How are you? The ordeal was scary for everybody."

"I'm fine, but my parents have come somewhat unhinged," Merritt answers with a nervous chuckle.

While I wait for her to elaborate, I try not to stare at her. I begin to mimic her behavior of playing in the loose dirt with my shoe.

"They want to leave Grayson," she finally says.

Her words send a shockwave through my body. From as early as I can remember, Merritt has been part of my life. By my side. There isn't a time in my life that she wasn't around, usually trying to convince me not to do something stupid. Every milestone. Every tragedy or celebration. I don't want to think about living life without her. Even with my own selfish desire to have Merritt in my life, though, I cannot fathom anyone wanting to leave the safety of the town.

I have no words, so she continues. "They feel like every family with daughters should leave."

"You're too young for Gallner." I reason.

"Do you really think he will consider age? He seems to be the type of man to take what he wants. Right or wrong. He is a monster without morals." Her voice trails off a bit.

I consider her words and realize she is right. The thought of her leaving is agonizing. The idea of her being forced into marriage with a monster like Gallner is unbearable. I must find a way underground whatever the cost.

Standing, now with even more determination, I gather my pack. "If you leave, how soon will it be?" I ask.

Merritt seems confused that I am departing so quickly after her revelation. She stands and replies, "Not sure. They have to think about what will happen to us if we are out in the wilderness with winter coming."

"Ok. That gives me a little time." I feel a tremendous sense of urgency.

"Time for what, Lukan?" she asks, her confusion growing.

"Never mind. Listen, if the Howlers come back while I'm gone, run into the woods with Dom and the others."

"How long are you going to be gone?" she asks with panic in her voice.

"Not long. Just overnight maybe." Part of me has a strong urge to stay out until I find a place of safety to lead everyone.

Merritt is nodding, apparently still concerned with my departure. With an attempt at a comforting grin, I cross the short rock wall. I feel her grab my pack and I turn to face her. Leaning in close, her lips lightly brush my cheek. A kiss on the cheek was an unexpected but welcome going away gift. I feel my face begin to burn with delight.

I know that my face is glowing red. Shyly, I say, "Um, thank you." My voice sounds awkward.

Merritt chuckles. "You are so charming." She is obviously amused by my embarrassment.

"If by charming, you mean bitter and complicated then yes, I am charming," I respond smiling.

She gazes at me for several seconds. "Be safe, Lukan," she finally says before walking away.

I stand just outside Grayson watching her walk away, wanting nothing more than to walk back into town with her. The forest and possibly an answer to our problems beckons me, though, and I turn and walk away.

*****

The trail is easier to traverse with a heart full of contentment. Yes, a huge burden has been placed on me by the new Howler Alpha. True, my community is living in constant fear and oppression.

The kiss, though.

Strange to think that something as delicate as a simple kiss on the cheek from Merritt is enough to at least temporarily relieve me from the anxiety I have been wallowing in. Stranger still is to think that just a few days ago any affection from Merritt, at all, would seem ridiculous. For reasons I can't explain or even understand, my friendship with Merritt appears to be transitioning to something greater. Why now? I can't help wonder…

I take the trail that will lead me to the window. My hope is that if I start at the window, I can write a note asking for help. Perhaps, whoever is living below will come out of their underground sanctuary to help us.

I am pleased that the air is clear today. No stench of death has invaded my nostrils yet. The thought makes me wonder the real purpose of the chimney in the meadow. It seems to be something to fear but not nearly as much as the Howlers.

My thoughts wander to Helix and his possible role in what is to come. I am conflicted with wanting to include him in Grayson but also fearing what the reaction of others will be. Ultimately, I conclude that I should let Helix decide. There is a fair chance that the strange blind man will choose to continue his wandering.

While I hike the familiar trail, I pause several times to pick flowers. My intention is to bring flowers to my mom as a thank you for allowing me to make this trip, and hopefully give her a little comfort during these difficult times. I decide, with an embarrassed grin, to pick some for Merritt as well. I feel myself blushing at the thought of giving her such a gift.

The sun edges its way higher into the sky as I hike. Birds sing cheerfully, and squirrels scamper across the freshly fallen leaves. Although still weighed down with the burden Gallner has placed on me, being in the forest seems to relieve some of the tension.

After walking for quite some time, I find myself at the edge of the woods. Although it remains hidden in the tall grass, I know that just in front of me lies the window. I scan the area for any signs of danger. Satisfied, I walk out of the forest towards the window.

The first thing that strikes me is that although my backpack is right where I left it, the bundles of medicinal plants are missing. Confused, I look around the area briefly. There are more plants along the trail that leads home. I can easily dig them up on my way back to Grayson.

With that matter settled, I focus on the window. The sun is high in the sky and reflects off of it harshly. Leaning down, with my hands shielding my eye from the glare, I gasp at the sight below me.

A girl.

Lia?

A frail, pitiful looking thing. The girl is asleep on the tattered blanket. She appears to be clutching her hand, which is bandaged. Her clothes are wrinkled and dull. Her greasy hair covers her face slightly. There is nothing spectacular about her. Nothing to make me believe that there is hope for Grayson beneath the ground.

I try to imagine what she must be going through. Her bandaged hand. Shabby, dull clothing. Greasy hair. By the looks of her, those that live below us are fighting their own battles for survival. What is happening below to cause the anguish that I can almost feel through the thick window? My hope for sanctuary withers as I look down on the depressing sight.

I gather my belongings to leave this area. To leave the girl, Lia, in her despair. There is nothing I can do for her. I notice the flowers I had picked for my mom and Merritt. Looking back at the window, where the dejected-looking sleeping girl lies cradling her bandaged hand, I make the decision to leave the flowers for her. Perhaps, waking up to fresh flowers will give the girl at least a tiny bit of comfort.

Chapter 15

The next few days in Grayson are uneventful. Although life returns to normal, moods remain sour. Husbands and wives quarrel relentlessly. Children act out in mischief and rebellion. Even the animals seem to feel the strain of the new threat that Gallner poses.

When I returned with the medicinal plants, the town was still in a state of panic over the Howlers recent visit. Apparently, Merritt's parents weren't the only ones thinking of leaving Grayson with their daughters. Their fear, although warranted, was causing them to make hasty, irrational decisions.

While I was away, two families fled Grayson in the middle of the night. They could have left during the day. The citizens that remain would have sent extra food for their journey. Why they decided to leave so abruptly proved that decisions were being made out of pure emotion and not logic.

Because of the emotional turmoil and rash decisions, some of the men call a town meeting. The entire town gathers inside the Community Building to discuss the recent visit of the Howlers. Everyone is desperate for answers. They demand assurances that their families will be protected. My instinct tells me that there are no assurances to be found within the walls of Grayson. We must look elsewhere. We must look below.

"This is no place for him," Old Man Parker barks to my father, pointing an arthritic finger at me. He blocks the doorway into the Community Building Auditorium.

My father looks at me and then back at Mr. Parker. He replies calmly, "Explain, please, Mr. Parker."

"He is an informant for the very maniacs we are having this meeting about," the crooked finger waggles at me with every word.

"That's not fair," Dom interjects with a hint of defiance in his voice. My father silences him with a look.

"It's true, sir. Gallner has commissioned Lukan," my father's smile is kind, and his voice is soft. "That is exactly why my son should be in this meeting. Gallner requires news of interest when he returns. If Lukan is kept away what is it that he will be able to deliver?"

"You want him to tell the Howlers what we are planning?" Mr. Parker is appalled at the thought.

"Absolutely not." My father's kind smile turns into a sly grin. "Lukan will tell the Howlers only that we met. The details of the meeting will be...slightly fictitious."

Mr. Parker ponders my father's words and finally seems to understand and accept the true meaning of my value as the town canary. I take in the conversation, amazed at my father's deviousness. There is no further discussion. I am immediately allowed in and even ushered to the front of the large auditorium.

It is apparent from the beginning, families are frightened and looking for answers. Without a clear leader, the meeting quickly becomes chaotic and disorganized. Several times, heads of households refuse to wait their turn to speak. It becomes a scene of men yelling over each other in an effort to be heard above the rest. Emotions are raw, and everyone wants their chance to be heard.

Most of the exchange centers around protecting the daughters. A lot of families are willing to leave Grayson in search of a safe haven from the Howlers. Others are just angry and lashing out because of the oppression the town feels from the fiends that threaten us. They don't have a clear plan on what should be done, so they do the only thing that comes naturally to them...place blame and point fingers.

The meeting continues in this manner for quite some time. There are a few men, my dad included, that sit silently while the mayhem proceeds unchecked. The noise almost becomes too much for me.

Nothing is being accomplished without order. I nudge my father, who sits next to me stroking his beard, but I keep quiet. Town Meetings are no place for children to speak. If they must attend, they are expected to sit quietly and listen.

Leaning into my ear, my father explains, "They need to say their piece. Even while they are shouting over each other, they are releasing anger and frustration. They will be ready to listen soon."

He is right. After awhile, the tension subsides, and the room begins to quiet. It appears that those that spoke out are much calmer now and ready to conduct the meeting properly. I'm not surprised when my father stands and turns to face the crowd. His level head and open mind make him a great candidate for leader. For his safety, however, he will never be given that task. Nobody will be named the leader of Grayson. Still, the town respects him and gladly give him their attention.

"This expansive room is almost too small to fit the incredible fervor of the citizens of this great town," he begins, with a calm smile. His hands are in his pants pockets in a casual manner. "Passion is defined as 'strong and barely controllable emotion.' There is a lot of passion in this room." The room is silent as he pauses briefly. "Usually when we say that somebody is 'passionate' about something, it is about an idea or about something they enjoy immensely. I have a tremendous passion for my wife. I am passionate about teaching my son and nephew how to be respectable men in this community. Many of you have the same passions regarding your own families."

My father is slowly moving through the crowd now. They stare at him intently, listening and hoping that his words bring the answers they desire. He makes a point to make eye contact with those he passes. As I follow him with my eye, I catch sight of Merritt. She is also captivated by his words. Even from this distance, I can see the shimmer in her eyes.

"We also have passion for the things that are unpleasant. Illness. Death. Winter. Howlers. Sometimes, it isn't conveyed as passion. Sometimes it is conveyed as fear or hate or anger. Tonight, we have spent a majority of our time needlessly bickering with each other. Why? Passion. If we would turn that negative passion into positive, a solution would present itself. Of that I am certain. Maybe not tonight. Maybe not even tomorrow. However, if we do not work together as a family, the solution will never be found, and Grayson will be lost. Our daughters will be lost."

He pauses once more, and I begin to think maybe he is done with his speech.

With one hand in his pocket and the other smoothing his beard thoughtfully, he continues. "Of course, the instinctive solution is to leave Grayson. Some have already done just that, and I fear for their safety more now than if they had stayed. Our ancestors called it 'fight or flight.' Take your daughters and run. Keep running until you find a place free of Howlers. There are two adversaries that make fleeing much more dangerous than staying. Winter and Howlers. First, if winter wasn't just a few short weeks away, you may stand a chance. However, we all know what a Grayson winter entails. Without proper shelter and food stores, you and your family are doomed. Second, it won't be Howlers that will threaten you, but it will be another formidable group. Perhaps with worse intentions. If history has proven anything it is this, whenever there is a catastrophe, there will be factions of those consumed with rage and greed. Bent on evil. Passionate about delivering their message of power. They will be in every corner of the earth. I implore you, stay. At least for the winter, stay with us. Let's take care of each other. Protect each other. The Howlers do not travel when the temperature drops. We have all winter to coordinate a plan that we can be *passionate* about. The Howlers refer to each other as "a pack." We, Grayson, are much more than that. We are a family."

Many are smiling and nodding their heads in agreement. It seems that my father's calming words of wisdom have brought the town together again. I feel a great sense of pride as he takes his seat between my mother and me once more.

*****

After the meeting, life in Grayson began to resume its normal pace. My father's words proved true. Although the town meeting had begun with chaos and yelling, it ended with a town once again united. Those that had been planning on leaving saw the wisdom in staying. At least through winter.

Before preparations for winter resumed, it was decided that Grayson would come together for a feast. We usually waited until after harvest to come together in this manner. However, in light of recent developments, the women of Grayson insisted such an event would be beneficial.

Not wanting to deplete the smokehouse, Dom and I set out on a quick hunting trip. With bows in hand and quivers strapped to our backs, we headed out of Grayson with the intent on bringing home some fat turkeys and as much small game as possible.

Along the trail, while setting the traps for rabbits and squirrels, I wasn't scolded once for heavy steps, as I had been on our first trip together. Although I still lack the experience that Dom has, I feel much more confident on this hunting trip than the last. The forest is a comfortable place for me. Natural. The song the leaves sing in the blowing wind is pleasing. The sound of it seems to break through and dust off the thick shell around my soul.

We work together and set the traps quickly. After setting the traps, we leave the area to give the critters of the forest time to find them. We will return in a few hours to collect what we have caught in the traps. With grumbling bellies, we decide to eat before stalking turkeys. My mother had packed some dried fruits and meats for the trip.

Looking around the area, I can tell Dom is pondering where we should eat our lunch and wait for the turkey to start moving. An idea comes to mind. I try to push it away, but for reasons I cannot explain, I have a longing to share at least one of my secrets with my cousin.

"I have a place we can eat without disturbing any of the wildlife," I offer.

Dom gives me a questioning look. "Is it close?"

Shrugging, I answer, "Close enough."

"Ok. Lead the way, cousin."

Smiling, I take the lead on the trail. I am both nervous and excited to be sharing this part of my life with Dom.

"This is the way back home," Dom acknowledges as he follows me.

We come to a fork in the trail, and I stop. Standing next to me, Dom scans the area. Before us is a small meadow surrounded by trees. Dom looks at me questioningly.

"Left or right?" I ask with a smile. He doesn't know what I know. To the left is the cliff with the blue lake at the bottom. To the right, the caves. Not wanting to reveal all my secrets, I give Dom the option.

He is obviously confused. His mouth is open slightly, and his eyes look in both directions. "Why not straight ahead?"

"Well, if you want to go home, then straight ahead is an option. If you want to see something you have never seen before, we have to go left or right."

Dom stares at me, trying to understand exactly what is going on. He looks back at the meadow, at his options. Turning back to me again, he asks, "What are you doing, Lukan? What is this?"

"I'm giving you an option. Left or right. Neither will disappoint, I promise."

He thinks for several more seconds before finally answering, "Left." A cautious smile spreads across his face.

"Good choice," Beaming, I give Dom a playful slap on the shoulder and head towards the cliff.

*****

"This is…This is…" Dom begins but seems unable to finish his thought as he stands on the cliff, looking out over the brilliantly blue lake below us. The wind gently blows his long brown hair off his shoulders. He doesn't seem to notice, though. Dom stands with mouth and eyes wide. Just like the first time I found this spot, my cousin is mesmerized.

Even now, after many visits to the cliff, I stand in awe of the beauty. The cliff, with the sheer drop to the water, is quite intimidating. Dom approaches the lip with caution. Shuffling his feet along the rock as if raising them to take a step will send him catapulting over. I, on the other hand, stand daringly close to the edge.

The water is a remarkable combination of blue and green. The wind we feel from this height is absent down below. Because of this, the sky reflects flawlessly off the water. Clouds float above us. The water gives the illusion of clouds floating below as well.

"This is…" Dom's words still falter him.

With a chuckle, I comment, "I didn't have any words the first time I saw this place either." As I think back to that day, remembering the loneliness and self-pity I felt, I add, "Of course, I didn't have anyone to share words with."

Dom glances over at me as I stare into the deep. "Why didn't you tell me? Why wouldn't you want to share this with me?"

Shrugging, I answer thoughtfully and maybe with a small amount of self-pity remaining, "You are Grayson's great hunter. You provide what others cannot. What I could not. Everything we do must be of some use to the community. Although beautiful, this place has nothing to offer as service to Grayson. I was afraid that the fact that I actually found enjoyment here, well, it would just add to the scorn I receive from those in town."

Dom considers my words while he stares at the side of my face. I feel his eyes boring into me as he contemplates how to reply to that. The words I just spoke to him are the most honest I have ever been with anyone. Although those closest to me have had to bear witness to my relentless brooding, I have never spoken of my depression to anyone. I hope he doesn't take my openness as weakness.

"The only scorn you receive is what you place on yourself." He finally comments.

I have no valid argument. His words are worth pondering.

We stare over the water for some time. Finally, I sit and unpack our lunch. Dom joins me, and we eat together in silence.

After a few minutes, Dom interrupts the stillness. "Have you brought Merritt here?"

His question surprises me. Merritt and I are best friends. When we were children, the three of us spent quite a lot of time playing and causing mischief around town. As we grew into the age of service for the community, Dom seemed to stay busy hunting and wasn't able to spend as much time with Merritt and me. Up until this moment, he has never asked me about her. I look at him without answering.

With a mischievous grin, he adds, "What? I know how you feel about her."

I feel my face turn red. "She's my best friend."

Dom nods and returns his attention to his food. He seems willing to let the subject go. I'm sure his willingness is only temporary, though.

"I haven't," I mutter. "Brought her here, that is."

"Why not? I would think she would love it here."

"She would love the beauty of it, but she is terrified of heights." I chuckle, thinking of her reaction to climbing trees. "When I told her that I jumped from the cliff, she nearly..."

"Wait. What?" Dom interrupts, obviously shocked by my words.

"Oh, did I forget to mention that sometimes I like to jump off the cliff and into the lake?" I ask slyly.

Dom stares at me with wide eyes. He shakes his head slowly, disbelieving. "I'm not sure if that is extremely stupid or extremely brave."

"I like to think...daring," I reply with a chuckle. "I don't know. Probably stupid. One thing I do know is it is extremely fun."

*****

My attempts to persuade Dom to dive off the cliff into the blue lake were unsuccessful. No matter how hard I tried, he could not be convinced. Although he did admit that he admired my "spirit," he just couldn't bring himself to take that plunge.

Without needling him any further, I dropped the subject, and we ate our lunch. Because neither of us wants to be away from Grayson for very long, we decide to split up again. While Dom goes in search of turkey, I am to check the traps.

Before leaving the cliff, Dom looks back at the area once more, from the tree line. The look of peace on his face confirms to me that he will remain in awe of the beauty that he saw here today. It will be difficult for him, I know, to return home and not be able to reveal his new secret. He will want to share this place with everyone. Maybe, in time, the citizens of Grayson will feel safe enough in this world to travel outside the walls. Then, they will be able to enjoy the beauty that surrounds them.

It doesn't take long for me to check the traps. They are empty. Dom had been worried that we had overhunted this area. It seems that he was correct. With plenty of daylight left, I gather up the snares and head farther into the forest.

As I walk further into the forest setting snares, I can't help but notice that the leaves on the trees are turning quickly from green to yellow, signifying the changing season. Soon, they will litter the ground, protecting the earth from the brutal cold. I begin to think about Helix. Where does a Wanderer go during the harsh winter season? How has he survived so long without a home to protect him from the elements? I try not to worry about my new friend. Obviously, he has survived many winters in solitude.

With all the traps set, I continue my hike down the game trail. It's important that I give the rabbits and squirrels time to find the snares before I come back to them. My mind wanders while I walk. I cannot seem to shake myself free from the image of the pathetic girl below the window. She is like an itch I cannot scratch. Since seeing her there, cradling her injured hand while sleeping, she has haunted me.

Lia.

She and her underground world remain a mystery to me. Perhaps, they always will. I had imagined a haven for Grayson to flee to. A place where Merritt could be safe. What I hadn't considered, though, was what the living conditions are in Lia's world. From the looks of her greasy hair and dingy clothing, her living conditions are meager at best. There are so many unknowns in the world below us; however, I can't help but think that our two communities can help each other.

My mind has wandered and so have my feet. Looking around, I realize that I have veered off the trail. Squirrels in the trees above me bark out their complaints. Obviously, I have interrupted their afternoon slumber.

Making my way through the tall trees, back to the trail, something catches my eye. Nestled in among the trees, is a structure. From this distance, it appears that it has two sides and a top. The earth is all around it, leaving an opening at the front. It reminds me of the ancient storm shelters some of the families have in Grayson. I am not too terribly alarmed by the sight of it. Only the placement of it in the forest.

I approach the shelter with caution. The storm shelters back home have heavy doors at the entrance. This concrete structure does not. As I approach, I see that there are moss-covered steps, also made out of concrete, that lead down into the ground. I contemplate following the steps. What lies at the bottom is protected by the shadows cast by the concrete structure.

Approaching cautiously, I glance over my shoulder nervously. Even though I know that I am alone in the forest, I feel as though icy fingers are snaking their way up my spine. As a slight shiver causes the hair on my arms to stand on end, I realize that I can just make out what hides in the shadows at the bottom of the concrete steps.

A gasp escapes me, interrupting the stillness of the forest, causing me to jump. What I see before me is just as inconceivable as the window and the chimney. The clouds drift away from the sun above me, casting more light on what is below.

A large metal door.

Without any doubt, I know that I am looking at the entrance to the underground world of Lia, the broken girl on the tattered blanket. The last time I saw the girl, I had come to the conclusion that life underground isn't the answer for the people of Grayson. Now, though, seeing the entrance in front of me, I can't help but think about the possibilities that lie on the other side of it.

Something more disheartening occurs to me, though. The stench of death that emanates from the chimney. The cries of agony that my blind friend, Helix, is able to hear sometimes. These seem like very real problems for those living underground. As real to Lia, as Howlers are to me. Those reasons are why I remain planted at the top of the steps, looking down into the shadows at the looming door.

I am as much drawn to the door to the underground as I am repulsed by it. Slowly, I back away from the stairway. I do not take my eye from the darkening shadows for fear that the door will swing open and I will be snatched away into the living tomb beneath the earth.

Chapter 16

Alone in the forest, slowly backing away from the metal door, I continue to stare down into the concrete stairway that leads to the underground world. A haunting moan that seemingly comes up from the shadows startles me from my stupor. I know I should flee, but I remain planted in this spot.

Along with the moan, a series of harsh clicks can be heard, followed by the sound of metal complaining as it is opened perhaps for the first time in ages. The sound echoes throughout the once serene forest. A cold shiver that cannot be attributed to the crisp weather crawls up my spine, causing the hair on the back of my head to stand on end.

The sound of the moan grows louder and slightly more menacing. I am aware that the sounds of the forest have ceased. The birds, squirrels, and even the annoying bugs that continuously buzz, have gone silent. They have been replaced by the sounds of the metal door at the bottom of the steps opening. Somebody or something is finding their way out from the underground world. The question is, is it an act of escaping the anguish below? Or is it an attack on me, the person that seems to have an unquenchable curiosity?

The scene before me becomes too much, and I am relieved when I find that my feet finally remember how to work. Turning quickly, I begin my escape from the forest. My legs pump hard, and my lungs work furiously to bring in enough air to fuel my escape.

"Lukan!" A voice, full of torment, screeches above the sound of my feet crunching on fallen leaves.

I stop abruptly. Although it is unnerving, it isn't the sound of my name being screamed out that halts my escape. No, it is the owner of the voice that is shrieking out my name that paralyzes me. I have heard this voice before. I am familiar with its tone and inflections. The voice of an angel. The voice of Merritt. Always full of hope, compassion, tenderness. Never like this - thick with despair and torment.

"Lukan!" Merritt's voice slices through the tranquility of the forest around me. This time with more anguish and desperation.

The pain in her voice sends a tremor through my body shattering the fear that had sent me running away from the door. Without thinking, I frantically run back towards the concrete steps and the sound of my friend being tortured. While I run, I try to think of how Merritt found her way into this forest. Why would she leave the safety of Grayson? Was she looking for me?

Her screams continue, piercing the serenity that the forest usually offers. For a brief, selfish moment, I desperately want to cover my ears to block out the sound of her agony. Merritt is no longer screaming my name. This should comfort me, but the gurgling sound that now fills the forest now is almost more than I can bear.

My lungs burn at the effort. How did I get so far away from the metal door in such a short amount of time? It didn't seem like I had been running very long when Merritt's desperate screams shattered the silence of the forest.

Suddenly, there is only silence.

I stop short of the concrete steps that lead down to the metal door. The silence is almost more excruciating than the sound of Merritt's screams. Standing at the top of the concrete steps, I begin to tremble violently. I don't want to step down into the darkness.

The silence becomes so heavy that I begin to consider that maybe the screams had been the product of my over-active imagination. Perhaps, Merritt is safely inside the walls of Grayson and not trapped underground with Lia and those being burned. Maybe she will not end up as ashes belched up from the ground through the chimney in the meadow and then scattered by the wind. It is conceivable that my mind is playing tricks on me. Toying with my emotions.

Closing my eye, I concede to the fact that I am actually losing my mind. This life has become too much for me. The feeble mind of this one-eyed boy simply isn't strong enough to handle this post-Langston world. Obviously, it is shutting down, and all I can do is allow it to happen.

The sound of metal grinding on metal interrupts me as I question my own insanity. I open my eye and immediately fall back onto my backside. The scene before me does nothing for my clouded lucidity.

Black smoke.

Snaking up from the now open metal door, black smoke approaches me. I know that I should begin to back away. I know that I should run away. My body has once again forgotten how to function, and I find myself lying on my back with black smoke swirling around my face menacingly.

The black smoke roils around, enveloping me. It blocks out the sun, and I am forced to strain to see the forest beyond. As if the smoke itself isn't horrifying enough, I am struck by the stench of it. Metallic and musky. Almost like leather being tanned over a flame. Helix told me what this horrendous odor is. It is the smell of death.

Somehow the putrid odor of death has found its way to me. Unable to control my reaction, I turn my head and vomit onto the ground. With my belly now empty of its meager contents, I continue to dry-heave violently. The death smoke looms above me like a snake ready to strike.

Staring up at it now, something else catches my attention. I close my eye, attempting to get a better perspective on what exactly is grasping for my attention. Because of the foullness of the stench, my eye waters profusely and my nose burns. Still, somehow, I am able to concentrate enough that I discern what exactly has caught my attention.

Whispers.

Deep inside the black smoke, whispers are barely audible. There is no explanation for this phenomenon. Yet, I still find myself planted to the ground rather than running. The whispers seem to be coming from several different voices, filled with agony. I close my eye tighter. The voices cry out. Screaming. Anguishing. Terrified. Although I cannot make out any words, I am sure that the voices belong to those whose bodies have been burned and were sent up into the smoke as ashes.

It is all too much for me, and I slam my hands onto my ears to block out the misery that boils around me in the black smoke of death. I roll on the forest floor, hands pressed against my ears, with my eye closed tightly. I weep for the lost souls that cry out to me.

"Lukan," I hear Merritt's sweet voice cry out to me. My eye pops open, and I stare into the blackness, seeing nothing through the smoke. "Help me, Lukan." My heart hammers loudly in my chest, but I am certain that it is Merritt's voice in torment.

I try to stand, but the black smoke coils and strikes at me. Falling back to the ground, I summon all my courage. Facing the smoke, a scream from deep inside of me pierces the darkness. The sound of it seems to startle the smoke. For a second, I sense that it has backed away from me slightly. Only for a second, though.

The black smoke begins to tremble, but I am sure it isn't from fear. Somehow, I have angered a thing that shouldn't have any emotions. Inside the now pulsating black smoke, the screams of agony have grown louder and more desperate.

"Lukan!" I hear Merritt scream shrilly.

The smoke descends upon me, suddenly. It holds me down somehow, and I thrash against the weight of it. I get the sense that the smoke itself isn't heavy. Of course, smoke is not heavy. No, what I am feeling is the weight of the agony felt by those that have been taken by the smoke. The burden of their torment is what weighs me down now.

As Merritt continues to scream, I writhe and weep. Suddenly, the weight is gone, and I open my eye. The black smoke is gone. Even the stench has disappeared from the forest. Lying on my back, trembling at what I have just experienced, I try to catch my breath. I look to my left. Nothing but forest.

I look to my right, and a scream escapes me as I back away.

Next to where I had been, Merritt lies motionless. She is beaten and bloody. Her eyes stare straight up into the sky. Although I know she is dead, I rush over to her. Cradling her, I weep uncontrollably. For several long minutes, I hold my best friend's dead body tenderly. Other than the light kiss she gifted me with, we have never been affectionate with each other. I regret that now. More than anything, I regret not revealing my true feelings for her.

I take a minute to look into her lifeless eyes, once brown and rich, now gray and dead. Leaning back, I take in the sight of her. Her face is bloodied, and I can see a horrid gash across her forehead. I try to imagine how she was when I left Grayson. I imagine what could have brought her out here.

Staring at her, my heart leaps into my throat when she turns her head toward me and screams, "Lukan!"

Chapter 17

"Lukan," I hear her say, as I struggle to flee from her lifeless body. "Lukan!"

Her voice is different. She doesn't sound like the Merritt I have known since I was a boy. The voice I know as almost melodious sounds odd to me now. Still somewhat pleasant, but strange nonetheless.

I continue to writhe under Merritt's dead weight.

"Lukan!" she shouts with more force in her voice.

A sharp pain on my cheek halts my thrashing. Opening my eye, I groggily become aware of my family staring down at me with concern. I begin to realize that I am not in the forest at all. Merritt, dead and cold only moments ago, is not lying in my arms with gray eyes. The light from daybreak is just beginning to peak through the curtains of my bedroom window. Although I can feel the chill in the morning air, my body is drenched in the sweat induced by the horrific nightmare.

My mother sits next to me on my bed. Her face etched with worry. Standing over her shoulder, my father doesn't seem nearly as worried. Reaching for my eyepatch, a wave of embarrassment washes over me as I realize that I must have been yelling out in my sleep and woke him up. Although he doesn't seem angry with me, he isn't exactly pleased to be awake at such an early hour either.

"Sorry, Lukan," Dom says. I turn my head slightly and see him standing by the door with an apologetic look.

"Did you slap me?" I ask slowly, still trying to discern reality from my nightmare.

Dom doesn't answer me. The look on his face tells me that he did. This adds to my embarrassment, and I feel my face begin to burn red.

"You were having a dreadful nightmare, Lukan. I tried to wake you gently. When I couldn't…" my mother explains softly, with a nervous glance in Dom's direction.

"I'm sorry I woke you all up," I apologize, still ashamed.

My family doesn't say anything for several seconds. They stare at me with curious eyes.

"I'm okay," I acknowledge, sitting up and swinging my legs over the side of the bed. "It was just a dream." I try to smile, but I feel no confidence in it.

"Come, Domenic. There is much to do today. It is a good thing Lukan woke us up early so we can ensure we finish everything for the feast." My father announces, urging my cousin out of the room.

My father and cousin leave, but my mother remains by my side. I feel like she is staring at me but when I look at her, I am surprised to see that she is gazing out the window. She watches as the morning light slowly consumes the darkness. I can't help but wonder where her thoughts are. She has had to endure her son's nightmares many times in the past. I'm sure the torment of it weighs on her.

"I'm okay, mom," I say with as much assurance as I can convey.

With kind eyes, she returns her focus to me. "Do you want to tell me your dream?"

I consider this briefly but decide against it. There is no reason in adding to my mother's worries. Besides, it was just a dream. A horrific, torturous, blood-chilling nightmare. Still, just a dream.

"Okay, then. We better start our day." She says with a smile. "I have lots of cooking to do."

With that, she stands and exits my room. Alone with my thoughts, the nightmare begins to replay in my mind. The black smoke of death. Merritt's piercing shrieks and then lifeless body lying on the forest floor. Merritt screaming my name, even in death. I keep telling myself that none of it was real. It was all just terrifying images that my mind created for the sole purpose of torture.

Well, one thing was real.

The metal door.

Finding the door sent an odd mixture of excitement and alarm sweeping over me. More than anything, I had wanted to believe there was safety for Grayson underneath this world of death and torment. Unfortunately, that was before I knew about the voices of anguish that filter up through the ground; before I had breathed in the air of death from the metal chimney in the meadow. The small twinge of excitement that I felt was fleeting. Hope slipped away just as handily.

I am burdened with terror at the thought of what I imagine to be lurking behind the door; however, the stench that is being belched up from the chimney in the meadow holds my fear in its grip like a vice. Still, my heart hurts for Lia, who seems stuck in the middle of the two nightmares. Without the ability to enter her underground world, and not entirely certain I want to anymore, there is nothing I can do to help the poor girl on the tattered blanket. She is as stuck in her world as I am in mine.

When we finished our hunt last night, I hadn't told Dom about my find. The secrets I carry with me now outnumber the truths I hold. He had sensed that I was troubled but only asked me once if there was something wrong. I gave him a fake smile and began to brag about his superior trapping skills. Of course, the subject of hunting sidetracked his focus away from me. My glum mood was immediately abandoned and not mentioned again.

I remained haunted by the possibilities of the underground even as we made our trek home. Dom respected my silence, though. There were no more questions. I'm sure now, after witnessing the torture I endure in the grips of my nightmares, Dom is relieved that I didn't answer him. Relieved that I didn't share my burden.

Attempting to rid myself of the pointless guilt I feel for the dilemma that lies beneath my feet, as well as Grayson's with the Howlers looming, I shake my head. The act is futile, of course. The predicament that we are all faced with weighs so heavily upon me that I almost feel the ache of it between my shoulders.

Nothing can be done for either situation, though. Not now, as I change from my night clothes into my handmade pants and buttoned shirt, in the security of my home, still reeling from the nightmare that I fear will forever haunt me. Both circumstances require action on my part. Action that will take careful consideration and planning.

Eventually, I'm sure I will have to confide my secrets to my father. Hopefully, in all his wisdom, he will have sound advice. It is quite possible, however, that he will find my claims to be further evidence of his son's eroding mental state.

Almost on cue, my father appears at my doorway. "Lukan, your cousin and some other young men are setting up tables and chairs for the feast. They could use your help, son."

"Yes, sir," I reply as I step into my mocassins. Feeling his eyes on me, I glance at him.

His look is no longer one of disapproval as it had been when I woke from the terror. Now, as he looks at me, I can see the questions that I can only assume burns deep in his belly. We share a smile as I stand and approach the doorway. I contemplate whether I should say something to him now as his gaze pierces through me. With preparations for the feast hurriedly being made throughout the town, I decide that today just isn't the day for revelations. Today is a day for celebrating the life the people of Grayson have built regardless of the threat of the Howlers.

*****

With the early autumn sun high in the sky, the citizens of Grayson assemble on the lawn of the Community Building. This gathering isn't being forced by the Howlers, though, which means that moods are cheerful. Spirits are high. Sounds of lively conversation and laughter can be heard throughout the town. While children chase each other around playfully, the women watch and laugh at their antics. The men, always planning, always serving, discuss the fast approaching season of frost.

A light breeze swirls the delectable aroma of the prepared food around our heads. Each family has contributed to the feast. Some brought small game, seasoned and smoked. There are dried fruits and sweet bread to enjoy also. The food that is provided is delicious. Nothing is left once bellies are full.

"You seem to be in a constant state of brooding these days," Merritt says as she approaches me with a crooked smile.

I act surprised to see her, but the truth is, I have been trying to sneak glances at her all day. When I look at her, I try not to see her as lifeless. Try not to see her mouth, rigid from death, stretch open wide as she screams my name.

Merritt sits in the empty chair next to me. I can smell the lavender in her hair. I welcome its soothing effect.

"I'm not brooding. I'm just watching the kids play while eavesdropping on the women's gossip." I return.

"Anything good?"

"Not really. I'm a little disappointed." I say with a slight chuckle.

"Why? Because you actually sat here and listened to them?" Merritt replies, amused by her own snarkiness. Realizing that I have gotten a little lost in the sound of her laughter, I nod awkwardly. "Good thing you have me here to save you from yourself." She nudges me playfully with her elbow. I'm sure she doesn't realize how badly I need to be saved.

She looks at me with her dark, gentle eyes. A strand of her hair gently sways around her chin with the breeze. Slowly, I reach for it and place it behind her ear. Her gaze doesn't leave mine, and I can feel myself begin to tremble. I think of all the things I want to say to her. The things I feel need to be said. It seems like a day like today, a day of celebrating and uniting as a community, is the perfect time to reveal my secrets to my best friend.

"Do you trust me?" I say quietly, only slightly unnerved by the thought of revealing my feelings.

She begins to nod, but her reaction is cut short by shouts of alarm. As one, Merritt and I turn our attention to the sounds of panic. In the street, I can see some Grayson women running towards the Community Building. Children that had been playing just minutes ago are now clinging to their mothers. The men run towards the chaos.

"Stay here," I say to Merritt as I follow the men down the street.

Running towards the commotion, I look to my left and see Merritt running beside me. Although annoyed that she could be potentially running towards danger, I'm not really that surprised.

"You need to stay with the women," I comment.

"Why? You already told me their gossip was boring. This seems much more exciting." A playful grin spreads across her face. Once again, that rebellious strand of hair is showing its defiance by not staying behind her ear.

Up ahead, I can see a group of men. They are huddled around something. I can tell by their actions that it isn't Howlers that have caused their alarm. This is something else.

I am stopped short when I hear the voice. Low, deep, throaty. Familiar.

"I am not a threat to you," Helix says calmly. Even surrounded by men on the verge of panic, my blind friend remains placid.

I rush to the middle of the circle of frightened men, placing myself between Helix and them.

"Back away from him!" I yell. "Back away. He's not a threat." I cannot imagine why Helix has come to my home. Even more, I cannot imagine how he found his way to Grayson at all.

"He's a Howler, Lukan. You back away from him!" I hear my father yell from somewhere in the crowd of panic-driven men.

"He isn't a Howler. He's my friend. Please just calm down." I beg.

The mob murmurs among themselves with questions and complaints. I make eye contact with my father and try to convey to him, without speaking, that Helix is not to be feared. At this moment, this group of frightened men is the only thing to fear. They seem close to hysteria which makes them highly unpredictable. At this moment, I can see just how close Grayson is to the edge of frenzy due to the treatment received by the Howlers.

"Back away," my father says to the crowd, calmly. "Let Lukan testify for the stranger."

The men slowly relent. Still complaining, they back away from Helix and me. I try to make eye contact with those closest to me. They need to see that if I am not fearful of this stranger, then they have no reason to be either. Their fear, however, fuels them. Their fear makes them vulnerable. Their vulnerability makes them angry.

I had thought that I wanted to share Helix with Grayson. Even though I knew there would be apprehension about his looks and the mystery that surrounds him, I still felt like they would embrace him as part of the community. This is not how I imagined introducing him. Wandering in. Surrounded by a scared and angry mob. As I take in the scene that surrounds me, I see the true potential of what this group of men can do when threatened. I can't help but wonder why they have never risen up like this against the Howlers.

"Lukan," my father says, distracting me from my wandering mind. With a nod of his head, he prompts me to explain why I am standing in front of this large blind man.

I glance at Helix. If he is frightened, his face doesn't betray him. Although the weather is still warm, he wears his thick fur. I imagine it is easier to wear it than to carry it. In his left arm, he cradles a bundle of neatly wrapped plants that I recognize to be medicinal. In an instant, I realize why Helix has traveled to my community.

His strong hand comes down on my shoulder gently.

"His name is Helix," I begin, facing the crowd once more. "He's my friend."

Although somewhat quieter, there is still an audible grumbling in the crowd. My father stands with narrowed eyes, stroking his graying beard thoughtfully. He waits for me to continue.

From somewhere in the crowd, I hear somebody yell out, "He's a Howler!"

"He isn't a Howler. He isn't." I respond. "He's a…" I'm not sure how to explain. When I had asked my family about "Wanderers," they had acted as if I was insane. Maybe I am. Still, I don't want to think of what this crowd of panicked men, pushed too far, will do to my wandering friend or me.

"A what?" Dom asks. I hadn't realized he had joined the crowd. Looking around, I see that women and a few children have joined their men.

Merritt stares at me with wide, curious eyes but I see no fear in them. Before I answer my cousin, I flash Merritt a nervous smile which she mirrors with one of confidence.

"What is he, Lukan? What is he if he isn't a Howler?" Dom persists.

"He's a Wanderer," I say slowly. I can hear the uncertainty in my own voice. More grumbling from the crowd. Women gasp and draw their children in closer as if a Wanderer is something to be feared.

"Please," Helix says from behind me. "There are many things in this world to fear. I am not one of them." His deep voice, soothing to me, has silenced the crowd. They all stare at him with wide eyes. "I'm not a Howler. I'm not really sure there is a name for somebody like me. I belong to no group or clan. My days are filled with wandering the countryside just trying to live my life in peace."

Slowly, one hand on his beard, the other in his pocket, my father approaches Helix and me. Somehow, Helix senses my father's approach and lowers his hand from my shoulder. He steps up to stand right next to me. Trying to match Helix's confidence, I stand tall and face my father.

"What did you say your name is?" my father asks my friend softly.

"My name is Helix, sir." My friend's deep voice that comes from deep inside his belly answers politely. "When I last saw Lukan, he had been retrieving plants that your community needed for healing. He left in quite a hurry that day because of the threat that was approaching your town. The plants were left behind. I didn't want your community to be without the medicines you need."

Looking between Helix and me, my father nods with understanding but says nothing.

"I have kept the plants wrapped in wet linens. They are still healthy, I'm sure." Helix says after some time.

"How did you find us?" Dom asks, now standing behind my father. "You're blind." I smile as I remember having the same reaction when I first saw Helix. Flabberghasted that a blind man could be capable of so much in a world that seems bent on harm.

"I could smell you," Helix answers, causing me to chuckle as the memory from our first meeting plays out further.

"Smelled?" Dom retorts, with raised eyebrows.

"The food. The smell of it is very inviting." Helix pauses, but I can discern the groan that resonates from deep in his belly. "I have been searching for Lukan for a few days."

The crowd that surrounds us is silent. Although still wary of the stranger, they no longer seem as scared as before.

"You must be hungry from traveling," my mother says to Helix as she steps forward from the crowd. "There is still plenty. You are welcome to it."

A broad smile spreads across Helix's sun-kissed face. "Thank you, ma'am."

With this invitation from my mother, the crowd relaxes, and some begin to disperse.

"No, Helix, we thank you for bringing us our medicine," my mother replies with a kind smile even though he cannot experience the beauty of it.

"You must forgive our precautions, Helix," my father begins. "We have been terrorized by a group known as Howlers for quite some time. Sometimes, our fear is greater than our ability to be the reasonable people that I hope you will come to see us as."

"Of course, sir. No apology needed." Helix responds as he holds out the plants for someone else to take.

"This is Luetta, my wife," My father explains as my mother gently takes the bundle from Helix. "Standing behind me is our nephew, Domenic. You already know our son, Lukan. My name is Avis. We are happy to welcome you to Grayson."

"Thank you, Avis. I appreciate your hospitality."

"Helix, if you don't mind me saying so, your speech seems quite refined." My father acknowledges.

Helix chuckles and explains, "My mother felt very strongly that her sons be civilized in this barbaric world."

"She sounds like a grand woman," my mother says.

Turning his head in my mother's direction, Helix replies with sadness in his voice, "She was."

Chapter 18

"Thank you, Luetta, for the delicious meal," Helix says to my mother after he wipes the last of the remnants of his dinner onto his napkin. "I haven't eaten this much in quite some time."

Pleased, my mother replies, "You are very welcome."

After the citizens of Grayson were confident that Helix wasn't a threat to the community, they welcomed him. Mrs. Clifton thanked him for bringing the plants. She offered to let him "clean up" in her bathhouse.

Being the only doctor in town has some perks. Having a bath house is one of them. Because there is no electricity, the only way to heat water is by warming it over a fire. The families of Grayson use the bathtubs in their homes for bathing and washing clothes. Mrs. Clifton's work requires that she have multiple areas for such a task. She must be able to wash soiled bed linens at the same time that a person is soaking to bring a fever down. The elderly need extra care and precautions so as not to put them in any more pain than their failing bodies already are so they are brought to Mrs. Clifton's and bathed where it is much more comfortable. She has herbs and spices that make the experience more endurable.

When Mrs. Clifton offered one of her bathtubs to Helix, he readily agreed and thanked her. I waited outside the bathhouse until he was done. When he walked out, with Mrs. Clifton escorting him, he smelled of the same lavender as Merritt always does. I found this odd since he has no hair to shampoo.

"I'm not sure what to think of the new aroma of my furs," Helix commented as we walked home. "She said she sprinkled it with lavender. What do you think of it, Lukan?"

With a smile, I assure him that it smells nice but will wear off soon. I can understand, being part of the forest that he would want to smell like the forest.

So, freshly bathed and smelling like lavender, Helix ate dinner with my family. It wasn't anything fancy. Mostly just leftovers from the feast. Helix devoured every morsel, though, while we watched with captivation.

Conversation, during dinner, was light. I am surprised but thankful that my parents never ask Helix or me how we met. If they did, I would have to give up my secret about the cave to them. Dom is aware of the cave since I had to retrieve my bow and quiver from their hiding place inside. I am thankful he has given me the respect of not telling anyone else about it.

"Will you be staying in Grayson?" My mother asks.

"No, I'm afraid I can't," he answers.

"Why not?" I ask, surprised that he wouldn't want to stay after a hot bath and nice meal. "Where will go you?"

Helix ponders this for several seconds before answering. "I never know. Just wherever my feet take me."

This idea seems preposterous to me. Grayson offers Helix food, shelter, friendship. Yet, he has no desire to stay.

"It's just as well," Dom quips. "If the Howlers come while he is here, there could be severe consequences."

"The Howlers visit often?" Helix asks.

"Not too often. Just often enough to keep everyone scared." I answer.

My mother has set bowls of strawberries and honey in front of each of us to enjoy.

"We are lucky to have Lukan," my father interjects. "He has a keen ear. The Howlers have never come into Grayson without Lukan hearing them well before they arrived. This gift has given us time to hide our boys, including Dom, and anything else we do not want to destroyed."

"They certainly do have a passion for destruction," Helix remarks.

Although he is unable to see, we all nod in agreement as we enjoy the dessert my mother provided for us.

"Dom is right. I should not be around when the Howlers return. It could prove dangerous." Helix expresses between bites.

"Especially with their new Alpha," Dom adds. "He is even more unpredictable than Ripley was."

"New Alpha?" Helix inquires.

Dom has just put a strawberry in his mouth, so I answer for him. "They came a few days ago to introduce us to their new Alpha. We had hoped that the change would be good for Grayson. We were wrong."

"How so?" Helix's voice has taken on a different tone. He seems troubled by the news of a new Alpha.

I don't want to get into too many details with my mother sitting at the table. I don't want her to have to relive the nightmare of that day. Especially the part where Gallner had his arm around her as he threatened her son. I ponder on how exactly I should answer.

"After the new Alpha killed Ripley right in front of everyone, he singled Lukan out and made threats against him and the community," my father explains.

"What was the purpose of singling you out, Lukan?" Helix asks me.

"He thinks that I can give him information about the community that his own scouts haven't been able to get. He knows we are hiding the boys. He just doesn't know where. Ripley never questioned our hiding place. He also never questioned if we have a leader. Apparently, Gallner has been more perceptive." I explain.

I can barely perceive Helix begin to groan as he thinks about what we have just disclosed. "Did you say, Gallner?" Helix asks with concern in his husky voice.

"Yes. Gallner is the new Alpha." I answer.

My father must sense the change in Helix's tone also. He asks, "Do you know him, Helix?"

I watch Helix's face as his mood obviously becomes one of sorrow. After several seconds, Helix finally answers, "I used to. He's my brother."

Chapter 19

We stare at Helix. I can't help but wonder what is more uncomfortable for him – the fact that he can't see us staring or the awkward silence that now engulfs the room.

"Lue, put on some coffee, please. We have much to discuss with our new friend, and I have a feeling it is going to be a late night." My father says, breaking the silence.

My mother nods and gets up from the table, collecting the dishes before she heads to the kitchen to make coffee.

"Gentlemen, I suggest we move into the living room. The furniture is much more comfortable than these hard chairs." My father recommends as he stands stiffly.

By the time I guide Helix onto the couch in the living room and get seated comfortably, the coffee is ready. My mom sets a tray that holds five steaming hot mugs of coffee, honey, and milk on the short table in the middle of the room. After everyone adds what they like to their coffee, we get comfortable and give Helix our attention once more.

Helix doesn't wait for anyone to prompt him. He begins to reveal his life secrets right away.

"I have never spoken any of this to another person. Please be patient with me as the memories return. Some are quite painful."

"Helix, you don't have to share with us. We are strangers to you. Memories are an intimate part of a person's soul that deserve protection." My mother says compassionately.

"It's important that you know. My story has more to do with Grayson than you realize." Helix pauses briefly and then continues. "My mother was taken when she was a young girl. The Howlers came into her community, killed her parents and brother. They took her when she was only ten years old." His voice is thick with sadness.

"Four merciless years later, she gave birth to me. I was not born from love. Quite the opposite. My mother was condemned to a miserable life of torture. Raped. Beaten. She suffered oppression in the worst, most cruel, sense of the word." Helix pauses, and I fear the memory of his mother's torment has become too much for him.

Across the room, my mother sniffles. Obviously, the story has already struck a nerve in her as a woman and most certainly as a mother.

"I also suffered at the hands of the Howlers but nothing like my mother. I believe she endured the brunt of the torment in order to protect me. I also think it was something else. Something about me. I was an oddity. Something strange and unknown. Nobody knows why but I never grew any hair. Not one strand." Helix says this with a light chuckle that does nothing to lighten the mood in the room.

"You can imagine that I was a pretty strange looking child. Slick headed. Lacking eyebrows. Not even hair on my arms or legs. Because of that, the Howlers didn't pay much attention to me. They seemed almost afraid of me because of the way I looked. Still, I was tormented. Day after day, I had to watch as my mother was beaten and tortured at the hands of the monsters. Many times, she became pregnant. Only two of her children lived long enough in her belly to enter this cruel world."

I hear my mom sniffle once more. I know her compassionate heart is breaking for Helix's mother.

"Ripley became Alpha, and our predicament became even more dire." Helix pauses. His head hangs for several seconds. We give him the time he needs. It's obvious that his life has been filled with more anguish than we could ever imagine.

"My mother, recovering from giving birth to Gallner just three weeks before, convinced me to leave the camp. I didn't want to leave her, but she was adamant that I escape and find a place of safety. She felt that if I found my way back to her community, the people there would be able to send help and we would be free. That wasn't the case, however. I did manage to escape the camp, but after a day of hiking through the forest alone, Ripley and a group of his madmen found me. I could have run from them. Could have gotten away. Ripley made me believe that I wasn't in trouble. He acted as if he understood what it was to be a mischievous boy. I followed him, telling myself that I would get another chance to escape. When we came over a hill, my mother and tiny baby brother were there. They were being held by some of Ripley's henchmen. I knew then that I was about to meet my demise. I had been tricked." Helix hangs his head once more.

"You don't have to continue, Helix," my father acknowledges. "there is no reason for you to disclose any of this to us."

"He's right, Helix," I comment. "I think we know how this story ends. We've heard it before."

Helix's head bobs slightly, surprised that we would have heard this story already. "No, I feel I must. Perhaps by speaking my anguish out loud, the wounds of my heart will heal"

"The consequences for escape are exact and savage. With tremendous malice, Ripley took my eyes. I can describe the pain I felt while he was gouging my eyes with a knife. Or even afterward while fighting the infection that set in as I stumbled through the forest. The most excruciating thing, though, was hearing the screams from my mother as she watched her child be mutilated. Of course, the pain was too much for me, and I passed out. When I woke up, still in a tremendous amount of pain, I was alone in the forest. Alone, to fend for myself. Blind. I was eleven."

"Oh, Helix," my mother whimpers, unable to hold back her compassionate tears for the boy who lost his eyes, his mother, and his brother all on the same day.

Although pained by his ordeal as a child, I am mesmerized by Helix's resilience. "Helix, I know that telling your story has been difficult. I have to ask, though, how did you survive the forest at such a young age and blind?" I ask.

"Miraculously," Helix answered matter-of-factly, and with a warm smile. "I'm not sure how long I wandered aimlessly through the forest. In my blindness, I had no idea when it was day or when it was night. With no food or water, I grew weak very quickly. Conceding to death, I curled up beside the base of a tree. When I woke up, I was shocked to find that I was being tended to. I could feel a cold damp linen washing the blood from my damaged eyes and face. I could hear a man humming a happy song. Although I was frightened, I didn't have the energy to struggle against the humming man. I spent several days under his care. He would speak to me, but I was lost in my pain and anger. I remained silent. Finally, he quit talking. Quit washing my wounds. I knew he was still there because I could hear him moving around in his little shack. One day, I heard the door open. I heard the man walk out. I knew the door was open because I could hear birds singing and bugs chirping. The more I listened, the more I could hear. The wind, whistling through the blades of grass. The sounds of baby birds nagging their mother shrilly for their breakfast. Everyday, my caretaker did this. Eventually, I gained the strength to walk out. When I first stood from the bed, I was surprised to find that I was able to walk across the room without any fear of stumbling over any furniture. You see, my brain had already begun to retrain the rest of my body. All the days that he had been walking around me, leaving the door open, my brain had been paying close attention. It knew what the sound of footsteps sounded like at different parts of the small space. Knew where to step without stumbling."

"Who was he?" My curiosity was getting the best of me.

Helix chuckles at my impatience. "His name was Avery. A recluse. Brilliant man, but quite odd. That is why he was never bothered by the Howlers. They feared him because of his peculiarity. He made them believe that he could summon spirits. It was all a farce, of course, but it worked to protect him. My favorite thing about Avery was his fascination with astronomy." Helix tips his head and points to his tattoos. "He marked my head with a map of the stars and planets."

"That must have hurt," Dom stated, and then thought better of it, "Of course, I guess after what you had been through, the pain was not so bad."

"Not so bad," Helix remarks with a smile. "Avery was afraid that the science of astronomy would be lost forever if he didn't pass on his knowledge. So, he passed it on to me."

"But you can't read it. Even if you had sight, you can't read what is on top of your head." Dom states the obvious.

"You can, though." Helix's mood seems to have improved since getting past the agonizing part of his life story. "You can copy the markings on parchment and then study them. That is how we pass on the knowledge." He smiles broadly, and his contented groan comes from his belly for the first time since beginning his story.

My father has been quiet, stroking his beard as he always does when in deep thought. "Helix, we thank you for divulging your story to us. I know that I speak for the rest of my family when I say that I am truly sorry for what you have had to endure. Please know that you have found a haven with us here in Grayson. We will ensure your safety."

The moan from Helix's belly almost sounds like a cat's purr as he says, "Thank you, Avis. I have wandered alone in the forest for so long that I'm afraid staying in one place will actually feel confining."

With a throaty chuckle, Helix adds, "Although that bath was quite pleasant, I must admit."

We all chuckle at Helix's admission.

"Well, please know that you are welcome back as often as you are in the area," my father adds.

Helix nods his appreciation.

"There is one more thing I must ask, Helix. I hope it isn't too painful." My father sits forward with his elbows on his knees. "Is there anything you can tell us about Gallner? Anything that will help our community?"

Helix thinks about this for several seconds before responding. "The last time I saw him, he was a newborn. Only a few weeks old. If I saw him today, I wouldn't even recognize him."

"Okay, thank you for your honesty."

"I would say this, Avis. I can't imagine the fury that is boiling inside of that man. To be born from rage, into a world of torment, it doesn't surprise me that he is demented. Ripley obviously saw something special in Gallner and groomed him into becoming the next Alpha. He just didn't realize that Gallner held so much resentment. I don't think Gallner's resentment will subside even now after he has killed Ripley. It's obvious that his anger consumes him. I am fearful that his anger will consume Grayson as well."

Chapter 20

The telling of Helix's life story left me with a sour taste of bile in my throat. As I had listened to him recount the horrors he has experienced, I couldn't help but feel shame for the self-pity I have wallowed in since childhood. Losing my eye, as well as my loved ones, is nothing in comparison to what Helix has had to endure, and yet I let the tragedy of it control my entire existence.

Leaning against one of the stone pillars at the entrance to Grayson, with the sun just beginning to peek over the horizon, I vow to find a way to rid myself of this guilt that I have carried; break out of this cage of misery that I have placed myself in. I realize that the process has already begun, thanks to Helix. He provided me with the tools I need to begin my escape from the prison I have put myself in. With his gift of the bow, I realized my potential as a valuable member of this community. With the telling of his story, I realize that the life I have been given is a blessing and not a curse.

"I imagine you had quite a bit of explaining to do last night," Merritt says, approaching me from behind.

Delighted to see her, I turn to greet her with a smile. "Why are you out so early this morning?"

"I could ask you the same thing?" she leans comfortably against the other pillar, gazing out across the dark field. Because of the chill of the morning, Merritt has a quilt wrapped around her shoulders.

For several minutes, we watch as the night concedes to the rising sun. It doesn't give up its charge right away. With its darkness and cold, the night clings desperately to the earth. The sun will not be denied, though. With fantastic brilliance and warmth, the sun advances, spreading its light across the landscape in dazzling hues of pink.

Merritt and I watch the display silently for several minutes. Neither of us speaks. We simply appreciate the scene before us. Eventually, I sneak a look in her direction. I am surprised to see that her eyes are on me. I give her an embarrassed smile, but she doesn't look away.

"I'm glad you came out here this morning," I say to her quietly. "I had hoped we could find time to talk today. Let's take a walk."

"Okay," Merritt says cautiously. She turns towards Grayson and begins to walk on the path.

"No, not that way," I comment. Waving my hand towards the meadow, I add, "Let's take a walk in the meadow."

Merritt's eyes widen. She has not been outside the walls. Although she is aware that the short rock walls have never protected our community from the threats that loom all around, she still holds great fear for what lies beyond the walls. Fear of the unknown.

I hold my hand out to her. Her wide eyes narrow at me. Slowly, though, she reaches out and takes my hand. Together, we walk through the rock pillars and into the meadow. I have much to say to her. At this moment, though, I want Merritt to experience the beauty that lies beyond Grayson without distracting her.

Looking out over the meadow, I begin, "I want to apologize to you, Merritt."

She looks confused but remains silent. We continue to walk, hand-in-hand, for the first time. In the distance, birds are beginning to greet the day. Without actually witnessing it, I know that all the animals of the forest are coming out of their dens and nests. They will work all day, feverishly, to prepare for the upcoming frost. A frost that, by the feel of this crisp morning, is sure to be upon us within the next few weeks.

"You have no reason to apologize to me, Lukan." Merritt's voice is soft, but I am strangely taken back to the nightmare I had.

Shaking off the chill that the memory sends up my spine, I continue. "For too long I have lived in a constant state of anger. Angry at myself for what happened the night I lost my eye. Ashamed that I have been a liability to the community instead of an asset. Last night, Helix sat in my living room and told us the unthinkable things he has lived through. I know you have questions about him. I don't blame you. I will say this about him, that man is rarely unhappy. He is always smiling." The thought of Helix's smile and thunderous laugh makes me chuckle. "After everything he has been though, that smile is always present."

"I have to admit that when Helix entered town, I was frightened. His furs. The markings on his neck and head. The cloth covering his eyes." She ponders briefly. "It was all very intimidating. But then he put his hand on your shoulder." Merritt stops and faces me. "You didn't even flinch under his touch. You seemed just as comfortable with his hand on you as you do holding mine. That's when I knew."

"Knew what?"

"When you lost your eye, you lost a lot. You lost your confidence, your sense of self." I look away from her. The words she speaks are more accurate than she realizes. With a gentle finger, she touches my chin and brings my attention back to her. "You gained so much more though. Nobody else can hear danger approaching. You can, though. Why? Because you gained the gift of perception. You perceive danger well before any of us can. If Helix were dangerous, you would have most certainly perceived him to be so. When he placed his hand on your shoulder, I knew he could be trusted. I knew he was important to you. I trust him because I trust you."

Her brown eyes gaze at me softly. I return her gaze until the notion to kiss her makes me uncomfortable, and I am forced to look away. The sensation is strange to me. Although she has kissed me lightly on the cheek, I have never felt the urge to kiss her. Until now.

Our brief near-intimate moment is interrupted as I hear my name being called. Looking back towards town, I am surprised to find how far Merritt and I have walked. At the entrance to town stands Helix and my father. Disappointed that the moment with Merritt is lost, I am not too terribly upset. There will be more opportunities.

Together, Merritt and I approach the men. Helix is carrying a pack over his shoulder. I can only assume that means he is leaving Grayson to resume his life of wandering once more.

"Good morning," Merritt greets cheerfully. My father returns her greeting.

Helix sticks out his hand and says, "Good morning. I am Helix." His deep voice is pleasant and cheerful.

Merritt shakes his hand, and I can't help but notice how small it looks in his.

"I am happy to meet you. I'm Merritt," Merritt remarks cordially. "Are you leaving town after such a short time?"

"I'm afraid I must. Rest assured, though, I will be taking the sound of your beautiful voice along for the journey, Merritt."

Merritt beams, while I shake my head and roll my eye, and my father chuckles lightly.

Looking at me coyly, Merritt says playfully, "You could learn something about romance and charm from Helix, you know."

Helix's boisterous laughter fills the countryside. The sound of it is contagious, and we all join in. I am thankful for the light moment we share before having to say goodbye to my friend.

Chapter 21

The hot days of summer are quickly replaced with the coolness of fall. Leaves, now brown and yellow, abandon the trees they have clung to for so many months. No longer will they whistle the sweet song of the wind. No longer will they provide shade when the sun is high in the sky. The role of the leaf, now lying on the ground, is now that of nurturer. Spread across the forest floor, the leaves will crumble under the feet of the wildlife that traverse the area. Their purpose now is to protect and feed the earth while winter assaults it with its cold blast. The life of the leaf, though short, is significant and purposeful.

The people of Grayson fall into the routines that signify the changing of seasons. It has been a couple of weeks since Helix made his surprise visit to my community. Although I miss hearing his deep voice speaking his wisdom to me, I have no doubt that I will see my friend again. He has a tendency to appear when I least expect him.

With all the work that must be completed during the harvest, I have had little time to spend with Merritt. We have gone on a few walks together, read the large book of Geography a few times, even went on a picnic once. Still, our time together always seems to be cut short due to the weariness this time of year causes.

The best thing about the past few weeks is the fact that Gallner, or any of the Howlers for that matter, have not terrorized our town. At dinner, last night, my father voiced his concerns over this.

"I fear that our citizens will be given a false sense of security. We are becoming unmindful as we go about our daily duties. The Howlers could arrive at any moment, and we will be caught completely off guard," my father explained.

"Not with Lukan around we won't," my mother countered with a proud grin.

I thought it strange that even in their absence, we found ourselves worrying about the Howlers. It seems that we will never truly have peace of mind in this world.

I have a strong urge to visit the window one more time before the cold arrives and I am forced to stay indoors. However, every day that passes without a Howler visit means that tomorrow could be the day. Not only does Grayson need me as their alarm system, which I am happy to do, but Gallner is expecting me to report something interesting to him when he arrives. If I am absent, the consequences for the town are certain to be disastrous. It is too risky for me to leave Grayson until the Howler's finally do show up again to cause havoc.

The day finally came.

Standing now, on the lawn of the Community Building, Gallner and his band of fiends, loom over us on the stage. After watching helplessly as the group saturated Grayson with their vileness, throwing rocks through windows, tearing down fences that we had just finished mending, toppling gravestones in the town cemetery, we followed them here and listened to a speech by Gallner that held my point. Now he is beckoning me to the stage so that I can "report in."

Slowly, I make my way to the stage. I take my time walking through the crowd, collecting my thoughts. If Gallner is as crazed as I believe he is, this report can go very badly for me. I wish my mother had stayed at home, so she wouldn't have to witness what is sure to happen to her son.

"Lukan, my friend," Gallner greets as I approach him on the stage. I try to stand tall, with square shoulders. He places an arm around my shoulder, and I look out over my community.

I find my parents. Naturally, my mother is overcome with fear, and my father holds her close. I try to convey with my eye that it will be alright. My father gives me a quick nod and then whispers into my mother's ear.

Scanning the crowd, I finally find Merritt. Her eyes are wide, and her mouth is set in anger. I wink at her in an attempt to calm her nerves. She does not return my wink. She doesn't even smile.

"What have you got for me?" Gallner asks, he has removed his arm from my shoulder. He rubs his hands together in excitement.

"Well, nothing really to get too excited about," I start. I glance at my dad. He nods his head once to assure me. We have discussed this. I have rehearsed what I need to say. Still, I do not look forward to the consequences.

"Right after you left, the town had a meeting. Naturally, some people didn't want me there. Others said I should listen in so I can report to you. Not a whole lot was really decided at that meeting, but one of the men there gave a really great speech about passion. I should have written it down for you. You would have been inspired, I'm sure."

I glance at Gallner. His eyes are narrowed. Obviously, none of his howlers have ever practiced sarcasm on him because he doesn't seem to understand that's what he is receiving from me.

"Then we had a feast. It was incredible. Really, it was. You should have been there…we had smoked squirrel. Have you had smoked squirrel? I feel you would really like it if you ever tried it. You missed out."

A hard slap across my face silences me.

"Do not patronize me, boy!" Gallner shouts at me. "You will speak to me with respect!"

Gathering my thoughts after the surprise of being slapped, trying not to be enraged and lashing back at the madman, I calmly respond, "I apologize if my words seemed patronizing." I pause for just a second. "If I may say so, Gallner, 'patronize' is a fancy word for somebody that wears a poorly prepared wolf skin just so you can intimidate his enemies. I mean, can you even smell yourself?"

The air is immediately knocked from my lungs, and I fall to my knees as he punches me hard in the belly. I choke, trying to suck in air. Faintly, I can hear my mother sob. I dare not look in her direction. The Howlers around me laugh and jeer as I struggle to find the oxygen my body requires. Closing my eye, I allow myself to feel the pain but only briefly. I struggle to stand to my feet, my lungs still burning as they search for air.

Through gasps, I say, "The only reason I bring it up is because there was a man here a few weeks ago that had a similar way of talking." Cough, wheeze. "When he was asked how he acquired such a broad vocabulary, he said his mother was adamant that her sons be educated." More coughing and wheezing. "He described his mother as grand."

I stare hard into his eyes as I hold my aching belly and continue to try to draw a deep breath. His eyes are wide and full of curiosity and surprise. I can see that his breaths are also coming in shallow gasps. This is the response my father and I were planning on. We have delivered a surprise attack on Gallner with something he isn't used to – emotions.

"This stranger also spoke of a brother. He would love to be able to see his brother again. He'll never get to though, because of his blindness." I never take my eye from his.

It's obvious that he is shaken by my words. Shaken at the thought of his brother being alive after being left alone in the wilderness, brutalized and mutilated. Shaken at the memory of his mother. Gallner begins to back away slowly which confuses the Howlers, but they begin to back away as well. Not sure exactly what to do with the emotions that are coursing through his body, Gallner looks at the crowd with shaky eyes. With a weak howl, he leaps from the stage. His madmen follow him as he races away from Grayson.

When I am sure they are gone, I collapse onto the stage. My insides burn, but I feel lucky that he didn't climb me like a tree and snap my neck the way he did his Alpha. My parents and Merritt are at my side in an instant.

"I'm okay. I'm okay," I assure them, fighting the urge to gag.

"Well done, Lukan," my father commends. "We have found Gallner's weakness."

"But at what cost?" my mother demands.

"A slap across the face and a punch in the gut is minimal," I respond, attempting a laugh to calm her frayed nerves. "Gallner is reeling from feeling emotions and reliving memories that have been groomed out of him. It is unlikely that we will see him again until spring. When he comes back, we will be ready."

Chapter 22

Once again, I begin my day just as the sun is beginning to kiss the horizon. Dawn has become my favorite part of the day. Leaning against the pillar at the entrance of Grayson has become my favorite daily routine. Sometimes Merritt joins me, and we talk about all the far-away places we would like to visit. Sometimes we just watch the sunrise in silence.

Today, though, I am thankful to be alone.

For many nights, I have been restless. Tossing and turning in my bed. Sleeping very little. Since Gallner's last visit, my mind has been wandering to the window. I am distracted by thoughts of Lia.

My thoughts of Lia are not the same as how I think of Merritt. When my thoughts wander to Merritt, as they so often do, I ponder on her beauty, charm, and wit. I think about her confidence. No, I do more than think of it. I envy her confidence. She is brave in so many ways that I am not.

When I think about Lia, the sad and broken girl on the tattered blanket, I think of anguish and misery. I want to know what it is in her underground world that has caused her so much trepidation. Is it the smoking chimney? My curiosity is getting the better of me. I must check on her one more time before winter arrives with a blast of cold fury.

With one last look at Grayson, I remove myself from the pillar that I was leaning against, pick up my pack and bow, and set out on my journey. In the distance, I can hear a pack of coyotes. Their frenzied howling signals that they have had a successful early morning hunt. I do not fear coyotes. When they howl, it doesn't mean the same as when the Howlers make the overexaggerated noise. Coyotes howl for the sole purpose of communicating with their cherished pack members. Howlers do it to intimidate and be obnoxious.

Before I went to bed last night, I announced that I would be leaving Grayson for a couple of days. Dom was a little curious since I didn't go into any more details. My mother was, understandably, worried. She begged me to stay. She didn't understand what could be on the other side of the walls that had such a pull on me. I wasn't ready to tell her.

"He'll be fine, Lue," my father said soothingly to her.

"But the Howlers?" she argued.

"The Howlers won't be back." Approaching his wife, my dad wrapped his arms around her and explained, "Lukan's curiosity is more than the walls of Grayson can contain, my love. I believe he gets that from you as you have been outside the walls many times gathering the flowers you love."

I watch my parents as they discuss me like I'm not there. It doesn't bother me, though. I stand amazed at their love for each other. Their gentleness with each other. For some reason, my mind wanders to Helix's mother. She never knew the loving embrace of a man. Never knew what it was to look into a man's eyes and have a meaningful conversation. She only knew torment and anguish.

Another thought occurs to me. If Gallner indeed chooses a woman to be his, that woman will be sentenced to the same life of torture. The thought causes my stomach to turn over.

"I must go, mom. I won't be gone long, and then I won't leave again. You'll be stuck with me in this house all winter long. By the time winter's over, you'll be begging me to leave." I say with a grin.

She relents, of course. We all knew she would. Even she knew she would. Sometimes I think she makes a fuss just because she is a mom and she is expected to make a fuss.

An owl swooping low across the meadow distracts me from my thoughts. I stop to watch him, admiring his grace. When he makes a couple of sweeps across the meadow, no doubt looking for a meal before he heads to his nest for the day, he flies up onto a nearby tree limb and lets out a loud hoot. He is answered shortly by another owl that I hadn't even known was there.

*****

It takes me almost the entire day of nonstop walking to reach the meadow with the window. When I get to the edge of the forest, I stop. I want to observe before stepping out into the open. Taking a deep breath, I realize that the air seems clean. No death smoke today.

While I watch the meadow, I take the dried fruit from my pack. My mother had packed a small portion of food for my journey. Just enough food for a one-night trip into the woods.

A twig breaking to my right causes me to flinch. My bow is in my hand in less than a second. Steadily, I aim towards the trees where the sound came from. Because both of my ears hear better than my one eye can see, I close my eye and concentrate on the sounds of the forest.

Birds chirping. Leaves giving up their hold on their trees and falling to the earth. Bugs skittering around underneath the leaves. The wind changing directions. A twig breaking under the weight of a….

"Come out," I say forcefully, still aiming my bow in the direction of the sound.

"Lukan, it's me. Put the bow down," I hear Dom shout.

Relaxing, I set my bow on the ground and watch my cousin walk out from behind a cluster of trees.

"Dom, what are you doing out here?" I ask with annoyance.

"I don't know. I just felt like I should follow you. You know, to protect you."

"Protect me from what? The birds? Squirrels?" My annoyance is building rapidly.

"I don't know, Lukan." Dom seems to be having a difficult time explaining himself. "I just want to know what draws you out here. Is it Helix? Are you looking for him?"

My patience is running thin. Glancing out towards the window, I take in a deep calming breath that does nothing to calm me.

"Being alone is what draws me here. In town, there is always somebody around. Out here, I can be by myself. I don't know. Maybe I have a Wanderer's heart like Helix. But no, I am not looking for him. When he wants to be found, he always finds me." I explain.

None of it is a lie. Living in the walls of Grayson does feel crowded sometimes, but that isn't why I'm here. I can't tell Dom the truth, though. Not about the window. Not yet.

Dom considers my words. I can see him looking over my shoulder, into the meadow.

"This is where you shot the buck, isn't it?" he asks. I'm not sure if he is trying to change the subject or if the memory just entered his head.

With a sigh, I answer, "Right over there."

To my horror, Dom starts to walk in the direction I just pointed. Right towards the window.

"Dom, wait!"

He stops abruptly and turns around. "What? What is it?"

I'm no good at this, I realize. I have no idea how to keep him from walking out into the meadow.

"Come with me. I'll show you what I'm doing out here," I concede, walking past him.

Together, Dom and I walk out into the meadow. Just before we get to the window, I turn to him.

"You know the cliff, right? The cliff I took you to and told you that I dive from?"

Dom nods.

"You know the cliff is important to me. I enjoy going there. Alone. Which is why I have kept that spot a secret."

"No, you kept the cliff a secret because Auntie would never let you leave the house again if she ever found out," Dom says with a sly smile.

He's right, of course.

"True, Listen, I like being part of a community. I also like having my secrets. This place is one of my secret places. I wasn't ready to share it with anyone, but here you are. What choice do I have?"

Dom is smiling broadly now. He loves that he has won. His enthusiasm just aggravates me that much more.

"I'm serious, Dom. You can't tell."

"I won't. I promise." He says.

"Fine. Come on."

Parting the tall grass, the window comes into view, and I hear Dom gasp. The flowers I had left the day I saw Lia lying on the blanket with her bandaged hand are still there. They are withered now. I hope when Lia woke up that day and saw the flowers, she felt at least a little comfort. The room below is empty now. Only the blanket remains.

"What is this?" Dom asks in a whisper.

"Not sure. I found it the day I killed the buck."

"Where did the flowers come from?"

I didn't want to tell Dom about Lia. I wanted to keep that bit of information to myself. Mainly because I am afraid of how he will react when he finds out there in another civilization living below our feet. Knowing about the underground world may also lead to another conversation where I have to disclose the information about the death chimney.

"Lukan?" I took too long to answer his question. I look up at him. "Where did the flowers come from?"

"I, uh, I put them there," I say slowly.

Dom's eyes narrow as he attempts to process this new information.

"Why?" he asks, looking at the window and then back at me.

I can't come up with an answer that will satisfy Dom's curiosity, so I stand in silence, staring down at the window.

"Lukan?" Dom exclaims. "Answer me. What exactly am I looking at here?" His patience is frayed even thinner than mine.

I still don't know exactly what to say. This is why I didn't want to talk to anyone about Lia or her underground community.

My silence only angers Dom. "C'mon, Lukan! I thought we were past the secrets and the lies. I thought we were getting closer."

"Oh, don't pull that on me, Dom. Just because we are cousins that happen to live in the same house doesn't mean you have a right to every one of my secrets." I say, exasperated.

"I don't want to know all your secrets. Just this one. Why is there a window in the middle of nowhere and why did you put flowers on it?" His voice isn't as loud. I can tell he is trying to reason with me.

I guess, with something as strange as this so close to our home, he has a right to know. Still, I wasn't mentally prepared to share this with anyone yet. I'm not trying to be unreasonable or selfish. I just don't want the people of Grayson to panic. They have a tendency of doing that when faced with the unknown.

"Please, Dom. Just trust me," I plead. "The window. I'm still trying to figure it out. That's why I came out here. I wanted to see it one last time before winter sets in. When I know more about it, I will tell you. I'll tell the whole town."

He looks at me with narrowed eyes. "The flowers?"

"I wanted to show our good will to whoever is living down there. A peace offering, I guess." It's only a partial lie.

Dom considers this. "A peace offering."

"Yes."

"To show good will."

"That's right."

"You think it's safe down there. Don't you? You want it to be so that the people of Grayson can have someplace safe to live." He has me, and he knows it. "Am I right?"

Nodding slowly, I acknowledge quietly. "You're right. You're right." My voice sounds more defeated than I mean for it to.

"Is it?"

"I don't know. I haven't found the way in." Still only a partial lie. Even though I did find the way in, I haven't found the way to get into it.

With this, Dom returns his attention to the window. He squats down to get a closer look. This is not how I saw this day going. I hadn't considered how I would feel to have to share it with anyone besides Helix.

"Dom, go back home now please," I say, interrupting his thoughts.

"Why?"

I don't have a good answer that doesn't sound completely selfish. After I think for a second, I come up with one that might work, though.

"Because my mom will be in hysterics if we are both gone for the night. Does she even know you're out here?"

Dom looks down, "No. I snuck out when you left. I'm sure she's worried."

"I'm sure she is, and it's going to take you all evening to get back. That's if you run."

"What are you going to do?"

"I'm going to camp out here tonight. Look around a bit. I'll head back in the morning, collecting plants for Mrs. Clifton along the way. I'll be back by lunch." I explain.

Dom nods. "Can I come back here with you in the spring?"

I hadn't considered this possibility. I hadn't considered that others might also feel the draw of the window and want to visit it.

"Of course," I'm not sure if it's a lie or not. Hopefully, by spring, Dom will be preoccupied with something else and be too busy to come back out to the window.

Nodding, he begins to walk back towards the woods. I breathe out a sigh of relief. Before he gets into the woods, he turns back towards me.

"I promise I won't say anything to anyone about this place. I know it's special to you, Lukan."

With a sincere smile, I reply, "Thanks, Dom. Be safe going home. I'll see you tomorrow."

"See you tomorrow." With that, Dom turns and disappears into the woods.

With just a hint of sadness, I watch the edge of the woods. I expect my cousin to walk back out. Now that I've sent him away, I realize that I will be spending the night in the very woods that terrorized me in my sleep just a few short weeks ago. I look around nervously, and the weight of loneliness settles heavily upon me.

*****

My sleep is once again interrupted.

Screams of terror pierce the night. I sit up shakily and look around frantically. Darkness envelops me with a thickness that I can feel in my chest. The forest and all of her inhabitants are silent. I cannot see them in the darkness, but I know the tall trees stand sentry around the place where I camp tonight. Sadly, the forest and the trees cannot protect me from the nightmares that haunt me. The chill of the autumn air, although frigid, isn't the cause of my goosebumps.

Although stoking the nearby fire would warm me and provide a comforting light in this darkness, my exhaustion takes over once again. Laying back into my bedding, I begin to dose once again. I think of Merritt and our enjoyable times together. Times when we were children, and we would play chase, or she would watch me climb trees while she stood on the ground demanding that I come back down. I think about her thick brown hair with the bouncy curls at the tips and the red strands that only like to appear when the sun shines on them just right.

Once again, screams shatter the silence, and I realize that I am not dreaming. Somebody in the distance is being tortured. I hastily make my way to the smoldering ashes of my campfire and begin stabbing at the remains with a stick. In the darkness, amidst anguished screams that now seem to surround me, I see a small ember begin to glow. Adding dried leaves, the ember births a spark which evolves into the fire I need to give me light and warm the blood that has turned cold in my veins.

The screaming continues. It seems to come from all around me as it echoes through the forest. When night first started to edge the day away, I had been afraid to fall asleep. Afraid of the nightmares that I was sure were going to haunt me. The screams that are echoing through the darkness now are far worse than the torment of the death smoke nightmare I had feared. I slam my hands over my ears in order to block out the anguish that resonates through the trees.

I am reminded of Helix telling me that the Howlers don't come into this forest. Hearing the screaming now, though, I'm sure he was wrong. If Howlers are nearby, I certainly don't want to announce my presence with a brightly burning fire. I begin throwing dirt onto it until it is smothered into a small flame. Just enough to keep the darkness at bay. I sit as close to the fire as possible as if its small light will protect me from the danger that I fear is all around me.

A hoot owl in a tree nearby voices his complaint about all the noise I am making on the ground. Or perhaps, my small fire is disrupting his night of hunting and he is voicing his displeasure. Either way, I jump at this new sound that comes from the forest. I realize, however, that the screams have ceased. Holding my breath, and closing my eye, I listen carefully for any sound that may not belong to the forest.

I hear nothing. Just the crackling of the fire.

Moments ago, I had longed for the silence. Now, though, it snakes up my spine eerily. With my arms wrapped around my legs, I huddle close to the small fire. My imagination runs rampant with thoughts and possibilities of who was screaming.

Soon, guilt sets in as I realize that I should have helped the person. What could I have done, though? Really? A one-eyed boy. I wish I had asked Dom to stay.

I long for the morning. For the light of day to crush the darkness. When it does, I will return to Grayson and apologize to Dom for my selfishness.

Chapter 23

With daylight, my sense of adventure returns. With the darkness gone, so is my fear of the unknown.

I slept the rest of the night fitfully. When I woke up, I groggily remembered my promise to rush home and apologize to my cousin. The higher the sun rose into the sky, the more confident I felt about remaining in the forest. Just a while longer, at least.

With the sun shining brightly, the screams I heard the night before seem like they were just a dream. Something my over imaginative brain conjured up. I know that isn't the case. I know that the screams were real, though. I fear I will hear them in the sleep for the rest of my life. That would be a fitting punishment for being too scared to help.

I return to the window. Nothing has changed. The blanket lays in the middle of the room. I wonder how long I need to stand in this spot before Lia, or anybody enters the small room below me. Sitting down, I cross my legs and wait. Waiting for a sign of hope from the underground.

The sign does not come, though, and I grow impatient as the day wears on.

Standing, I decide to head home. This decision isn't easy. I know I won't be returning until spring. I could go to the metal door, but the nightmare of the death smoke is still too fresh and haunting. My adventurous side and my frightened side argue over the prospect of going to the door. Frightened side wins out, and I set my course for Grayson.

*****

As I near Grayson, I can see a figure leaning against one of the entrance pillars.

Merritt.

When she sees me, she does something that stops me in my tracks. She leaves the comfort of Grayson and runs through the meadow, towards me. The trek has taken me all day. I'm tired, hungry, and probably just a little irritable. However, seeing that dark hair bounce as Merritt makes her way towards me, those troubles seem insignificant.

As she nears, however, I see that her face conveys something besides happiness to see me. I rush to meet her.

"Lukan, you're okay!" Merritt says when she reaches me. Her arms wrap around my neck. I can feel her violently thumping heart against my chest.

"Of course, I am," I reply, confused at her reaction. I have been outside the walls many times.

Releasing me, she looks me in the face. The fear that is etched on her face causes panic to begin to grow in my belly.

"What is it?" I ask, fearing that my mother's warning about the Howlers coming during my absence had been correct.

"Is Dom with you?"

I think about her question. The strangeness of it.

"No. He was with me yesterday, but he left me in the forest. He said he was coming back here." A strange prickling on the back of my neck causes me to shiver. I brush at it with my hand even though I know there is nothing there.

"He didn't come back." Her eyes are wide. 'He's missing."

Although a bit odd and slightly alarming, I am not ready to panic over my cousin being out in the forest for one night. He knows the forest. Knows how to traverse it safely.

"I'm sure he's fine. Probably decided to take advantage of a few more days of hunting before winter comes," I try to calm her nerves. "I guess my mom is pretty worried?"

Merritt nods and her curls whip back and forth freely, distracting me slightly.

"You better get home and try to calm her down," she advises.

Together, Merritt and I enter Grayson.

When we enter my house, my mother rushes to me.

"Please tell me Dom is with you."

"He was for awhile, but then he left to come home," I explain, already feeling the guilt settling between my shoulders for leaving town. Losing Dom or me to the forest has always been a tremendous fear for her. "I'm sure he is hunting, mom. Give him a little longer." I try to calm her nerves.

"He didn't even tell us he was going," she says to nobody in particular as she makes her way to a chair and sits.

The fact that he didn't tell anyone he was leaving Grayson, even for a bit, is odd for Dom, and slightly annoying. I know, however, that he didn't want anyone to know he was following me.

"Mom, I'm sure he's fine."

"Lue, Domenic is fine. He has more experience outside these walls than anyone else in Grayson." My father says to console his near-panicked wife.

His words irritate me. What my parents don't realize about me is that I have spent a lot of time in the forest. I have walked the same game trails that Dom and the other hunters have used to stalk their prey. I have taken more risks outside the walls of Grayson than Dom has. The forest is my safe place from this maddening world of judgments placed on me by my disability.

I work to hide my annoyance but my mom notices.

"What? What is it Lukan? Do you hear something?"

"No. No, I don't hear anything." I reply, shaking my head. "I'm tired. I need to get these plants to Mrs. Clifton."

My mother's face contorts into a sob while my father attempts to console her. Jealousy rises in my throat like bile as I watch the spectacle of their worry over a boy that isn't even their son. Turning, I stomp to the door. Merritt leans against it. I had forgotten she was here. She has witnessed the entire scene. Her eyes are narrowed, and I can sense her displeasure.

"What?" I say with more annoyance in my voice than I had intended.

Merritt shakes her head slowly but says nothing.

"Listen, if he isn't back tomorrow, I will go back into the woods and search for him."

"If he isn't back by tomorrow, he could be dead." Merritt hisses at me.

"It's just the forest. There isn't anything in the forest that will hurt him," I am almost shouting now. Even as I say the words, the image of the black smoke of death that haunted me in my sleep and Merritt's lifeless body screaming my name. I tell myself that was just a nightmare.

With a sharp shake of her head, Merritt steps away from the doorway. I take one last look at my parents and then Merritt before I walk out.

As I walk to Mrs. Clifton's home to deliver the plants she will use for medicine, I am plagued with swirling emotions of anger and regret. Angry that my parents and Merritt are making such a fuss over my cousin. Angry that he didn't tell anyone that he was leaving

Grayson and now his actions are falling on me to answer for. Angry that everything is always about Dom.

There is also regret.

Regret that I wasn't more sensitive to the feelings of my parents and Merritt. Regret that even after all these years, I still feel jealousy. Most importantly, regret that I wouldn't allow Dom to stay with me last night.

As I walk, citizens of Grayson greet me cordially. They are unaware of the turmoil that my family is enduring right now. A dog, somebody's pet, walks beside me for a bit before being distracted by a smell that has caught his attention.

In the distance, a sound stops me in my tracks. A scream. This is playful screaming, though. Just children playing tag or a boy pulling a girl's braid to gain her attention. Still, just playing. The sound of it halts me, though. I am reminded of the scream I woke up to the night before. The scream of agony that seemed to come from all around me, penetrating the tranquility of the forest.

I don't want to think that the owner of the screams was my cousin. I don't want to, but I must consider the possibility.

My breath seems stuck in my throat as I imagine Dom being tortured while I sat by the warmth of the fire. A tremble begins in my hands and then quickly moves up my arms. As I struggle to breathe, a darkness creeps in. I feel myself falling. Although my mind is screaming at me to block the fall, my body refuses. Before I can do anything to stop myself, I am on the ground and blackness takes over.

*****

"When was the last time you ate?" I hear Mrs. Clifton ask.

Sluggishly, I become aware of lying in my bed with a cool towel on my forehead. Mrs. Clifton sits next to me. She has just asked me something, I think. I couldn't concentrate on her words, so I don't know what the question was. I struggle to recall it so I can answer her correctly.

"Lukan, when was the last time you ate?"

Oh yeah, that's what it was. Now, to get my mouth to work so I can answer.

"Um, last night, I think," I reply slowly.

"That's what I thought," she replies kindly. Turning to somebody else in the room, she adds, "He's fine. Just too much exertion with too little to eat. Once he eats, he will feel better."

Rolling my head to the side, I see Merritt standing against the wall. Her arms are crossed. Obviously, she is still perturbed with me. The scowl on her face makes me wish I had stayed passed out just a bit longer.

"Thank you, Mrs. Clifton," Merritt says.

With that, our town doctor stands. Before she walks from the room, she turns back to me and says, "Eat something, Lukan. The town needs you. We can't have you passed out on the street." With a kind smile, she walks from the room.

Knowing that I am about to be chastised by my best friend, I pretend to have fallen back asleep. Once again, though, nothing gets past Merritt.

"Oh, quit it, Lukan," she demands. "I know you aren't asleep."

Opening my eye, I sit up in the bed and remove the cool towel. I make a mental note to thank Mrs. Clifton for having the kindness to leave my eyepatch on.

"Are you trying to kill yourself? Is that what all this is?" Merritt asks sharply.

"Kill myself? No. Why would you think that?" I am appalled that she would think that of me.

"I don't know, Lukan. You are always doing things that could get you killed. You are bitter and jealous and angry with the world because of an accident that happened nine years ago. I just want to know what is going on in your head." Merritt's eyes brim with angry tears.

I ponder her words. The sneaking off. The cliff-diving. Befriending a stranger who very much looks like a Howler. Spending time away from Grayson. I can see how all those things could seem like I have a death wish.

"No, Merritt. I don't want to kill myself. Maybe I have a death wish, but I don't want to kill myself." I answer.

"What's the difference, Lukan? Either you want to live, or you want to die." The tears that have been threatening to fall, now do.

Nodding, I say, "I want to live, Merritt. I do. I promise you."

Merritt wipes the tears from her cheeks.

"Good." She says quite simply.

We spend the rest of the afternoon together. She makes sure I get something to eat and then helps me with Dom's chores. My mother, although still worried, carries on with her day like any other. Merritt helps my mom prepare dinner and the four of us sit down to try to enjoy it together, all while worrying about Dom.

Even though Merritt explains that she doesn't need me to walk her home that night, my father insists that a gentleman never lets a lady walk home alone. When we reach her front door, she turns to me.

"What do you really think has happened to Dom?" she asks. "I can see it on your face. I can hear it in your voice. There's something you're not saying."

I can't hold her gaze. Looking down at the ground, I answer honestly, "Dom followed me into the forest. After we had a discussion, he said he was going home." I pause, unsure if I should divulge any more information. Tired of the secrets, I continue, "In the middle of the night, I woke up to screaming." Merritt gasps. "I couldn't tell where it was coming from in the dark."

"Did you hear howling?" she asks in a whisper.

"No."

Merritt takes in a deep breath and asks, "Do you think he's dead?"

"No, I don't. I really don't." I assure her. "I will give him until tomorrow, and if he isn't back, I will go looking for him."

Merritt reaches for my hand and says, "Please, be careful. I don't need you to go missing too. I couldn't live with that."

I look into her eyes and try to convey my feelings for her without actually speaking them out loud. I find it strange that I was ever able to summon the courage to dive from a cliff into the blue lake yet I am too afraid to tell my best friend how I feel about her. I tell myself that when the time is right, Merritt will know my true feelings.

Chapter 24

It is midday, and I prepare to go on another journey outside the walls of Grayson. This will not be a journey to the caves or the cliff. Not to the window, metal door, or chimney. Dom is yet to return, and I have the task of finding him and bringing him home, whatever his state.

At the entrance to Grayson, which is my exit, My mother clings to me. With fearful tears, she packed my bag full of food. Enough to last several days. She doesn't say so, but I get the impression that I'm not supposed to come back until I know the fate of my cousin.

Just as I am about to depart, Merritt grabs my arm. Thinking that she is going to give me a "goodbye, my brave prince" speech, I turn to her. Her eyes are wide, and she looks out over the meadow. When I see what has caught her attention, I hand my mother the pack she just placed on my shoulder and through gritted teeth, I tell them to run home and warn everyone they see along the way.

They see the danger. Howlers are approaching. They do not howl. They do not wrestle with each other along the way. They seem all business as they steadily gain on our town.

"There is still time to warn everyone and get the boys out of town," I yell as I race away to do my duty.

Running.

Shouting the alarm.

The citizens of Grayson send their boys into the forest frantically and then wait for the wrath of Gallner and the Howlers to pass them by. The Howlers are upon Grayson much quicker than normal, even though they are walking. As they walk through the streets, they do not destroy. Today, they are all business.

When they reach our house, I am appalled to see that they have Dom. Between two large Howlers, he is bound and requires help. I can see that his face is badly bruised. My anger boils, but above all else, emotions must be kept in check or the consequences could be fatal. I glance a look at my mother. She must understand this as she stands stoically as the Howlers pass by with her nephew. She gives no indication that the boy belongs to her.

The whole town gathers on the lawn of the Community Building. The scene before us is like something from my nightmares. Ten Howlers, clad in wreaking wolf skins. Although silent before, now they howl and pace back and forth behind their leader and their hostage. The Howler Alpha, Gallner, stands behind Dom. He's holding him up. From my vantage point, it's unclear whether Gallner holds Dom in submission or if he holds him because my cousin is simply too weak to stand on his own. The wounds on his face and hands, as well as his bloody clothes, lead me to believe he has been tortured and is too weak to stand on his own.

I hate to think of what Dom has been through in the past two days at the hands of the Howlers. One of his eyes is black and swollen shut. He has wrappings that ooze with blood on his arms. His head bobs at times, making it evident that his strength has left him. The fact that he isn't dead, though, gives me some comfort. The Howlers are a vicious and unforgiving group. They thrive on the power they hold over this land through their brutality. If they wanted to kill him, I reason in my mind, then they would have killed him already.

Although he already has our attention, Gallner raises his hand to an already silent crowd.

"Since I was little, the Howlers have been collecting boys for their pack," he begins. "Then, one day, there were no more boys. The women were only giving birth to baby girls. Every town we went to…only girls." He shrugs as he says this and then purses his lips. "So, two days ago, we find this," he says, motioning to Dom with one hand as he continues to hold him up with his other. "A boy. Can you imagine how surprised we were? I mean, years of only girls and now… At first, we were thrilled to have a new potential pack member. Even though he wasn't thrilled about the idea at all." A maniacal chuckle before he continues, "But then the question, where did he come from? None of the towns have boys. We asked our new guest. I mean, we asked nicely." A look of sincerity crosses his face briefly before returning to one of anger. "The boy refused to answer. Sadly, as you can tell by looking at him, he refused to answer many times. So, now here we are." A look of determination as he squints his eyes and seemingly looks at each one of us in the crowd. "Now, we are asking you. Grayson, where did he come from? Which town does he belong to? Does anyone want to claim him?"

The town is drowning in silent horror at the sight before us. I stand in the crowd with my parents. My father has his arm around my mother's waist. Mrs. Watkins, a good friend of my mom, is holding fiercely to my mom's hand. Both are attempting to comfort her as she cries silent tears, looking upon the boy she has raised as her own. I want to reach out to her, but I know the act will only draw attention.

"No?" Gallner bellows, interrupting my thoughts and causing me to flinch. "Nobody wants to claim this boy?" He looks at Dom, who is still struggling to stand. "Nobody wants to claim you. You must be as worthless to them as you are to me."

Although Dom is taller than the Howler Alpha, Gallner's muscular frame and oversized wolf skin give the illusion that he is the larger of the two. I search Dom's face for a sign. Any sign that he wants his town to intervene for him. He gives me nothing.

Gallner and his band of degenerates are growing increasingly restless. It seems that the longer they go without destroying something, the more agitated they become. Gallner's eyes flicker back and forth across the crowd as if he is looking for something. Eventually, his eyes land on their prey.

Me.

When Gallner finds me, a maniacal smile spreads slowly across his face. I have always thought that his thin mustache, always curling up at the ends, was amusing. Now, though, as it curves into a malicious grin, I am terror-struck.

Gallner's eyes do not leave my face. I look on in horror as he pulls a knife from the back of his pants. As one, the entire community gasps at the sight. Dom barely reacts. His head continues to bob, but he does seem to shift his weight away from Gallner and the rusty blade that he has produced.

Gallner finally shifts his eyes away from me and addresses the crowd once more, "Are you trying to insult me?" Of course, nobody answers him. To his pack he comments, "I think they're trying to insult me." The Howlers that continue to pace and fidget behind him begin howling again.

When they quiet back down, Gallner continues, "I do so enjoy being insulted. That means I don't have to be nice anymore."

He says this last part with his eyes on me once more. In my anger, I feel a solitary tear snake its way down my cheek, and I am ashamed. His evil grin returns as he brings the knife up to Dom's throat.

Fear turns to anger, and I feel my body react. Just as I start to charge the stage, I am stopped by a nightmarish scream. For an instant, I thought that Dom had finally regained his energy enough to put up a fight. His limp body and the startled look on Gallner's face prove otherwise. The scream has come from somewhere in the crowd behind me.

With a subtle twitch, Gallner motions for the owner of the scream to be retrieved from the crowd by his Howlers. Even without looking behind me, I already know. My mind is trying to prepare me, but my heart is unwilling to accept it.

Coming from behind me, I can hear the struggle as they drag the culprit through the crowd. I don't have the nerve to watch. Closing my eye tight, I hang my head, wrapping both arms around it in an attempt to squeeze this day away. The struggle continues. As the melee passes by me, I am shoved out of the way, causing me to look up. My stomach turns over, and I feel bile rise into my throat. When the chaos finally reaches the stage, Gallner releases Dom, allowing him to fall, and yanks her into his arms violently, placing the knife to her throat. My biggest fear is looming over me on the stage.

Merritt, held by Gallner.

Merritt. She has been my best friend since childhood. She knows me better than anyone in this town. My heart, the part of me that chose her before the rest of me figured out what was going on, breaks as I look at her. Her eyes are wide with fear and anger, but she continues to struggle against Gallner's grip.

"Young lady, weren't you taught not to interrupt the grown-ups when they are talking?" Gallner laughs savagely as Merritt struggles.

The arm that has been wrapped around her waist drops and she begins to turn towards him. Her anger is in full control, and her body is simply reacting. Gallner reaches behind her and grabs the back of her head, pulling her hair viciously. She cries out and begins to settle a bit.

"You're insane!" Merritt spits out in anger.

"I know," Gallner replies with hysterical laughter. "Isn't it great?" He leans his head back and releases a howl that is returned by the pack that paces behind him.

I try to formulate a plan as I watch this unfold. If I had my bow, I'm sure I could end Gallner quickly. I would have his pack to worry about, but hopefully, while their attention is on me, Merritt and Dom could get away.

I could rush the stage, but Gallner's pack is standing around him now. It's as if they know….

"Apparently, the boy belongs to you," Gallner says to Merritt. "Finally, somebody is claiming the little scamp."

His smile gone, with Merritt still in his grips, Gallner turns to the crowd and says, "The rules have always been simple. Your boys. That's it. Obviously, by the looks of this one, you have been hiding boys for years. So, I can only assume that you have more boys hidden even now." Gallner scans the crowd before continuing. "Grayson doesn't come free. You have to pay the rent. Sometimes, rent will be in blood."

With this, Gallner raises the knife above Merritt. Just as he is about to bring it back down on her, he is halted by a voice in the crowd.

"No, brother!" I hear the familiar throaty voice of Helix shout from the back of the crowd. "Don't do this."

Gallner is understandably caught off guard at this newcomer shouting at him from the crowd. He scans the crowd until he sees the man, cloaked in his own coat made of animal furs, standing in the back.

Helix doesn't wait for Gallner to respond. Using his guide stick to assist him, he begins walking through the crowd and towards the stage. The crowd parts and allows him to pass by with ease.

Gallner watches Helix with wide eyes. For the first time since Gallner has been terrorizing Grayson, I see something new in his eyes. Fear.

"Please don't do this," Helix repeats.

"How dare you approach our Alpha!" One of the Howlers bellows and charges towards Helix.

"No!" Gallner yells, causing the Howler to halt. "Leave him."

The Howler backs away, obviously surprised that his Alpha chooses to have mercy on this blind man.

"I have no brother," Gallner says with a shaky voice. He still clings to Merritt but seems distracted.

"You do. Our mother gave birth to you just a few weeks before your former Alpha, Ripley, did this to me and left me for dead in the forest."

"My brother fled. When he was caught, he received a just punishment."

Helix considers this and takes a different tactic, "What happened to our mother? Surely, she is no longer alive. I can't imagine she would approve of this life you have chosen."

Gallner flinches at the mention of his mother. I can't help but wonder if this approach is too much for him to handle emotionally.

"My mother had a purpose. She outlived her usefulness. Do not mention her again or I will bury this knife into your belly!" Gallner is clearly coming unhinged. I fear for Merritt's safety.

Sensing the unraveling nerves, Helix apologizes and bows slightly. I am thankful that the exchange is over. I'm not sure what Helix hoped to gain from it.

"People of Grayson, listen to me. I have been patient with you even when I know that you lie to me. There will be no more lies. I have no more patience to give. Today, you will learn what it means to respect your Alpha." Gallner declares.

In one fluid motion, Gallner brings his knife down and plunges it into Merritt's belly. From where I stand, the sickening sound of the impact along with the gasp and yelp that comes from Merritt bounces around in my head causing me to feel dizzy. Still holding the knife, blood already pooling around it from the devastating wound, Gallner slices up. As he pulls the blood-soaked knife from her belly, blood is slung from the wound and onto those closest to the scene. Releasing her hair, he allows her to fall to the ground.

The silent crowd has been undone. Weeping and moaning, and even sounds of people unable to keep from vomiting at the sight, fill the air around the Community Building. Merritt doesn't make a sound as she lies writhing on the stage. Her hands attempt to cover the wound but still her blood pools around her. Merritt's parents, distraught at the sight of their daughter, have to be physically held back, so they do not storm the stage.

Gallner stands over her, watching her life slip from her until her blood begins to reach his feet. He steps away and looks back at the crowd. His voice is quiet but demanding as he addresses the citizens of Grayson once more.

"I will be back. Soon. When I come back, I'm bringing my army. You will see. You will see what your boys could have become if you hadn't hidden them from me." He pauses and purses his lips in thought. "If you hide your boys, my army will search the woods around Grayson. They will find them." His eyes are wide with fury, and he nods his head as he speaks, "Your boys will be brought up on this stage and," Gallner rubs his mustache in thought, "Well, you know what will happen." He makes a subtle motion towards Merritt. His blood-soaked knife hangs loosely from his hand. It drips the blood of the girl I love onto the stage.

Gallner yells to Helix, "And you, blind man! You better be gone when we come back!"

Looking down at Merritt, he continues, "Get this cleaned up. It will attract predators."

The Howlers behind him laugh at this last statement. Gallner howls and exits the stage, and the rest of his pack join him. Keeping my eye on the stage, I listen as the Howlers make their way out of our community. They are making much more noise leaving than they did arriving. Not only are they howling but the sounds of windows breaking and other raucous activities cause those around me to flinch and weep harder.

When I feel the madmen are far enough away, I dash through the crowd and leap onto the stage. I make my way to Merritt, slipping a bit in her blood and fighting the urge to vomit at the smell. Falling to my knees next to her, I gently gather her into my arms. Her body is limp, and I fear she is already dead. The image of her in my nightmare floods my mind.

There is so much I want to say to her. So much I should have said already. I can feel the regret begin to wreck me. Cradling Merritt in my arms, I bring my mouth to her ear and whisper my true feelings for her. I whisper my admiration for her strength, beauty, and charm. I whisper the intentions that will never be accomplished because now one-half of me is forever lost. I whisper my gratitude for her wit and snarky comments that, even though annoying at times, always made me smile and most definitely gave me the courage to bury my self-pity and become what this community needs. Lastly, I whisper my love for her.

Sobbing now, I lean her head back and look into her face. I take it all in and try to remember her features without blood smears. Closing my eye to concentrate and attempt to gain control over my emotions, I see her leaning against a tree she was too afraid to climb. She smiles at me because she knows she doesn't have to be brave enough to climb it. I will climb it for her and then describe everything I see from the top. Her eyes dance with delight as I climb back down and paint a picture for her with my words. The breeze blows her hair across her face slightly, and her petite hand pushes it back behind her ear. With my eye still closed, holding her bloody body, I see Merritt the way I've always seen her but was never brave enough to say.

When I open my eye, I am startled to see that Merritt's eyes are open too. Through heavy lids, she peers at me and attempts a weak smile. I return her smile, but the tears continue to roll down my face. Her parents, weeping and attempting to apply pressure to her massive wound, are with us now. Mrs. Clifton also makes vain attempts to stop the bleeding. The gruesome wound is much too extensive to be mended. I can hear my parents behind me tending to Dom.

Merritt's mouth moves slightly, and I lean my ear closer to make out her words. She tries to gather the strength she needs to speak. Finally, and slowly, she does. "Gallner does *not* know how to treat a lady. I'm starting to think he may have mommy issues."

A weird chuckle-sob escapes me as I realize that even in her dying moments, Merritt's true personality is shining.

"Lukan, listen to me." She continues weakly. "Don't let them take our community. You can stop this. Stop them. They think you are weak because that's what you let them believe. You aren't." Merritt closes her eyes and struggles to take in a breath. My heart crawls up into my throat as I fear this is the end of her. Surprising me again, she opens her eyes, "There is a strength in you that you haven't let anyone see. Let them. Protect our home." Her eyes begin to roll back, and she struggles to regain control of them. "Love you, Lukan."

*****

Running.

Blades of grass, sharp on the edges, tug at my pant legs as I run. Running from the Community Building. Running from the scene of my best friend's murder. Running from the loss of my love. Certain of what I am running from but with no clear picture of where I am running to. Just running.

The tears of loss flow hot down my blood-smeared face. Not only tears of sadness but tears of hatred and fury. They do not subside. They flow freely. It is as if the heartache of my entire life is being released at once. I do not fight it. I get the sense that I am being cleansed. Although my grief will never end, I'm sure the tears will. When they do, the cleansing will be complete, and my greater purpose will be revealed. A purpose I have missed because I have had an insatiable need to be cleansed.

Running.

My mind replays the scene of Merritt's death. Her last words to me bounce around in my head.

"Love you, Lukan."

As she said them, I could feel her life leaving her bloodied body. Merrit's mother wailed, and I placed her body in her open arms. Standing, I looked over at Dom who was still lying where Gallner had dropped him. Mrs. Clifton was there, already cleaning his wounds. My parents looked up at me. My mother had tears in her eyes, but I could tell that her tears were for Merritt. Dom was battered, but his wounds would heal.

Standing in Merritt's blood, I took in the scene around me. Merritt, lifeless. Dom, tortured. Rage began to edge out the anguish. My breaths came quicker. My vision started to turn red.

"Lukan," I heard my mother say, with worry in her voice.

Looking down at her, I saw worry etched on her face. A mother knows her son's intentions even before he does. She knew where my head was. In my mind, I already had my bow and was on my way to take revenge on the Howlers.

Shaking her head, my mother said, "No, Lukan."

Her words were meaningless to me. Without responding to her, I jumped from the stage.

Before I can get through the crowd, though, I am stopped by Helix. With a strong hand, he clutches me by the elbow. His face is stern but compassionate.

"Do not allow rage to consume you, my friend," Helix says in a deep voice that isn't much louder than a whisper. "It will only produce more pain. Nothing will be accomplished. Your hurt will not be healed. You are at the precipice of something greater than your anguish. Something that is sure to heal all of Grayson."

With a violent jerking motion, I wrenched my elbow from his grasp and ran towards my house. Blood pumped hard through my veins as I ran home, retrieved my bow and quiver, jumped across the wall and out of town. I'm not sure when the tears began to fall again.

Running.

I run without any real sense of direction. No plan. Just hate and thoughts of murderous revenge. I have no idea where the Howlers have gone. No idea where their camp is. It seems like I would have run into them by now. Slowing to a walk, I look around to see where I am.

A defeated chuckle escapes me as I realize that I am on a familiar trail. My anger was leading me to the Howlers, but apparently, my heart has other plans. Standing at the edge of the forest, I walk out into the meadow. For reasons I cannot explain, I feel as if I am walking towards something greater than my anguish. Greater than Grayson's fear. I consider that maybe Helix was right. It's almost as if I am walking towards…hope.

Wiping tears from my face, I walk towards the metal door that leads to the underground. The door of my nightmare. Since this day is a waking nightmare, it makes sense that this is where I belong.

A plan begins to form. The plan that has been brewing all along. Get the people of Grayson to safety. Get my family to safety. After I am sure they are safe, I end Gallner and the Howlers once and for all.

My mother's story from long ago creeps into my mind.

"Somewhere far away, there is a safe place. A place where people don't have to worry about the outside monsters. They have food and water."

Realizing what I must do, I rush down the steps that lead to the door. With a thudding heart, I slowly reach my hand out and touch the metal. It's cold and lifeless, and I am immediately reminded of Merritt's body lying in blood. I shake the image from my mind before I am overcome with emotions again. Once my people are safely underground, and the Howlers are exterminated from our land, I will take the time to mourn.

A brief thought of what or who is waiting on the other side causes me to pause. I know my nightmare was just that. A nightmare. Not real. Just the overactive imagination of a teenage boy. There is no real threat on the other side of that door.

As soon as I get the door open, I plan on declaring that I mean the inhabitants of the underground no harm. Hopefully, I can talk to whoever lives beyond this door, explaining our situation and they will welcome the town of Grayson. We have strengths and abilities to offer, as well as food from our gardens and smokehouse.

Grasping the handle, I give it a twist and shove.

Nothing.

It seems stuck. Driving my weight into it, I push harder.

Leaning my head against the cold metal, I close my eye as I grasp the handle firmly. The tears threaten to fall once more as I feel defeated. My heart is ready to mourn all that has been lost. With a deep breath, I deny the emotion. There will be a time for mourning. Now is the time for action.

I try the door once more.

Nothing.

Frustration sets in, and I begin shoving the door frantically.

Taking a step back, I look the door over. There are no key holes. It doesn't appear to be locked. However, something is indeed keeping it from opening. I begin to wonder if it is blocked from the inside. It makes sense that whoever is living beyond it would take precautions to ensure their own safety.

The events and emotions of the day begin to take their toll on my mind and body. Turning, I put my back against the door. The cold finds its way through my sweat-soaked clothing easily, making me shiver.

I find my breaths coming rapidly as the realization of this predicament becomes clear. With my back against the door, I slide down to the ground, pulling my knees up close to my chest. I rest my forehead on my knees and place my hands on the back of my head. The uncomfortable position seems to help clear my thoughts.

The window.

I can leave another message for Lia on the window. She can speak to whoever is in charge. Speak on my behalf. On behalf of Grayson. Once they hear that we are peaceful and are in need of a safe haven, they will surely open the hatch and let us in.

The thought spurs me to my feet, and once again I am running.

It doesn't take me long to reach the window. Once there, I look down at the room below my feet. What I see on the gray side of the window causes me to break out into a barrage of hysterical giggles. I had felt that the window held hope. A safe haven for my family. What I see, though, looks like what I am feeling.

Despair.

Anguish.

Below me, lying on the tattered blanket that has laid vacantly during all but one of my other visits, is a girl.

Lia.

Just like the last time I saw her here, her plain clothing is thin and without color. She has blonde hair that seems soaked in sweat and is in need of a brushing. She doesn't see me standing over her. Her face is covered with one arm. It's obvious to me that she is crying. She seems lost in her misery. As I watch her, a feeling of guilt overcomes me. I wouldn't want to be stared at as I grieve. I can't help wonder what, in her safe place, has brought on her sorrow.

The plain girl moves her arm from her face and reaches for something that lies beside her. Following her eyes, I see that she has a book with her. She seems to be reading it while she weeps, constantly drying her eyes on the sleeve of her shirt.

To my astonishment, she looks up. For a brief second, I feel the urge to jump out of her view. Not because I am fearful of her but because I don't want her to think that I have watched her raw and vulnerable display of emotions.

Our eyes meet. Her eyes, still wet with tears, widen. On the sunny side of the window, through tears of my own, I gaze down at her. I feel something that I haven't felt in a very long time. Hope.

This girl on the tattered blanket, in the dark room, has given me hope.

This girl from the underground.

This girl named…

Lia.

<u>Dedication Page</u>

This book is dedicated to all those who have a disability.

May you know peace and find the strength that lies within you to rise above and know your worth in this world. May you surround yourself with people that see the true quality of your nature.

May your dreams be grand, and your determination be fierce.

"Strength does not come from physical capacity. It comes from an indomitable will." - Gandhi

Sneak Peak into Secrets Revealed: Book 3 of the Secrets Series –

Chapter 1

Lia

My eyes, burning with hot tears of anguish over the death of my mother, have a difficult time focusing. My breath catches in my throat as I realize that I am not alone with my pain. He stands over me, on the other side of the window. The young man that I believe to be Lukan stares down at me with one wide eye. His other eye appears to be covered. I have a hard time making out his features through my tears and with the sun shining brightly behind him. What I am able to discern, though, is a boy about my age with dark shoulder-length hair. His clothing is much different than mine. My attire is bland and without color. Lukan's clothing seems to have a personality all its own. Colors, patterns, and textures melded together in a way that makes it seem as though there is a story to be told with each article.

We stare at each other through the window for several seconds. Lukan seems just as startled to see me as I am him. I continue to wipe the tears from my face as I try to formulate a plan to communicate with him. I am certain the boy from the outside world is here to save me from this world of misery. I can see his wide eye narrow as he takes in the sight below his feet.

How pitiful I must look, laying on the floor, face wet with tears of mourning and desperation. I have imagined being able to see Lukan since the day I saw the bloody handprints. That day seems like ages ago now. I imagine that when he left the arrow, and the flowers, his image of me was much different than the sobbing girl he sees now.

Suddenly, Lukan falls to his knees and places his hands on the glass. When he does, I am able to see his face much more clearly. I know that I should find the fact that he only has one eye worrisome; however, the thing about him that bothers me the most is that it appears he is covered in blood. So much blood on his clothing and hands. It also seems that he has been crying. What has happened, in his world, to cause him the pain that is so obvious on his tear-streaked face?

Lukan's mouth begins to move, and his face is consumed by a look of desperation. He is trying to say something to me, but the glass is too thick. I unable hear his words. I can only sit and stare at him, shaking my head.

Sitting up now, I watch as Lukan tries to communicate with me. The longer I watch him shouting into the glass, the more unnerved I become. Taking my eyes off Lukan, I scan the small room in search of a way to communicate with him. Tearing an empty sheet of parchment paper from my mother's journal, I reach my finger into some muck on a nearby pipe and write the only thing that comes to mind.

HELP

I hold the paper up as high as I can reach, desperate for Lukan to see. His mouth quits moving immediately. He stares at the word for a long time. I lower the paper back down to my lap. Lukan shakes his head slowly, and a look of sadness passes over his face.

I look away as my tears begin to fall once again. The realization of my situation tumbles over me with tremendous weight. Lukan cannot help me. Nobody can help me. More importantly, I cannot help the people of Terra Convex. We are doomed to this living tomb for eternity.

Above me, Lukan begins to pound on the window, startling me from my despair. Looking up once more, I can see that he is pointing and mouthing a word. I shake my head to communicate that I do not understand what he is trying to communicate. He is obviously becoming aggravated. I'm surprised at how much emotion he can convey with just the one eye.

He stands and walks away from the window. I fear that he has abandoned his communication with me and a wave of anxiety rushes over me. Seconds later, he returns with dirty fingers. Stiffness begins to settle into my neck; still, I continue to stare up at him. With a mud-covered finger, he continues to try to communicate with me. He writes out one simple word.

ROOD

Even though the word he writes with his finger is backward, I know that he is trying to tell me to go to the hatch door. So Lukan knows about the hatch. Apparently, Lukan knows more about Terra Convex than I had realized. I wonder if he knows that the metal door is locked, with a combination that I do not know. He seems adamant that I go there, so I reluctantly stand and walk over to the door that leads to the hallway. Looking back at the window, I see that Lukan is already gone. Obviously, headed towards the hatch. Hoping against hope that he knows a way in, I also make my way to the only way in or out of Terra Convex.

Lukan

Although I had hoped to see Lia, I hadn't expected to. We stare at each other for several seconds. Lia's tear-streaked face is a mixture of misery and astonishment. I imagine the look on her face is much like my own. Matching Lia's movements, I wipe my face dry of the tears that I thought would never cease.

I am curious as to what has caused her so much anguish. The image of the chimney, belching up the horrid stench of death, scratches at the back of my mind. I try to ignore the irritation it causes, but I can't help but wonder if the chimney of death is the cause of her turmoil.

Now that I have actually made eye contact with the girl from the underground world, I seem to be at a loss for what to do besides stand above her and stare awkwardly. Her eyes are probably a lovely shade of blue when she isn't crying. At this moment, though, they are blood-shot and charged with torment. Even while witnessing Lia's anguish, I am still confident that there is safety for Grayson on the other side of this window. There has to be.

Lia's eyes grow wider with every second that she stares up at me. I can only imagine what a frightful sight I must be to her. A one-eyed boy. Face and hands smeared with dirt, sweat, tears, and the blood of the girl I love. Looking down at my clothes, I can see that there are rips and tears that are the result of running through the forest without regard to the trees, bushes, and briars that attempted to hold me back.

Suddenly feeling that time is slipping away for Grayson, I fall to my knees and place my hands on the glass. I hope she can see the desperation on my face and let me in. If I can just explain the events that led me here, I know that she will have pity on me and then, hopefully, my people. In my mind, I can see the large metal door opening. Lia is just inside, beckoning me into her world with a smile and a welcoming wave of her hand.

The door is the key. It is the gateway to the survival of my community. With great desperation, I tell Lia to go to the door. I point and say the word repeatedly. She only sits and stares at me. She shakes her head, and I realize that the glass is too thick for me to be heard beyond it. I grow increasingly unnerved by the whole ordeal, but I am determined to communicate with her.

Lia begins to look around the small room. She seems to be searching for something. Why does she not go to the door? Surely, she must know of its existence. Suddenly, Lia tears a sheet of parchment paper from the book in which she has been clinging. She reaches behind the pipes that are closest to her and begins to smudge her fingers across the paper. When she holds up the paper, my hopes shatter.

HELP

I stare at the word for a long time. When I first saw her, I could tell that she was going through something dire. It hadn't occurred to me that her situation might actually be something she needed help escaping. Shaking my head slowly, I regretfully try to convey to her that I have no help to give. Lia lowers the paper back to her lap and her tears resume.

I am surprised by the burden I feel for this stranger. Her despair floods over me with tremendous weight. I feel guilty for giving Lia hope. Perhaps my guilt is because I wasn't able to help Merritt when she needed me the most. More importantly, if I am unable to get into the door, I cannot help the people of Grayson. We are doomed to a life of servitude and torture at the hands of the Howlers.

The significance of the situation - the situation Lia and I share - becomes too much for me. In anger and frustration, I strike the window. Lia flinches and looks up at me once more. I yell into the window and point in the direction of the metal door. Lia merely shakes her head. She obviously doesn't understand what I am trying to convey. I become increasingly aggravated.

Another thought occurs to me, and I stand and walk away from the window. I find a patch of dirt nearby and spit into it until it becomes mud. Dipping my fingers into it, I quickly return to the window and try a different type of communication. With dirty fingers, I hastily write one simple word on the glass.

DOOR

Looking down on the word, and Lia beyond, I immediately realize that the word she is looking up at is ROOD. Still, she seems to understand the meaning. With a noticeable look of dejection, Lia slowly stands and walks over to the only door in the tiny room. This seems like progress, and I race away from the window and toward the large metal door that represents my salvation.

Works by Amy M. Ward & Olivia Cayenne:

Secrets Series:

Secrets Above

Secrets Below

Secrets Revealed

Long Ago Secrets (coming end of 2018)

Works by Amy M. Ward

Myra: Changed (an ebook short story)

CPSIA information can be obtained
at www.ICGtesting.com
Printed in the USA
LVHW050322030320
648719LV00005B/526

9 780692 110508